12TH
OF
NEVER

JAMES PATTERSON is one of the best-known and biggest-selling writers of all time. He is the author of some of the most popular series of the past decade – the Alex Cross, Women's Murder Club and Detective Michael Bennett novels – and he has written many other number one bestsellers including romance novels and stand-alone thrillers. He lives in Florida with his wife and son.

James is passionate about encouraging children to read. Inspired by his own son who was a reluctant reader, he also writes a range of books specifically for young readers. James is a founding partner of Booktrust's Children's Reading Fund in the UK. In 2010, he was voted Author of the Year at the Children's Choice Book Awards in New York.

Also by James Patterson

A list of more titles by James Patterson is printed
at the back of this book

12TH OF NEVER

JAMES PATTERSON

AND MAXINE PAETRO

arrow books

Published by Arrow Books in 2013

3 5 7 9 10 8 6 4 2

Copyright © James Patterson, 2013

James Patterson has asserted his right under the Copyright, Designs and
Patents Act, 1988 to be identified as the author of this work

First published in Great Britain in 2013 by Century

Arrow Books
Random House, 20 Vauxhall Bridge Road,
London SW1V 2SA

www.randomhouse.co.uk

Addresses for companies within The Random House Group Limited can
be found at: www.randomhouse.co.uk/offices.htm

The Random House Group Limited Reg. No. 954009

A CIP catalogue record for this book
is available from the British Library

ISBN 9780099574255
ISBN 9780099574262 (export edition)

The Random House Group Limited supports the Forest Stewardship Council®
(FSC®), the leading international forest-certification organisation. Our books
carrying the FSC label are printed on FSC®-certified paper. FSC is the only forest-
certification scheme supported by the leading environmental organisations,
including Greenpeace. Our paper procurement policy can be found at:
www.randomhouse.co.uk/environment

Typeset by SX Composing DTP, Rayleigh, Essex, SS6 7XF
Printed and bound by CPI Group (UK) Ltd, Croydon, CR0 4YY

Suzie and John, Brendan and Jack

PROLOGUE

A DARK AND STORMY NIGHT

One

I WOKE UP to a sharp report, as if a gun had gone off next to my ear. My eyes flew open and I sat straight up in bed.

I yelled *"Joe,"* but my husband wasn't lying next to me. He was in an airplane, thirty-five thousand feet above the heartland, and wouldn't be home until the morning.

There was another ferocious crack and my bedroom brightened with lightning that snapped and wrapped around the windows. A boomer shook the window frames and sheets of rain lashed the glass. I was so distracted by the vicious storm that it took me a second or two to register the wave of pain that came from my belly and washed right through me.

3

Oh, man, it hurt really bad.

Yes, it was my own fault for gorging on refried beans for dinner, then chasing down the Mexican leftovers with rigatoni marinara at ten.

I looked at the clock—2:12 a.m.—then jumped at the next seismic thunderclap. Martha whined from under the bed. I called to her. "Martha. Boo, honey, whatchoo doin'? It's just a storm. It can't hurt you. Come to Mama."

She flapped her tail against the carpet, but she didn't come out. I swung my legs over the bed and flipped the switch on the bedside lamp—and nothing happened. I tried a couple more times, but damn it—the light wouldn't go on.

The power couldn't be out. But it was.

I reached for my Maglite, accidentally knocked it with the back of my hand, and it flew off the night table, rolled under the bed, and went I don't know where.

Lightning branched down and reached across the black sky, as if to emphasize the point that the lights were out as far as the eye could see.

I grabbed the cordless phone and listened to dead air. The phones were out, too, and now I was feeling that weird wave of stomach pain again. *Yowee*.

I want to be clear. I was feeling a wave, not a contraction.

My age classifies me as an "elderly primigravida," meaning over forty, pregnant with my first child. I had seen my doctor yesterday morning and I'd checked out fine. The baby had checked out fine, and wasn't due for another week.

I had booked a bed on the birthing floor at California Women's Hospital, and although I'm not the organic granola type, I wanted to have the whole natural childbirth experience. The truth was, this baby might be the only one Joe and I would ever have.

Another wave of pain hit me.

To repeat, it was *not* a contraction.

I staggered out to the living room, found my handbag—an item I hadn't needed in several weeks—and dug around until I found my iPhone. The battery bar was showing that I had only 10 percent of a full charge. Too damned little.

I leaned against a wall and went online to see what kind of storm was beating up San Francisco.

The squall was even worse than I thought. Twenty thousand families were in the dark. People were stuck in elevators between floors. Signs and other detritus had been flung through windows. Cars had skidded across roads, crashed, and flipped. All emergency vehicles had been deployed. Emergency rooms were flooded with patients and downed power lines were sparking on the streets.

This was shaping up to be one of the worst storms in SF history. Headlines quoted the mayor: STAY IN YOUR HOMES. THE STREETS ARE UNSAFE.

Martha slunk over and collapsed on top of my feet.

"We're going to be okay," I cooed.

And then that pain came over me. And it flipped me out.

"Go away," I yelled at Martha. "Go away."

She ran.

"I'm sorry, Boo," I said to my whimpering dog. "These are false contractions. If they were real, I would know it."

I grabbed my knees—and that's when my water broke.

No way!

I could not comprehend what was happening

6

—it could not be happening. I wasn't ready to have the baby. It wasn't due for another week. But ready or not, this baby was coming.

God help me.

My little one and I were really in for it now.

Two

I WANTED TO abandon my body.

Yes, that sounds insane, but that's how I felt—
and it was all that I felt. I clicked the light switch
up and down, picked up the landline.

Still no power and no phones; neither would
be restored until the sun threw some light on the
situation. I had five minutes of battery left on my
iPhone, maybe less.

I speed-dialed my doctor, left a message with
her service, then called the hospital. A nice woman
named Shelby asked me, "How often are your
contractions coming?"

"I don't know. I didn't time them. I didn't even
know I was having them."

"Lindy?"

"Lindsay."

"Lindsay, your water breaking means you'll be in labor for a while yet. You could deliver in three hours or three days, but don't worry. Let me explain about three-one-one."

I knew about 311. But still I listened as Shelby explained that 311 was the rule for what to do when your contractions come every three minutes, last for one minute, and that pattern repeats for at least one hour: you go to the hospital.

"Are you kidding me?" I screeched into the phone. "Because, listen! I'm alone and I've never done this before."

"Do *not* come in until you're in active labor," Shelby said. "Stay home, where you're comfortable."

I yelled, "Thanks!," snapped off my phone, and walked my enormous baby bump to the window. I was breathing hard as I looked up Lake Street in the direction of my chosen hospital. There was no traffic, no traffic lights. The street was closed.

A tremendous burst of lightning cracked the sky open and sent Martha skittering under the couch. It was crazy, but I was starting to like the storm, even though it had sucked all the air out of the room.

It was hot. Damned hot. I kicked off my XXL pj's and another painful wave took my breath away. It was as if a boa constrictor had wrapped itself around my torso and was squeezing me into the shape of a meal.

I was scared, and it wasn't all about the pain.

Babies got strangled by umbilical cords. Women died in childbirth. Elderly primigravidas were more at risk than younger women, and old babes like me weren't supposed to do childbirth by themselves. What if there were complications?

Claire Washburn is my best friend. She is San Francisco's chief medical examiner—a forensic pathologist, not an obstetrician, but hell. She'd had three babies. I knew she could talk me through this. At least she could try.

I dialed and Claire answered with a groggy "Dr. Wazjjjbrn."

"Claire. It's too soon to go to the hospital, I know, but *yow*. I think I can feel the baby's head down there. What should I do?"

"Don't push!" my best friend shouted at me. "I'm calling nine-one-one right now."

I shouted back at her, "Call a private ambulance service so I can go to the Women's Hospital! Claire, do you read me?"

Claire didn't answer.

My phone was dead.

Three

MY RAGING RIVER of hormones was sending a single, unambiguous message.

Push.

Claire had said, "Don't push," and that sounded both insane and impossible, but I got her drift. The baby was safe inside me until help arrived.

It must have taken me ten minutes to ease my throbbing, hurting self into bed.

I knew that Claire wouldn't let me down, that she had probably thrown the weight of her office behind the 911 call. I put my birthing instincts in park and thought with my entire being, *I'm in God's hands now. All I can do is make the best of this and hope that the baby is safe. That's all I can do.*

Martha got up on the bed and curled up next to me. I put my hand on her head and I resisted my contractions. I heard noises, someone calling "Helloooo"—sounds that were far outside my tunnel of pain. I put my hands up against blinding flashlight beams and then, like a force of nature, all the lights went on.

The power was back.

My bedroom was filled with strapping men standing shoulder to shoulder in a line that stretched from the door to the bed and ran along both sides of it. There had to be at least twelve of them, all with stricken, smoke-smudged faces, all in full turnout gear. I remember staring at the reflective tape on their jackets, wondering why a dozen firefighters were crowding in on me.

I shouted, "Where's the fire?"

A large young man came toward me. He was at least six four, with a buzz cut, a still-bleeding gash on his cheek, and a look of deep concern in his eyes.

He said, "I'm Deputy Chief Robert Wilson. I'm called Robbie. Take it easy. Everything is going to be okay."

Really? Then, I realized that a fire rig had been

closer to the apartment than an ambulance and so firefighters had answered the 911 call.

I said, "This is embarrassing. My place is a mess."

I was thinking about my clothes strewn all over the place, dog hair on the bed, somehow forgetting that I was completely naked with my legs spread apart.

Robbie Wilson said, "How are you doing, Sergeant?"

"I'm having a baby," I said.

"I know. You take it easy now."

He fitted an oxygen mask to my face, but I pushed it away.

"I don't need that."

"It's for the baby," he said. He turned to the gang of firemen and shouted, "I need boiling water. I need towels. A lot of them."

Did I have any clean towels? I didn't even know. I pushed the mask away again and grunted at Robbie, "Have you ever delivered a baby?"

He paused for a long moment. "A couple of times," he lied.

I liked him. I trusted him. But I didn't believe him.

He said, "You can push now, Sergeant. Go ahead and try."

I did it. I pushed and grunted and I lost track of the time. Had an hour passed?

It felt as though the baby were grabbing my rib cage from the inside and holding on with both fists. The pain was agonizing and it seemed that I would never get Baby Molinari out of my body and into the world. Just when I thought I had spent my last breath, my baby slid out of my body into Robbie's baseball-glove-size hands.

I heard a little cry. It was a sweet sound that had the special effect of putting the pain behind me, hugging me around the heart.

"Oh, wow. She's *perfect*," said Big Robbie.

I peered into the light and said, "Give her to me."

I wiggled my fingers in the air as someone cut the cord and cleaned up her little face. And then my baby was in my arms.

"Hello, sweet girl."

She opened her eyes to little slits and she looked right at me. Tears fell out of my eyes as I smiled into my daughter's face. A bond was formed that could never be broken; it was a moment I would never, ever forget.

My little girl *was* perfect and as beautiful as a sunrise over the ocean, as awesome as a double rainbow over swans in flight.

It's too bad the word *miracle* has been overused, because I swear it's the only word that fit the feeling of holding my daughter in my arms. My heart swelled to the size of the world. I only wished Joe had been here.

I counted my baby's fingers and toes, talking nonsense to her the whole time.

"I'm your mommy. You know that, baby girl? Look what we've *done*."

But was she really okay? Was her little heart beating at the right pace? Were her lungs filling with enough air?

The big dude said, "You should both have a thorough checkup. Ready to go to the hospital, Sergeant?"

"We're going in the fire rig?"

"I'll make room in the front seat."

"Oh, *good*," I said. "And please, amp up the sirens."

BOOK I

THREE WEEKS LATER

Chapter 1

YUKI CASTELLANO PARKED her car on Brannan Street, a block or so away from the Hall of Justice. She was lucky to have gotten this parking spot, and she took it as a good sign. Today she was glad for any good sign.

She got out of her car, then reached into the backseat for her briefcase and jacket. Then she set off toward the gray granite building on Bryant Street, where she worked as an assistant district attorney and where, in about an hour, she would prosecute a piece-of-crap wife and child killer named Keith Herman.

Keith Herman was a disbarred attorney who had made his living by defending the most heinous of slime-bucket clients and had often won his cases by letting prosecution witnesses know that if they testified, they would be killed.

Accordingly, witnesses sometimes fled California rather than appear against Herman's clients.

He'd been charged with witness tampering, but never convicted. That's how scary he was. He was also a registered sex offender, so that made two juicy bits of information Yuki couldn't tell the jury because the law said that she couldn't prejudice the jury by citing his prior misdeeds.

So Yuki had been building the case against Herman based on evidence that he'd killed his wife, dismembered her body, and somehow made his young daughter disappear, arguably a harder charge to prove because the girl's body had not been found.

Yuki had been doing nothing but work on the Herman case for the last five months and now, as the first day of the trial arrived, she was stoked and nervous at the same time. Her case was solid, but she'd been surprised by verdicts that had gone against her in cases as airtight as this one.

As she turned the corner onto Bryant, Yuki located the cause of her worry. It was Keith Herman's defense attorney, John Kinsela, who, right after Keith Herman, was probably the sleaziest lawyer in the country. He had defended legendary high-profile killers and had rarely lost a case.

And he usually destroyed the reputations of opposing counsel with innuendo and rumors, which he leaked as truth to the press.

Yuki had never gone up against Kinsela before, but Kinsela had shredded her boss, Leonard "Red Dog" Parisi, in a murder trial about two years ago. Parisi still hadn't gotten over it. He was pulling for Yuki, giving her his full support, but it wasn't lost on Yuki that he wasn't trying the case himself.

Red Dog had a bad heart.

Yuki was young, fit, and up for the challenge of her life.

Yuki walked quickly toward the Hall, head bent as she mentally rehearsed her opener. She was startled out of her thoughts by someone calling her name. She looked up, saw the good-looking young guy with the blond cowlick and the start of a mustache.

Nicky Gaines was her associate and second chair in this trial. He was carrying a paper bag.

"Damn, you look good, Yuki."

Gaines was five years younger than she was, and Yuki didn't care whether he really did have a crush on her or if he was just flattering her. She was in love. And not with Nicky Gaines.

"You have coffee in there?" Yuki asked.

"Hot, with cream, one sugar. And then I've got the double espresso for you."

"Let's go straight to the courtroom," Yuki said.

"How are you feeling about this?" Gaines said, walking up the steps along with her.

"Like if I don't get a double-barreled conviction, I may kill Keith Herman myself."

Chapter 2

WHEN JENNIFER HERMAN'S dismembered body turned up in eight separate garbage bags, and when seven-year-old Lily Herman hadn't been found despite the exhaustive police search conducted over a six-month period, Keith Herman was tried in the press and found guilty of murdering them both.

The intense media attention had whipped up a lot of hatred toward Keith Herman. It made it nearly impossible to find a jury who hadn't watched the network specials, hadn't seen the rewards offered for information about the missing child, and hadn't formed an opinion as to the guilt of the accused.

And so jury selection had taken almost three weeks.

Now the press filled half the gallery in court-room 202, Superior Court of California, County of San Francisco. The other half of the room was filled with citizens who had lined up early enough that morning to have scored one of the precious seats.

At 8:23 a.m. Yuki was at the prosecution table in the blond-wood-paneled courtroom. Her laptop was open and as she went through a long e-mail from Red Dog, she hoped all her witnesses would show up to testify—that they hadn't been silenced or intimidated (or worse) by the opposition.

Across the aisle, at the defense table, sat two ordinary-looking men who were actually two of the scariest people Yuki had ever met. Keith Herman was paunchy, bald, and had black eyes that looked like bullet holes in his unlined, babyish face. Not all psychopaths look homicidal, but Keith Herman did. Herman had never shown any remorse, not while identifying the sections of meat that had once been his wife, not while discussing his missing daughter.

Herman's attorney, John Kinsela, was tall with thinning gray hair and a bloodless complexion that made him look as though he climbed out of a coffin at night. Unlike his client, Kinsela was smooth. He expressed sadness and regret. He listened thoughtfully and spoke well and persuasively on camera. He passed as a reasonable facsimile of a person. A little digging into his past had turned up five divorces and the ownership of a Glock semiautomatic, which he carried at all times.

Yuki had been with these ghouls through countless hours of depositions and felt that she knew them too well.

She had dressed this morning in a bright red suit because she had a slight build, could look younger than her years, and because of the fact that red made her look and feel more powerful.

You couldn't hang back in red. You couldn't hesitate. You really had to live up to red.

She also wore a gold star on a chain around her neck, a graduation-from-law-school gift from her mother, who had been murdered several years earlier.

Wearing the star kept Keiko Castellano present in Yuki's mind and might even help her to win.

She had to win.

This was a tremendous opportunity to get justice for the victims, to become a hero to female victims everywhere. It was also an opportunity to be humiliated by a savage attorney and his perverted, murdering client.

It was her job to make sure that Keith Herman didn't get out of jail—ever.

The buzz in the gallery intensified, then cut off suddenly as the door leading from the judge's chambers opened behind the bench and Judge Arthur R. Nussbaum entered the courtroom.

Chapter 3

YUKI HALF LISTENED as Judge Nussbaum instructed the handpicked jury of six men, six women, and four alternates, who were as diverse a group as could be imagined: black, white, brown, white-collar, and blue-collar.

Nussbaum had been a clever trial lawyer, but the judge was new at his job and Yuki was sure he would play this one by the book.

When he asked her if she was ready to begin, she said she was. Gaines whispered, "Go get 'em," and Yuki stood, greeted the jury, and walked confidently to the lectern in the well of the courtroom. Then, without warning, she blanked. She couldn't remember the first sentence in her opener, the key that would unlock her carefully wrought statement.

Yuki looked over at Gaines. He smiled, nodded, and her mind unfroze.

She said, "The defendant, Keith Herman, is a killer, and the evidence in this case will show you that the people who depended on Mr. Herman, the ones who looked to him for protection and love, are the people who should have feared him the most."

Yuki paused to let her words sink in, looked at every member of the jury, and began to lay out her case.

"On March first, a day like any other, Keith Herman tucked his daughter's lifeless body into the backseat of his Lexus, and she was never seen again. Jennifer Herman, Keith Herman's wife, never reported her daughter missing, because as her husband was driving off with their daughter, Jennifer Herman was already dead by her husband's hand.

"You will hear testimony that before she disappeared, Jennifer Herman told a friend on several occasions that she was afraid of her husband and that if anything ever happened to her, the friend should go to the police. Which this friend did. Had Lesley Rohan not called the police, they wouldn't have looked for Jennifer Herman and her body would have been buried under several tons of garbage in a landfill.

"You will hear testimony from another witness, an undercover police officer, who will tell you that he was offered one hundred thousand dollars by the defendant to kill Jennifer Herman."

Yuki's mind unclenched. She knew that she had gotten into the rhythm and the beat of her perfectly choreographed and well-rehearsed presentation. She was in a great groove.

She told the jury about the witnesses she would introduce—the sanitation worker who found the body of Jennifer Herman in eight separate garbage bags and the forensic pathologist who would talk about Jennifer Herman's cause of death.

She walked to the counsel table and picked up an 8 x 10-inch color photo of a young child with dark wavy hair and a captivating smile. Carrying the picture in both hands, Yuki showed it to the jury as she walked along the length of the railing.

"This beautiful child is the defendant's daughter, Lily, who has been missing for over a year. You will hear from a neighbor's housekeeper, Maria Ortega, that a month before Lily disappeared, she became moody and withdrawn and that there were bruises on her arms and legs. Ms. Ortega will testify that she reported her suspicions to the police.

"The state," Yuki said, keeping eye contact with the jury, "does not have to prove motive, but if I were sitting in the jury box, I'd be asking, 'Why would the defendant, a man with wealth and means, decide to put his entire life in the toilet? Why would he kill the beautiful woman who was his wife, and the wonderful little girl who was his daughter?'

"Did Mr. Herman abuse his little girl, and did his wife catch him at it and try to protect their daughter?"

Kinsela shot to his feet. "Your Honor, this is argument."

"Overruled."

Yuki didn't hesitate.

She stepped on the gas.

She said to the jury, "Did Mr. Herman physically abuse his little girl? Did Mr. Herman kill his wife when she tried to protect their daughter? What was his motive for murdering his loved ones?

"That question is going to haunt me for the rest of my life."

Chapter 4

WHEN SHE STOOD behind the lectern, Yuki felt like a little kid peering up over the edge of a table. So she stayed close to the jury box and spoke loudly enough for everyone in the courtroom to hear.

"We can't know what was in the defendant's mind when he took the lives of his wife and daughter, and the victims can't tell us," she said.

"We don't have to know or prove motive, but we do have a witness, Ms. Lynnette Lagrande, who will testify that the defendant wanted to ditch his family. She will testify that she was in love with Keith Herman, that Mr. Herman said that he loved her and wanted to marry her. And so Ms. Lynnette Lagrande, a model citizen, patiently waited for

Mr. Herman to make good on that promise for the last three years."

There had been no coughing in the gallery, no shuffling in the jury box, and even when the defense team attempted to distract the jurors and the audience, Yuki had kept all the attention on herself.

But when she said that Lynnette Lagrande would give evidence proving that the defendant wanted to leave his family, John Kinsela snorted —what passed for laughter in his corner of the underworld. Yuki's cheeks burned, but she didn't even flick her eyes in opposing counsel's direction. She had to bring her opening home.

She moved her glossy black hair away from her face, hooked it around her ears, and said to the jury, "The defense will tell you that there is no evidence connecting the death of Jennifer Herman to Keith Herman. They will say that Keith Herman's fingerprints and DNA were not on the garbage bags—that in fact, Mr. Herman never saw his wife or daughter the day our witness saw him leave his house and put his daughter into his car.

"The defense will impugn the character and the veracity of Mr. Herman's lover.

"They will tell you that the defendant was misidentified by his neighbor and will maintain that since the body of Lily Herman has never been recovered, there is no evidence that she is even dead.

"So I ask you and I ask them," Yuki said, pivoting so that she was staring the defendant and his counsel down. "Where is Lily Herman? Where is that little girl?

"The defense will tell you that the people's case is all based on circumstantial evidence. We have nothing to hide. We cannot put a gun in Mr. Herman's hand. But circumstantial evidence is real evidence.

"If you go to bed one night and in the morning you see snow in your front yard and there are footprints in that snow, that is circumstantial evidence that snow fell during the night and that someone walked across your yard. You don't have to actually see the snow falling to conclude that there was snowfall.

"So why are we all here today, ladies and gentlemen?

"We submit to you that Keith Herman did brutally kill Jennifer and Lily Herman so that he

could, for once and for all, be free to pursue his life
as a wealthy widower and come to the party with
no baggage and no financial overhead.

"We cannot let him get away with it. At the
conclusion of this trial, you will have evidentiary
proof that the defendant did callously commit two
premeditated murders."

The words were just out of Yuki's mouth when
John Kinsela laughed noisily again and once more
drew the eyes of the jury to himself.

Yuki sharply objected.

Judge Nussbaum sustained her objection and
Kinsela apologized for the interruption. But he had
stolen her moment, broken the mood. And he had
the jury's rapt attention as he stood to make his
opening statement.

Chapter 5

JOHN KINSELA BUTTONED his jacket and ran his hand across the lower half of his face. He achieved a look of contrition, as though he was sorry for the interruption.

It was all theatrics.

Yuki hoped the jury could read him as the drama whore he was.

"Folks, again, I'm sorry to have made light of the state's opening statement. It was rude, but unintentional. The prosecutor is doing her job, a very difficult one, I assure you, because there is no evidence linking my client to any crime."

Kinsela put his hands into his pockets, sauntered out into the well, and continued his conversation with the jury.

"As the prosecutor said, there is no blood, no DNA, no gun in Mr. Herman's hand. There is no direct evidence against Mr. Herman, because my client didn't kill anyone, and the circumstantial evidence, such as it is, does not tie him to the death of his wife.

"Mr. Herman is one of the victims here. He loved his family and is devastated by their loss. And yet, as Ms. Castellano told you, he was having an affair with Ms. Lagrande.

"For a married man to have an affair may be bad behavior, but it's not a crime. If it were a crime, about sixty-five percent of married men in the United States would be in the slammer."

There was a riffle of laughter in the courtroom, which Judge Nussbaum banged into silence with his gavel. He admonished the audience, and told them that he could have individuals removed or the entire courtroom emptied.

"You are here at my discretion," Nussbaum warned. "Go on, Mr. Kinsela."

And Kinsela did.

"Ms. Lagrande has a little cottage in the woods a few hours up the coast. She and Mr. Herman drove up there in her car on the afternoon of February twenty-eighth. My client was spending the night with Ms. Lagrande when the crimes presumably took place. They didn't see anyone and no one saw them. That is often the nature of a clandestine affair.

"Now, Ms. Lagrande is going to tell you that she was not with Mr. Herman the day that Jennifer Herman's body was found, the day Lily Herman tragically disappeared. She'll say Mr. Herman is making that up to give himself an alibi.

"Why is she going to betray Mr. Herman? Because they fought that weekend and Mr. Herman ended the affair.

"Ms. Lagrande is a woman scorned, and she's not just my client's alibi, she is the prosecution's entire case.

"The neighbor misidentified Mr. Herman and a car that is the same model as the one Mr. Herman owns. Lily Herman did have bruises, but she had them because she had a temper tantrum. Her father wouldn't buy her a dress she wanted and she flailed and kicked at Mr. Herman and he tried to restrain her. There was no beating, no call to the police, nothing like that.

"If he could, he would buy her a million dresses now.

"Mr. Herman did not report that his wife and daughter were missing on March first because he didn't know it. He was occupied with Ms. Lagrande at the time of this tragedy, which has unquestionably destroyed his life.

"That's it, folks. That is our case. Mr. Herman didn't kill anyone. This trial is about whether or not you believe Ms. Lagrande beyond a reasonable doubt."

John Kinsela thanked the jury and sat down. For a second, Yuki couldn't quite believe that Kinsela had singled out her star witness, shot a cannonball at her, then took a bow.

Yuki had hoped he would do exactly that. It was now in Kinsela's best interest to strip Lynnette Lagrande's testimony bare, break her, and throw her bones under the bus. He could only do that if she testified.

Her witness would appear.

Lynnette Lagrande, a woman with an exotic dancer's name, was in fact a grade-school teacher, twenty years younger than the defendant, and possessed of a spotless reputation. She'd never gotten so much as a parking ticket in her life.

Gaines showed Yuki the cartoon he had

doodled on his iPad. It was a Yuki character dunking a basketball into a net. Yuki never liked to say that a case was a slam dunk.

But the battle was shaping up and Yuki liked the look of the field.

"We're good," she whispered to Gaines as the judge called the court into recess. "We're looking good."

Chapter 6

JULIE HAD BEEN wailing since we left the hospital, hardly stopping before revving her engine and howling again. It had been going on for weeks and I was mystified and a little alarmed.

What was wrong? What was she trying to tell us?

It was just about 8:00 p.m. when Joe settled me into the big rocker in Julie's room. I reached up and Joe handed me our screaming little bundle of distress. I tried to nurse her again, but as usual, she refused me.

What was I doing wrong?

I said, "Please don't cry, baby girl. Everything is okay. Actually, everything is perfect."

She took in another breath and cried even

harder. As much as her first cry felt like a hug around my heart, now her cries felt like my heart was being squeezed in a vise.

"What is it, darling? Are you hot, cold, wet?"

She was dry.

"Joe, she's hungry. Okay, she might nurse a little bit if we wait her out. But listen, she clearly prefers the bottle."

"Be back in a sec," Joe said.

I rocked my daughter. Even with her fists waving and her little face as pink as a rose, she was a spectacular, fully formed human being made from love. I was in awe of her perfection. And more than anything, I wanted her to feel good.

I jounced her in my arms and sang a nonsense song that I made up as I went along. "Ju-lee, you're breaking my heart. What can I do for my bay-bee?"

I fished an old Irish lullaby from the vault of long-buried memories, and then hauled out a couple of nursery rhymes. Mice ran up a clock, cradles rocked, but nothing worked.

Joe appeared, like a genie, with a warm bottle of formula. I tested a drop on the back of my hand, and then I tried the bottle on Julie. And—thank you, God—she began to suck.

I was elated. Euphoric. Ecstatic. Julie was eating. Joe and I watched our daughter pulling at the bottle with intense attention, and when a few ounces had gone down and she turned away from the bottle, Joe said, "I'll take her, Blondie. You go to bed."

He put Julie over his shoulder and burped her like a pro.

"I love you, Julie Anne Molinari," Joe said to our baby.

"You've told her twenty eleven times today. She knows it," I said, standing up and kissing my husband.

"She can't hear it too much. This is the happiest I've ever been in my life."

"I believe that. But I think something is bothering you," I said.

"God. I can't sneak anything past you, Blondie. Even when you're dog-tired. Even when you shouldn't notice anything but Julie's fingers and toes."

I felt the first frisson of alarm.

"Is something going on? Tell me now."

Joe sighed. "How can I put this delicately? I got fired."

42

"*What?* Come on. Don't kid with me about this."

I was searching his eyes, looking for the joke.

"Really," Joe said. He looked embarrassed. Honest to God. I'd never seen this look on his face before.

"I got axed. It's being chalked up to cutbacks due to the financial deficit. Naturally, freelancers are the first to go. Don't worry, Linds. I know things about homeland security very few people know. As soon as the word gets out, I'll get calls."

My mouth was dry. My heart was thudding almost audibly.

I make a cop's salary. It isn't bad money, but it wouldn't support our airy three-bedroom apartment on Lake Street, which Joe had rented when he was working for the government as deputy director of Homeland Security.

When he was making a ton.

"How much money do we have?"

"We'll be fine for quite a few months. I'll find a job before we run dry. We'll be fine, Lindsay," he said. "I'm not going to disappoint my two fabulous girls."

"We love you, Joe," I said.

Our little daughter started to cry.

Chapter 7

YUKI WAS NAKED, lying flat on her back on the bedroom carpet, panting, her pulse slowing after her heart's wild gallop over the hills during the morning's romp.

She turned her head and looked at her gorgeous and in every way fantastic lover.

"I'm sorry," she said. "I tried, but I was distracted. Thinking about other things."

Brady laughed.

He rolled toward her, put his arm across her body, and pulled her to him. "You're too much fun. I'm crazy about you, you know that?"

She knew. She was crazy about *him*. Was this just the best sex she'd ever had? Or were she and Brady traveling in lockstep toward the real deal?

She touched Brady's mouth and he kissed her palm. She swept his damp blond hair back from his eyes and kissed the side of his mouth.

He took her face in one hand and kissed her lips and she felt him start to get hard again. He grabbed her by the shoulders and shook her gently, saying, "I hate to do it, but I've got to leave."

Brady was Lieutenant Jackson Brady, head of the homicide squad, SFPD, Southern District. Yuki reached down and ran her fingers up his leg, stopping at the round pink scar on his thigh, where he took a bullet that nicked his femoral artery. It was sheer good fortune that he had gotten to the hospital in time.

She said, "Me, too. I've got court in an hour."

Yuki got up, pulled her robe from the bedpost, and started for the kitchen of the condo her mother had left her. In a way, Keiko Castellano still lived here. She often talked to Yuki, although not out loud. It was as though Keiko's voice, her opinions, her experiences were so embedded in Yuki's mind that Keiko was just always *there*.

Now her mother said, "You good girl, Yuki-eh, but foolish. Brady still married. Look what you doing."

"You shouldn't be watching," Yuki muttered as she picked pillows off the floor and threw them onto the bed.

"I can't help myself," Brady said. He zipped up his fly and reached for his shirt. "You're so very cute."

Yuki grinned, slapped his butt. He yelled, "Hey," grabbed her, lifted her into his arms, kissed her.

Then Brady said, "I wanted to tell you about this case."

"Start talking."

As Yuki made coffee, she mentally rebutted her mother's commentary, telling Keiko that, as she well knew, Brady was separated, and his soon-to-be-ex-wife lived in Miami, as far across the country as possible.

Brady was saying, "You've heard of Jeff Kennedy?"

Yuki poured coffee into Brady's mug.

"Basketball player."

"He's a 49er, sweetie. His girlfriend turned up dead in her car, couple miles from his house."

"Homicide? And you think this Niner is the doer?"

Brady laughed, shook his head. "You're a tough talker."

Yuki put her hands on her hips and grinned at him. "It's been said more than once that I'm one tough cookie."

Brady took a sip of coffee, put the mug in the sink, put his arms around Yuki, and said, "Kill 'em in court today, Cookie. I'll call you later."

He kissed the center part in her hair and went for the door.

Chapter 8

AT NINE THAT morning, Dr. Perry Judd walked through the swinging half door at the entrance to the homicide squad room and demanded the attention of a detective, saying, "I want to report a murder."

Rich Conklin had walked Dr. Judd back to Interview 2 and had been trying to get a straight story ever since.

Dr. Judd said that he taught English literature at UC Berkeley. He was fifty, had brown hair, a goatee, and small eyeglasses with round frames the size of quarters. His jacket and button-down shirt were blue, and he wore a pair of khakis with a pleated front.

He had seemed to be a solid citizen.

"I was going into Whole Foods on Fourth Street last night," Judd said. "There was a woman right in front of me and it just happened that I followed her into the store. She said hello to one of the cashiers. I got the feeling she was a regular there."

The professor then described the woman in extraordinary detail.

"She was blond, about two inches of black roots showing. She was about forty, a 'squishy' size ten, wore a white blouse with a ruffled neckline and a necklace. Green beads, glass ones."

Judd had gone on to say that the woman had been wearing sandals, her toenails painted baby blue.

Then the professor had gone completely off-road. He began quoting from obscure books, and although Conklin seriously tried to get the connection, the guy sounded psycho.

Conklin liked to let a witness lay out the whole story in one piece. That way he could shape and sharpen his follow-up questions and determine from the answers if the witness was telling the truth or talking crap.

Dr. Judd had stopped talking altogether and was

staring into the one-way glass behind Conklin's back.

Conklin said, "Dr. Judd. Please go on."

The professor snapped back to the present, then said to Conklin, "I was thinking about *The Stranger*. You know, by Camus. You've read it, of course."

Conklin had read *The Stranger* when he was in high school; as he remembered it, the story was about a murderer who had separated from his feelings. Not like a psychopath who didn't feel—this killer had feelings, but was detached from them. He watched himself commit senseless murders.

What could this 1940s novel by Camus possibly have to do with a woman shopper at Whole Foods?

"Dr. Judd," Conklin said. "You said there was a murder?"

"This woman I described went to the frozen-foods section, and I was going there myself to get a spinach soufflé. She reached into the case and pulled out a pint of chocolate chip ice cream. She was turning back when three muffled shots rang out. She was hit in the back first, then she whipped around and was hit twice more in the chest. She was dead by the time she hit the floor."

"Did you call the police?"

"No. I didn't think to do it until now."

"Did you see the shooter?"

"I did not."

"Were there any other witnesses?"

"I honestly don't know," Judd said.

Conklin was a patient guy, but there were eleven open case files on his desk, all of them pressing, and Perry Judd was a waste of time.

Conklin said to the professor, "You said you teach writing. You're also a creative writer, right?"

"I write poetry."

"Okay. So I have to ask you—no offense—but did this murder actually happen? Because we have had no reports of any kind of homicide at any supermarket last night."

"I thought I had said I dreamed it last night. It hasn't happened *yet*," said Perry Judd. "But it will happen. Have you read *Nausea* by Jean-Paul Sartre?"

Conklin tossed his pen onto the table, pushed back his chair, and stood up.

He said, "Thanks for your time, Professor. We'll call you if we need to talk with you again."

There was a knock on the mirrored glass.

Conklin got up, stepped outside the room.

MacKenzie Morales, the squad's extremely attractive summer intern, looked up at him and said, "Rich, could I talk to Dr. Judd for a minute? I think I can get to the bottom of this."

Chapter 9

MACKENZIE MORALES, A.K.A. Mackie, was twenty-six, the single mother of a three-year-old boy. More to the point, she was smart, going for her PhD in psychology. She was working in the homicide squad for no pay, but she was getting credit and doing research for her dissertation on criminal psychopathy.

Conklin was finished with Perry Judd, but what the hell. If Morales wanted a shot at making sense out of crap, okay—even though it was still a waste of time.

Morales took a chair next to Dr. Judd and introduced herself as Homicide's special assistant without saying she was answering phones and making Xerox copies. She shook Judd's hand.

"Do I know you?" Professor Judd asked Morales.

"Very doubtful. I was going through the hall-way," she said, pointing to the glass, "and I heard you mention Sartre's novel— "

"*Nausea.*"

"Oh, my God, I love that book," Morales said. "I'm a psych major, and the protagonist in *Nausea* is the very embodiment of depersonalization disorder, not that they called it that back then."

"Depersonalization. Exactly," said the professor. He seemed delighted. "Separation from self. That's what this dream was like. If it *was* a dream. The imagery was so vivid, it was as if I were having an out-of-body experience. I watched a woman die. I had no feelings about it. No horror. No fear. And yet I know that this dream is prescient, that the murder *will* happen."

Judd was hitting his stride now, saying intently to Morales, "Do you remember in *Nausea* when the protagonist says about himself, 'You plunge into stories without beginning or end: you'd make a terrible witness. But in compensation, one misses nothing, no improbability or story too tall to be believed in cafés'?"

"Are you saying this has happened before?"

"Oh, yes. But I never reported those dreams. Who would believe that I saw a future murder? But I had to report this one or go crazy. Because I think I've seen the victim before."

"Tell me about the victim," Morales said. "Do you know her name?"

"No. I think I've just seen her at Whole Foods."

Conklin sat back and listened for any changes in the tall story he had heard before. Dr. Judd told Mackie Morales about the woman with the blond hair with roots, the sandals, and the blue-painted toenails choosing a pint of chocolate chip ice cream before she was gunned down—at some time in the future.

"I heard the shots but I didn't wake up," said Judd. "This woman put her hand to her chest, then took it away and looked at the blood. She said, 'What?'

"And then her legs went out from under her and she slid down the door of the freezer, but she was already dead."

Morales said, "And do you have any idea why she was—I mean, why she will be shot?"

"No, and I don't think she saw the person who shot her."

Perry Judd sighed deeply, put his hand on Morales's arm, spoke to her as though they were alone together in the room.

"Miss Morales, this is what it is like for me, exactly what Sartre wrote in the voice of Antoine Roquentin: 'I *see* the future. It is there, poised over the street, hardly more dim than the present. What advantage will accrue from its realization?' You see? This is how it is for me."

Conklin was disgusted. This whole story was about Dr. Judd. He was a flaming narcissist, a diagnosis that didn't require a degree in psychology to make.

Conklin said, "What's the address of the store?"

Dr. Judd gave the address in SoMa, only a few blocks away from the Hall, definitely a case for Southern District—if the murder ever really happened, or would happen.

For the second time in ten minutes, Conklin thanked Dr. Judd and told him that if they needed to speak with him again, they'd be in touch.

"He's a hard-core nutcase, right?" Conklin said to Morales when Perry Judd had left the squad room.

"Yep. He's delusional. Could be he's crazy enough to kill someone, though."

Conklin thought Morales made a fair point. But if Judd was getting ready to kill someone, there was no way to stop him. You can't lock someone up for having a dream.

Chapter 10

MERCIFULLY, JOE AND the baby were both sleeping. In the same room. In the same bed. At the same time. It was unbelievable, but true.

I filled Martha's bowl with yummy kibble and brought in the morning paper from the hall.

The headline read: FAYE FARMER DEAD AT 27.

I didn't stop to make coffee, just spread the paper out over the kitchen counter. The shocking story had been written by my great friend Cindy Thomas, charter member of the Women's Murder Club, engaged to marry my partner, Rich Conklin, and a bulldog of a reporter.

Unrelenting tenacity can be an annoying trait in a friend, but it had made Cindy a successful crime reporter with a huge future. Her story on

Faye Farmer had shot past the second section of the paper and was on the front page above the fold.

Cindy had written, "Fashion designer Faye Farmer, 27, known for her red-carpet styling and must-have wear for the young and famous, was found dead in her car last night on 29th Street and Noe.

"Captain Warren Jacobi has told the *Chronicle* that Ms. Farmer had been the victim of a gunshot wound to the head. An autopsy has been scheduled for Tuesday."

It was almost impossible to believe that such a bright, vivacious young woman was dead, her promising life just . . . over. Had someone taken her life? Or had she killed herself?

I kept reading.

The article went on to say that Faye Farmer lived with football great Jeffrey Kennedy, who was not a suspect and was cooperating fully with the police.

I'd watched Jeff Kennedy many times from the stands at Candlestick Park. At twenty-five, he was already the NFL's best outside linebacker. His defensive skills and movie-star looks had made him an immediate fan favorite, and at a guaranteed thirteen million dollars a year, he was the league's fifth-highest earner.

Faye Farmer had been photographed with Kennedy frequently over the last couple of years and had been quoted as saying she was going to be married—"to someone." The way it sounded, she wanted to get married to Kennedy, but he wasn't at the until-death-do-us-part stage.

I was dying for more information. This was what's termed a suspicious death, and my mind just cannot rest until a puzzle is solved. Of course, from where I was sitting at the kitchen counter, I had no more information than anyone else who had read the *Chronicle*'s front page this morning.

I was just going to have to tamp down my curiosity and get over it.

I put down the paper, then dressed quickly and quietly. I leashed Martha and went down the stairs, thinking I'd start off slowly, see if I could run a half mile, melt off a little of the twenty-five pounds of baby fat I'd added to my 5-foot-10-inch frame. I'd always been a bit hippy. Now I was a bit hippo.

Not a good thing for a cop.

The sun was still coming up over the skyline when I locked the front door behind me. But as I was about to set out, my attention was caught by a woman who was sitting behind the wheel of a rental car parked at the curb. She spotted me, too, got out of the driver's seat, and called my name.

I had never met her, never wanted to.

And now she'd waylaid me.

There was no place to go. So I stood my ground.

Chapter 11

I DIDN'T KNOW June Freundorfer, but I knew who she was. My eyeballs got small and hard just looking at her in the flesh.

She wore a slim gray custom-tailored suit, had perfect wavy brown hair, and a smile as bright as if she soaked her teeth in Clorox. In brief, she was an attractive forty-five-year-old power babe and she had history with my husband.

Here's the history.

Agent Freundorfer had been Joe's partner at the FBI. She was promoted to the FBI's Washington field office about the same time Joe was hired as deputy director of Homeland Security, also in Washington, DC.

June still lived in DC and until recently, Joe had

been flying there regularly to see his government-agency client.

I hadn't known about June, but a few months ago, while I was pregnant with Julie, a photo of Joe and June appeared in the *Washington Post*'s society page. June was looking up at Joe with twinkling eyes, a flirty look, and they were both in evening wear.

Joe insisted that there was nothing to the photo, just a charity benefit he'd gone to under pressure. He'd caught a flight back to San Francisco that same evening.

Then June called Joe's cell phone and I picked up. I announced myself, asked a couple of pointed questions, and June admitted that she was involved with Joe, but that Joe really did love me.

I went bug-nuts.

Joe said that June was lying, that she was trying to make trouble for us out of jealousy, and I can honestly say she wasn't just trying, she succeeded.

I threw Joe out of the house and changed the locks. He slept in his car, which he parked outside the apartment, just about where June's car was parked now.

It took a while for me to believe in Joe again, but

I love him and I had to trust him. And I totally do.

But now, those old suspicions returned as the beautiful Ms. Freundorfer came toward me, carrying a little turquoise shopping bag from Tiffany.

Martha read my body language and stood at my feet with her head lowered and ears back, ready to spring.

"Lindsay? You are Lindsay, aren't you?"

"Joe isn't around, June. Did you call?"

"So I don't have to introduce myself. Joe always said you were smart. Anyway, I brought a gift for the baby," she said. "Did you have a boy or girl?"

"We have a daughter."

June smiled graciously and handed me the bag. And I took it because to keep my hands at my sides would have been childish. I even thanked her for the gift, a thank-you that was less than sincere and wouldn't fool anyone, especially an FBI agent.

June said, "What's the baby's name? I'd love to see her."

"It's not a good time, June."

It would never be a good time.

She said, "Oh. Well. Best of everything, Lindsay. Best to all of you."

She returned to her car and after she'd waved good-bye and her taillights had disappeared around the corner, I opened the turquoise bag and undid the white ribbon around the small box inside.

June had given Julie a sterling silver rattle.

Very nice.

I took the rattle, the wrappings, and the unopened card and dropped it all into the trash can on the corner. Then I went for a run with Martha.

I ran. I hurt everywhere, but still I ran. Three miles later, Martha and I were back at our front door. I was soaking wet, but I felt something like my old self. It was a beautiful morning. I was married to a wonderful man and I was the mother of a healthy baby girl.

June Freundorfer be damned.

Chapter 12

THE COURTROOM WAS so packed that members of the press were standing together like matchsticks at the back of the room. TruTV cameras rolled, and Yuki saw Cindy Thomas sitting four rows back on the aisle.

Cindy winked at Yuki, who smiled before turning to say, "Your Honor, the people call Mr. Graham Durden."

A tall black man in his late fifties entered the courtroom from the rear, looking straight ahead as he walked purposefully up the aisle and through the wooden gate to the witness box. He was sworn in, then took his seat.

Yuki greeted her witness and began with

questions that established his identity and his role in the case.

"Mr. Durden, what is your address?"

"Fifty-seven Lopez Avenue."

"Is Mr. Keith Herman your neighbor?"

"Yes. He lives directly across the street from me."

Yuki noticed that Durden's hands were shaking. It was understandable. The man was a witness against a killer. If Keith Herman got off, Graham Durden would still be living directly across the street from him.

"Mr. Durden, did anything unusual happen on the morning of March first last year?"

"Yes. I'll never forget it."

"Please tell the court about that morning."

"I had gone out to get the newspaper off the porch and I saw Mr. Herman carry his daughter's dead body out to his car. I could tell that Lily was dead. He put her into the backseat and drove away."

There was a gasp in the gallery, a satisfying intake of breath, and the jury appeared absolutely gripped by what they had heard.

"Did you call the police?"

"Yes, I did."

"Did the police question the defendant because of your phone call?"

"Yes. The day after I called nine-one-one, I was asked to come into the station for a lineup. I positively identified the man who put the body of Lily Herman into his car."

"Do you see that man here today?"

Durden said he did, and at Yuki's request he pointed to the man sitting next to John Kinsela at the defense table.

"How well do you know Mr. Herman?" she asked.

"I've known him for about five years. I knew Lily since she was three. She likes my dog, Poppy. They used to play on my lawn. I know the man's car, too. Lexus. A 2011 four-door sedan."

"So you are absolutely sure that the man you saw on the day in question, the man putting Lily Herman into the back of the Lexus, was the defendant, Keith Herman?"

"Yes. I'm sure."

"Thank you, Mr. Durden. I have no further questions."

Yuki returned to her seat at the prosecution

table. There was some foot shuffling in the gallery, and people coughed on both sides of the aisle.

Judge Nussbaum scratched his nose, made a note on his laptop, then said, "Mr. Kinsela, your witness."

Chapter 13

JOHN KINSELA STOOD. He didn't snort or mug for the jury. In fact, he looked quite grave as he faced the witness.

"Mr. Durden, have you ever testified in court before?"

"No, sir."

"It's a little nerve-racking, isn't it?"

Yuki thought it was a question meant to rattle the witness, but it allowed the jury to see defense counsel as sympathetic, treating the witness with respect. If she objected, she could irritate the jury.

"I'm feeling fine," said Graham Durden. He folded his hands in front of him.

"Good. Now, Mr. Durden, you swore to tell

the truth, and yet in truth, you weren't a hundred percent sure that the man you saw on March first was Mr. Herman, isn't that right?"

"It was Mr. Herman. I know Mr. Herman."

"You told the police—and I'm reading from the transcript of your phone call to nine-one-one— 'I'm ninety percent sure that the man getting into the car was Keith Herman.'"

"I said that, but it was a figure of speech. It was definitely him. And Keith Herman was carrying Lily out to the car. Put her body into the backseat."

"What kind of car was that again, Mr. Durden?"

"A late-model Lexus sedan, 2011."

"And what color was the car?"

"Black."

"Now, you told the police it was a dark-colored Lexus, isn't that correct?"

"Black is dark. I should know."

There was a smattering of nervous laughter in the gallery. Yuki wasn't concerned. Graham Durden was a high school principal. He was about as credible a witness as there was. He had described the car as "dark." And yes, black was dark. He had told the police he was 90 percent sure he saw Herman. He was being careful.

"So just to be sure we're both on the same page," Kinsela said, turning to give the jury a good long look at the gravity of his expression. "You saw Mr. Herman put his daughter into a dark Lexus sedan on the street outside his house."

"That's right."

"Did you get the license plate number?"

"That car is always parked right there. I *know* the car."

"Yes or no: did you get the license plate number of that dark Lexus, Mr. Durden?"

"No."

"Now, as to the body of the girl you say you saw the defendant bring out to the car: did you one hundred percent identify that body as Lily Herman's?"

"One hundred percent," Durden said angrily. "One hundred percent."

"And how do you know she was dead?" Kinsela asked mildly.

"Her head was hanging back. She was limp."

"Could she have been asleep? Did you feel her pulse?"

"What?"

Yuki said from her seat, "Your Honor, counsel is badgering the witness."

Judge Nussbaum said, "Overruled. Mr. Kinsela, pick one question and ask it again."

Chapter 14

YUKI FELT TREMORS as the ground shifted beneath the witness box. Graham Durden darted a look in her direction, and she could see from the tight set of his lips that he was angry.

Durden didn't like to have his integrity questioned. And Kinsela was working him over with the finesse of a fishmonger wielding a boning knife. Yuki had rehearsed with Durden, warned him that Kinsela would try to impeach his testimony. Durden had assured her that he felt confident and steady, saying repeatedly, "I know what I saw."

Kinsela said, "Okay, Your Honor. I apologize for running on like that. Mr. Durden, how did you know that the child was dead?"

"She looked dead."

"She *looked* dead. And how far were you from the man who put the child into a dark sedan?"

"I saw them from my front steps. Fifty yards."

"Fifty yards." Kinsela paused to let the jury think about fifty yards. A hundred and fifty feet. Kind of far away. Then he said, "And did you have an unobstructed view, Mr. Durden?"

"Yes."

Kinsela walked to an easel, yanked down a piece of paper, and revealed an aerial photograph of Lopez Avenue between Sotelo and Castenada. The easel was positioned so that both the jury and the witness could see the image clearly.

Kinsela said to Durden, "Is this a photograph of your street?"

"Yes."

"And this house marked A—is this your house?"

"It is."

"This house marked B. It's Mr. Herman's house, isn't it?"

"Yes."

"What do you see between your house and Mr. Herman's house?"

"The street."

"Yes, we all see the street. And do you see trees? A line of trees on both sides of the street?"

"I could see Keith Herman plainly, carrying his daughter in his arms, putting her into the backseat of his Lexus—"

"You saw a man putting a girl into which side of the car, Mr. Durden? The side of the car facing your house? Or did he open the door on the side closest to the Herman house, so that the car was between you and the action you've described?"

"I saw Keith Herman carrying Lily."

"Please answer the question, Mr. Durden."

"He put her into the car on the side nearest his house."

"Okay. Thank you. Now, after that . . . when the man you saw that morning got into the driver's side of the car, his back was to you, wasn't it, sir? How could you possibly tell that it was Keith Herman, and not another man of average height and build, getting into a dark sedan?"

Kinsela paced in the well, head down as he continued with his battery of questions.

"Isn't it possible, sir, that you saw a car like Mr. Herman's car parked in front of Mr. Herman's house, and from that you drew an understandable conclusion that the man was Mr. Herman? Isn't it possible that you actually saw the *kidnapper* taking the child, not Mr. Herman?"

"Your Honor, I object to Mr. Kinsela bombarding the witness with questions. Again, if there is a real question in there, what is it?"

"Sustained. Please phrase *one* question, Mr. Kinsela. That's a warning. Don't do this again, or you will be fined."

"Sorry, Judge. I got carried away. Mr. Durden, given the distance, the visual obstacles, and that there are over sixty thousand dark Lexus sedans in San Francisco, could you have been mistaken when you stated that Keith Herman brought his daughter out to the car parked across the street from your house?"

"I saw Keith Herman," Durden said doggedly. "I saw him. I saw him one hundred percent."

"I have no further questions for this witness," Kinsela said, turning his back on Graham Durden.

Judge Nussbaum said, "Ms. Castellano?"

Yuki stood.

"Mr. Herman, you're wearing glasses. Were you wearing them on the morning of March first?"

"Yes, I was."

"And what is your vision when you're wearing your glasses?"

"Twenty-twenty."

"Have you ever been diagnosed with a mental disorder?"

"No. Never."

"Thank you. That's all I have, Your Honor."

"The witness may step down," said the judge.

Chapter 15

YUKI ELBOWED HER way out of the courtroom, smiled at the members of the press who were jamming the hallway, and said, "Hi, Georgia. Yeah, thanks. All's well, Lou," then, as John Kinsela and his client stood in the hall for an impromptu interview, Yuki headed for the fire stairs with Cindy Thomas on her heels.

"Aren't *you* popular?" Cindy said, going through the door behind Yuki.

"Sooo popular," Yuki said, her voice ringing in the cement-lined stairwell. "By the way, Cindy, you'd better behave yourself. Every word I say to you is off the record."

"You think I don't know that?"

"Yeah," Yuki said. "You've been known to

forget. So I'm saying it loud and clear. Don't mess with me."

"When did I ever mess with you? When?"

The door on the ground floor, behind the back wall of the grand lobby, swung out into the daylight under the flat of Yuki's palm and she and her blond-haired, determined friend filed out onto Harriet Street.

"Where to?" Cindy asked, catching up with Yuki.

Fringale was a cute, cozy bistro just a few blocks from the Hall of Justice, a little slice of France on the corner of 4th and Freelon Streets.

When Yuki walked through the door into the little place with its eggshell-colored walls, the aroma of rosemary and thyme filling the air, she felt the stress of the trial fade—all but the hard stone of worry in the part of her skull right between her eyes.

Could she really convict Keith Herman?

Had she forgotten what kind of lawyer John Kinsela was? Kinsela had *eviscerated* Red Dog Parisi.

The two women ordered salads as entrées, and when the waiter left the table, Yuki asked, "How bad did he hurt us?"

"You talking about how Kinsela gored your witness?"

"'Gored' him? It was that bad, huh?"

"Actually, Yuki, I think it made Kinsela look like a bully and a dirtbag. But did it discredit Durden? Yeah, I think so. Depends on what else you have. I take it Lynnette Lagrande is going to put you over the top."

The waiter placed a salad in front of each of them: a beautiful dish of frisée with bacon dressing, pine nuts, and a poached egg. Yuki broke the yolk with her fork, speared a leaf of lettuce, chewed it, and sipped her water.

"I feel good about my case. It's solid. But let's face it, John Kinsela has about twenty years of criminal law to my three."

"Lay out your case for me," Cindy said.

Yuki told Cindy the details of her case in the rapid, machine-gun style she was known for. She talked about the bruises on the child, and the fact that Jennifer Herman had confided in a friend, saying that her husband might harm her. She cited Keith Herman's paramour, Lynnette Lagrande, who not only refuted Herman's alibi for the time of Jennifer Herman's murder but would also testify to and document the fact that Keith Herman wanted out of his marriage.

"It's a good case," Cindy said. "What does Red Dog say?"

"He says that I've got Herman nailed on the evidence, and that he has total faith in me," said Yuki.

She and Cindy both nodded, Yuki wishing that she weren't remembering cases she'd lost.

"It's always about life and death," Yuki said.

"I have faith in you," said Cindy. "You can do this."

Yuki saw doubt in her good friend's eyes.

Chapter 16

CLAIRE WASHBURN DIDN'T mind putting on a dog and pony show as long as nobody sneezed or puked on the body. A high-profile case like this one would be scrutinized for mistakes, and the last thing she wanted was to have to explain to the court how random DNA got on the victim.

There was a bark of laughter outside the frosted glass of her office door. Claire sighed once, forwarded her phone calls to the front desk, then went to the conference room.

The twelve people who were waiting for her turned as one.

Claire couldn't stop herself from laughing. To a man, and to a woman, her visitors were dressed in baby-yellow paper surgical scrubs and Tyvek gowns. Most hilarious of all was Rich Conklin, Mr. September in the 2011 Law Enforcement Officers Beefsteak Calendar.

Great big handsome man, outfitted like a hospital kitchen worker.

Claire said, "Good morning, Easter chicks," and she laughed again, this time joined by the group of cops, junior techs from the crime scene unit, and law school grads from the DA's office who were getting on-the-job education this morning.

She caught her breath and said, "If we've never met, I'm Dr. Washburn, chief medical examiner, and before I begin this morning's autopsy, please introduce yourselves."

Claire had everyone's attention, and when the introductions were concluded, she began a condensed lecture on the purpose of an autopsy—to discover the cause and manner of death.

"You'll see that the victim will be wearing what she had on when she was recovered from the scene. She'll have bags on her hands to preserve any DNA she may have scraped from a possible attacker. She will have a complete external exam, including total body X-rays, before we do an internal exam, which I'll conduct.

"If Ms. Farmer's death is determined to be a homicide— not saying it *was* a homicide, but if the evidence leads to an indictment—the defense may try to prove that our evidence was contaminated, that we're a bunch of fumble-fingered idiots. Remember O.J.? Protecting the integrity of this postmortem is critical to catching and holding a bad guy. Because of lousy forensics, there are innocent people in jail for crimes they never committed and murderers walking the streets.

"To the dead, we owe respect. To the living, we owe the truth. Nothing less, nothing more, no matter where the evidence leads us.

"House rules: keep your prophylactic outerwear in place. Masks must be worn in the surgery and kept on. Understand? If you forgot to turn off your cell phone, do it now. Save your questions until I ask for them. When I'm done, I'll memorialize my findings for the record. Everything you see or hear from now on is highly confidential and leaks will not be tolerated.

"Are there any questions?

"All right, then. If we're all clear on the house rules . . ." Claire turned to her assistant, the fetching Bunny Ellis, her hair done up to look like mouse ears, reverent eyes turned toward her boss.

"Bunny, will you please wheel Ms. Farmer into the autopsy suite? Everyone else, follow me."

Chapter 17

CLAIRE HIP-BUTTED THE swinging door and entered the autopsy suite. The cops and junior-grade personnel behind her were excited, speaking in whispers that seemed to cut loose, rise in volume, loop around her, then die down to a hush again.

Conklin had the summer intern under his wing. Mackie Morales seemed bright and eager and maybe a little bit too much into Richie—the way she looked at him, the way he was a little puffed up, explaining things to her. Cindy would not be happy if she saw this.

And not too much escaped Cindy.

Claire laughed quietly but didn't say anything to Conklin. She went to the far corner of the room and pushed the button that turned on the video camera. The light on the camera didn't go on. She punched it a couple of times and still the little red eye was dark.

That was weird. The camera had been fine yesterday.

She pressed the intercom button, said, "Ryan, check the video setup, please."

"Yes, ma'am. It was unplugged. It's on now."

"Why was it unplugged?"

"I don't know. I just found it this way."

Bunny entered the room from the door that led to the morgue. She signaled to Claire as if to say, I need to talk to you.

"What's the holdup, Bunny?"

"I need to see you for a second, Doctor."

Claire sighed, crossed the room, and followed Bunny to the morgue, a refrigerated room lined with stacks of stainless steel drawers, each designed to hold a body. Some of Claire's patients had recently checked in. Some had been waiting for months for someone to ID them before they were buried as nameless corpses.

"What is it, Bunny?"

The girl's blue eyes were shifting and her lips

were trembling. Claire didn't get it. What the hell?

"I can't find her," Bunny said.

"What are you talking about?"

"Faye Farmer," Bunny said. "She's gone."

"What's her drawer number?" Claire asked, exasperated. She went to the whiteboard, ran her finger down the list.

"Twelve," said Bunny Ellis.

Claire turned away from the whiteboard, crossed to the wall of drawers, pulled the handle of number 12. The drawer slid out smoothly, bringing the corpse into view. There was a tag tied to the big toe. Claire saw instantly that there had been a screwup. Faye Farmer was not and had never been a seventy-year-old black man.

She said, "Who mixed up the bodies? What drawer is this man supposed to be in?"

"Seventeen," said Bunny. "Dr. Washburn, I already checked."

Claire reached down, opened drawer number 17. It was empty. She started pulling out drawers, slamming them closed, each body in its assigned box except for the black John Doe in Faye Farmer's drawer.

Bunny was crying now. She was a competent young woman and liked to do a good job.

"Stop that," Claire snapped. "Think. Did you see Ms. Farmer's body after she was checked in yesterday?"

"Not after I logged her in. She's supposed to be in twelve."

"Who moved John Doe one thirty-two out of box seventeen?"

Bunny shrugged miserably. "Not me."

The body couldn't have left the premises.

That was impossible.

Chapter 18

CLAIRE WONDERED WHAT she was supposed to tell the gang of junior law enforcement personnel. *We've been robbed?* She returned to the autopsy suite, clapped her hands, and said, "People, we've encountered a problem that I need to address right away. Sorry about this. We'll get back to you as soon as we can reschedule."

Conklin stood like a tree in a stream that flowed around him as grumbling law enforcement trainees shed their outerwear and filed out. He said to Claire, "What's going on?"

"Ms. Farmer's body has been misplaced. I want to make a joke about how she didn't like the accommodations, Richie, but there is nothing funny about this. If we don't find her in three minutes, I'm going to have a cerebral hemorrhage."

"Tell me what you know, from the beginning."

"The beginning: Faye Farmer was logged in last night at eight seventeen p.m. and stowed in drawer twelve. We've got double records and triple logs on that. When I left last night, Faye was tucked in. I came in this morning, ready to do the post, as you know, and overnight the body vacated the morgue.

"She's a one-hundred-and-thirty-five-pound dead woman. I can't see her anywhere. She's totally missing."

"Okay. Calm down, Claire. She didn't walk out of here, did she? She was positively dead?"

There *had* been a few instances in which people who appeared to be dead had regained consciousness after a stunning head injury or after having been in a coma. And a few of them had sat up on an autopsy table and walked out. Claire had no personal knowledge of these cases, but there were stories. This couldn't be one of them. Faye Farmer had a bullet through her head. Through and through.

It was cool inside the morgue, and yet Claire was sweating through her clothes and her lab coat.

Sweat seemed to be pooling in her shoes. She had never lost a body before. This was unimaginable.

"She was dead, Rich. Dead dead. Ten minutes ago I was worried about someone sneezing on her. Now, at the very least, we've lost chain of custody, which is plenty bad enough. Worst case is, we don't recover the woman's body and we never learn what killed her."

"Okay, okay, Claire. We'll find her."

Morales and four kids from the crime lab strip-searched every part of the medical examiner's office—the morgue, the back rooms, the supply closet, the administration bull pen.

Meanwhile, Claire and Conklin took the AV tech, Ryan Perles, into Claire's office, shut the door, and questioned him.

"I came in at about eight this morning," Perles said. He looked smug, Claire thought. Or as though he liked the attention, which he didn't normally get.

"I had a lot of things to do when I got in and I was busy doing them when Dr. Washburn paged me. I looked and saw that the cord to the video system was unplugged from the battery backup. When I left last night, it was plugged in and A-OK."

"Let's see the disk from last night," Conklin said.

The young tech opened the CD drawer. It was empty.

Claire put her hand on the back of a chair to steady herself. The conclusion was inescapable. Whoever took Faye Farmer's body had access to Claire's lab; most likely it had been someone who worked for her.

She could already visualize a video of Faye Farmer in some obscene pose in a car or a Dumpster posted on YouTube, going viral.

"Ryan, you came in this morning through the side door?" Claire asked him.

"Yes. Same as always."

"It was locked?"

"Yes ma'am. Of course it was locked."

"You're sure?"

"Do you mind if I ask what's wrong?"

"Ryan, let's take this conversation upstairs," Conklin said. "Sometimes a change of scene can help a person remember something he didn't know he forgot."

BOOK II

OFF THE BENCH

Chapter 19

IT HAD BEEN a long, loud, fussy night, but Julie had finally worn herself out and gone to sleep on Joe's chest. His clock projected the time on the ceiling in bright red digits. It was 4:54. I reorganized my blanket and settled in for what I hoped would be maybe forty-five minutes of deep sleep.

But Joe was wide awake. He said, "Let's talk about this again, Linds. I think in this case I know what's best for you better than you do."

I yawned, fluffed my pillow.

"I can't go back yet, Joe. I'm only going to be thinking about you and Julie, anyway."

"In case you've forgotten, I'm the oldest of seven. I have burped and changed a lot of nephews and nieces, and while it might hurt your feelings,

I'm good with Julie. I can take fine care of her."

"Okay."

"Okay what?"

"Okay, yes. I'll go back to work."

"Wait."

"What am I waiting for?"

"I had some persuasive arguments I haven't used yet."

I started laughing. "I'm persuaded. You did a good job, Joe."

"But you said you didn't want to go back to work."

"You won, sweetie. Don't be a spoilsport."

He laughed and I fell asleep without saying another word. I woke up at seven, snuck out of bed, and showered. After that, I felt around in the dark for my blue blazer; I found it and my trousers in plastic wrap on hangers in the closet.

Since my trousers seemed to have shrunk, I picked out a big shirt—one with pink pinstripes — and hung it out over my waistband, which I would have to do until I was a size 10 again.

Get used to it, everyone.

I buckled on my shoulder holster, got my gun out of the nightstand, then hung the chain holding my badge around my neck.

I air-kissed Joe and Julie so that neither of them woke up, carried my shoes out to the hallway, and put them on as Martha did a happy dance.

I took my dog for a short walk. I mean *short*. As soon as she did what she needed to do, I took her back home, then went back out to the street and looked for my car.

Did I feel guilty leaving Julie?

You bet I did. I thought of my baby girl, and it was like an umbilical bungee cord was connecting us, pulling me back toward home.

But I had gotten a compelling, nearly irresistible call from my former partner, Warren Jacobi, now chief of police. He had said, "I'm not saying drop-kick the baby and come in right away. It's like this. Brady is short-staffed and overwhelmed. He needs your help."

My old blue Explorer was parked a half block down from our apartment. I got in, turned the key in the ignition, and the engine started right up, almost as if it had been waiting for me.

I pulled out onto Lake Street and the car shot away from the curb, tires screeching. I could not wait to get to the Hall.

Chapter 20

BRADY'S GLASS-WALLED OFFICE is about the size and shape of a votive candleholder. He was sitting at his desk, dwarfing it with his bulk, his head bowed over an open file, phone clapped to his ear.

I no longer felt steamed that this once was my office when I was squad lieutenant. I had wanted to work hands-on, on the street, and I wanted that badly enough to ask for a demotion to sergeant. I rarely regretted that decision.

I knocked on the glass door and Brady looked up, said into the phone, "I'll call you later." He hung up, got to his feet, reached across the desk, and shook my hand.

"Good to have you back, Boxer. You feel okay?

Want desk work for a couple of weeks? Kind of ease back into things?"

"I'm good, Lieutenant. I've been running. Doing tai chi. I'm good."

He nodded, said, "Sit down. I think the chief told you—Peters asked for time off. Oxner transferred to Vice, so I'm down a team. I've been working with Conklin but he needs a real partner. I have to manage the bullshit going on around here."

"Sure. I understand."

As Brady sat back down and began patting down his desk, I thought about how much we'd been through since he joined the squad a year and a half ago. His first day, he told me to my face that I was nowhere on my current case. That I was sucking swamp water. He wasn't running for office, that's for sure, and I didn't like him.

About a week after that, we were bringing down a freaking serial psycho killer together. Bombs went off and Brady took a stance in front of a moving car and unloaded his gun.

Six months ago—another killer, a different day—Brady took two bullets during another act of profound bravery.

Jackson Brady didn't give good eye contact.

He didn't sugarcoat anything. I didn't love his management style. But I did respect him.

He was a good cop.

He found the file he was looking for and started filling me in on the death of Faye Farmer, former *Project Runway* winner and late, great designer to the stars.

"Take a look," Brady said. He handed me a sheaf of crime-scene photos of the victim in the driver's seat of a late-model Audi, slumped against the car window. Close-ups of the gunshot wound made it look to me like the shot had been delivered at close range.

Brady said, "You and Conklin are on this case. He'll bring you up to speed."

"Sure thing."

"I wish it was a sure thing," said Brady. "Conklin will tell you. The DB has vanished from the morgue."

"Vanished how?"

"Vanished—poof," Brady said. "The case of the purloined corpse. The media is going to go nuts when they find out. Claire says doors were opened with keys. Surveillance disk was jacked. It had to be an inside job, so talk to her. We find out why her body went poof, we've got a lead into who killed her. It goes without saying I want to be kept posted."

Brady was already back on the phone before I left his office to find my partner.

Chapter 21

MARIA ORTEGA WAS a naturalized American citizen, but she looked scared, as if Immigration were waiting to deport her when she stepped off the witness stand. Yuki knew that Ortega was timid, but even if Kinsela crushed her on cross, her story would be on the record and firmly in the jurors' minds.

Yuki smiled at the young woman in the demure navy-blue dress and walked toward the witness box.

"How are you today, Ms. Ortega?"

"Fine," she said in a near whisper. "Thank you."

"Will you tell us where you worked in December of last year?"

"I work for Mr. and Mrs. Sean Murphy on Lopez Avenue."

"And what did you do for the Murphys?"

"I clean their house every day."

"And is the Murphy house near the house where Keith Herman lived with his family?"

"Yes. They live three houses away."

"Okay. Mr. Kinsela, you mind if I borrow your overhead view of Lopez Avenue?"

"Since you're unprepared," Kinsela said.

"Thank you, Counselor," Yuki said, smiling for the jury. She pointed to the house three doors north of the Herman house. "Ms. Ortega, is this the Murphy house?"

"Yes."

"So can you tell us about a certain conversation you had there with Lily Herman? And please speak loud enough for the jury to hear you."

"I was sweeping the walk and Lily was riding her bike on the sidewalk. She stopped to say hello."

"What made this conversation memorable to you?"

Ortega wrung her hands. "Lily looked like she had been crying. She got off her bike and it fall to the ground. She ran to me for comfort. Into my arms."

"Please go on, Ms. Ortega."

"I hugged her and she started to cry some more.

She said her father shook her. She pulled up her sweater. She showed me bruises on her arms," Ortega said. "They look like they were from fingers. Squeezing hard."

"She had these bruises on both arms?"

"Yes. And on her neck. I saw marks."

Yuki counted to ten, letting Ortega's words soak into the room before she spoke again.

"And did you ask Lily about these marks?"

"Oh, yes."

"And what did Lily say?"

The witness followed Yuki with her eyes, as if Yuki were a clock and Maria was desperate to know the time.

"Lily told me that her father grab her. And that he shake her. And that he tell her he would like to kill her."

"Objection, Your Honor. This is hearsay and it is prejudicial. I move that the testimony be struck and the jury be instructed to disregard it."

Nussbaum said, "I'm still the judge, Mr. Kinsela. Both you and Ms. Castellano come here so that we can have a quiet chat."

Yuki and Kinsela crossed to the bench and Yuki said, "Your Honor, the witness reported this incident to the police on the day Lily spoke to her. It's in the police report. Opposing counsel knows this and the sole purpose of his objection is to intimidate the witness."

"No more shenanigans, Mr. Kinsela. Ms. Castellano, continue with your direct."

Yuki went back to the witness and asked Maria Ortega if she had called the police to report the incident. Ortega said she had. Yuki asked her the name of the police officer and she said, "Officer Joseph Sorbera."

"When Officer Sorbera came to the Murphy house in response to your call, what happened?"

"I talked to him for a minute, then Mr. Murphy told the officer that I was confused. That I was . . . 'hysterical.'"

"What happened after that?"

"They fire me," she said.

"Did they give you a reason?"

"I not supposed to make Mr. Herman mad."

Yuki said, "Were the Murphys afraid of Mr. Herman?"

Kinsela said, "Objection. Leading the witness and also inappropriate as hell."

"Sustained."

Yuki said, "I withdraw the question. Ms. Ortega, did you ever talk to Lily again?"

Ortega burst into tears. Yuki handed the young woman a tissue, and after a moment, asked her if she could continue.

Ortega nodded and regained her fragile composure. She said, "I never saw her again." She said it more strongly the second time. "I never saw her *again*."

"Thank you. Your witness," Yuki said to Kinsela.

Kinsela had turned his back on the witness and was talking behind his hand into his client's ear.

"I have nothing for Ms. Ortega," Kinsela said over his shoulder.

Yuki felt a rush of elation. Kinsela knew he wouldn't be able to shift Maria's testimony, so he put on a show to say she was unimportant. She was sure Maria's testimony had moved the jury.

Point to the prosecution. She was ready when Nussbaum said, "Ms. Castellano, please call your next witness."

Chapter 22

YUKI CALLED PATROLMAN Joseph Sorbera, the cop who responded to Maria Ortega's call regarding Lily. Sorbera was a solid guy, had been on the job for fifteen years, and Yuki knew he would be a very credible witness.

Sorbera told the jury about his brief interview with Maria Ortega, who had told him about the bruises on Lily Herman's arms and neck. He also verified that Sean Murphy, Ortega's employer, did tell him that Ortega had what he referred to as post-traumatic stress disorder from an attack when she was a teen—and that she couldn't be believed.

"And then what did you do, Officer?"

"I went to the home of Keith Herman."

"Did you speak with Mr. Herman?"

"No. He wasn't there. I spoke with Jennifer Herman, his wife."

"And what did she tell you about the reported incident?"

"She said that her husband yelled at the child for breaking a glass, saying she could have hurt herself, but that he hadn't touched her."

"Did you ask to talk to Lily?"

"Yes. Mrs. Herman brought the little girl to the door. She said that she hadn't been hurt and that she didn't know what Ms. Ortega was referring to."

"How did these two people seem to you, Officer Sorbera?"

"They both seemed scared out of their freaking minds."

"What did you do next?" Yuki asked.

"I gave Mrs. Herman my card. And I told her that if she remembered anything, or wanted to talk to me for any reason, she should call me."

"Did you report the incident to Family and Children Services?"

"Yes. But without corroboration from the child or the wife, they considered the incident closed."

Yuki said, "Did you consider the incident closed?"

"Pretty much," Sorbera said. "I didn't hear from Mrs. Herman, but when the bags of human remains were identified as her body and the child was reported missing, I went to my captain and told him about the incident."

"Thanks, Officer. I'm done, Your Honor."

When Kinsela had no questions for Sorbera, Yuki called her next witness to the stand.

Chapter 23

GARY GOODFRIEND WORE a fringed buckskin jacket, distressed jeans, and a plaid shirt. He swaggered as he came up the aisle, then walked through the gate as though he were bellying up to a bar.

Yuki took a sip from her water bottle and watched as Goodfriend was sworn in. The man was cocky. He had an ego. But he had also come forward and volunteered to testify for the prosecution.

He was an uncontrollable yet important witness, and Yuki had decided to take a chance on him.

When he was seated, she greeted him and asked him about his business.

"I'm an FFL. A licensed gun dealer. I have a store over in Castro Valley."

"Do you know the defendant?"

"I met him at a Calgun firearms show. I had a booth there. I talked to him for about ten, fifteen minutes."

"Did you sell him a gun?"

"Yes. I sold him a Beretta Px4 Storm. It's an exceptional weapon. Mr. Herman had a CCW and he paid cash."

"Can you tell us what CCW stands for?"

"Carrying a concealed weapon—a permit."

"Did you sell more than one gun at the gun show?"

"About fifteen guns that day. Another dozen the following day."

"And what was it about Mr. Herman that made him stand out in your mind?"

"He was talking to another customer while I rang up a sale. Something he said just stayed in my mind."

"And what was the nature of that conversation?"

"Two guys shooting the bull about guns. What they owned. What they liked. What they liked to shoot at."

"And what did Mr. Herman like to shoot at?"

"Mr. Herman told the other guy that he had a rat problem."

"Do you know the name of the other guy?"

"No, I didn't sell him a gun. I never saw him before or since."

"So you overheard Mr. Herman say he had a rat problem. What did the other guy say to that?"

"He said, 'Rat problem? You mean like a snitch?' And Herman over there said, 'No, a rug *rat* problem.'"

"What did you take 'rug rat' to mean?"

"A rug rat is a kid. A child. At the time, I thought he was just, you know, joking, but when I heard about his wife turning up dead and his kid going missing, I remembered what he said and it got me worried."

"Did you call the police?"

"Yes."

Yuki showed the police report to the judge and to Kinsela, then handed it to the clerk along with the sales receipt for the gun. These items were entered into evidence.

Then she thanked Gary Goodfriend and turned him over to the defense for cross-examination.

Chapter 24

JOHN KINSELA GOT to his feet behind the prosecution table and stayed there. He looked bored as he questioned Yuki's witness from across the room.

"Mr. Goodfriend, you say you sold thirty guns, more or less, at the gun show that weekend. Is that right?"

"Yes. More or less."

"And presumably you talked to more than those thirty people who bought guns from you."

"Oh, sure. I talked to hundreds of people."

"But you've told us that you remember Mr. Herman distinctly two years later. Is that right?"

"He's a memorable person."

"Memorable because he said he had a rug rat problem. Is that correct?"

"Yes, it is."

"And as I understand it, you took that to mean that he was buying a gun to kill a child?"

"You could take it to mean that."

"Seriously? But you didn't notify the police at that time, did you?"

"No. It just sounded like bull. Creepy bull, but bull."

"Did the defendant also tell you directly that he had a rug rat problem?"

"Nope."

"Would it surprise you to hear that, in fact, Mr. Herman's house did have rodents? And that he hired an exterminator?"

"If you say so, I believe you."

"Thanks. Now, apart from the overheard conversation, and whatever you two said during the gun transaction, did you have any conversations with the defendant at any other time?"

"Nope."

"So apart from the joke he made with this 'other guy,' you had no additional reason to believe that Mr. Herman meant to harm his daughter."

"No. Not really."

"That's all, Mr. Goodfriend. Thanks for your testimony."

Goodfriend leaned forward and addressed Kinsela's back. "Just his reputation as a criminal defense lawyer who is said to eliminate prosecution witnesses. Which means I'm putting my life on the line here."

Kinsela spun around to face the judge. His face was red and he was clearly surprised by Goodfriend's postscript.

"Your Honor, move to strike. The witness's remark is hearsay on its face and highly prejudicial."

Yuki was ready with a response.

"Your Honor, Mr. Goodfriend answered Mr. Kinsela's question and now he's objecting to the witness's answer."

"He offered his opinion on my client's character, which was *not* asked for," said Kinsela.

"All right, all right. Mr. Kinsela, before I instruct the jury, do you have any other questions for Mr. Goodfriend?"

"No, Your Honor."

The judge told the clerk to strike Goodfriend's last comment from the record. Then he instructed the jury that the witness's characterization of

117

Mr. Herman and his further opinion that his life was in danger were not evidence and that the jurors were not to consider it during their deliberations.

Yuki controlled herself, but she was elated. Nicky Gaines nudged her. He was grinning like a jack-o'-lantern. Another point for the prosecution. Hey: Team Yuki was on a roll.

Chapter 25

I LEFT BRADY'S office and crossed the fluorescent-lit, twenty-by-thirty-foot bull pen/obstacle course, getting hugs and high fives from cops I'd known for a long time. At the front of the room were two gray metal desks butted head-to-head. One of those desks was mine. The other belonged to my partner.

A cute young woman with dark wavy hair, wearing a white T-shirt and tight jeans, was sitting in my chair. She was in deep conversation with Conklin, who got to his feet when he saw me.

"Boxer, *hey*. Good to see you."

He gave me a gender-neutral hug, but a good one, and then said, "Meet Mackie Morales, our summer intern. Mackie, my partner, Sergeant Lindsay Boxer."

Morales got out of my chair and reached out to shake my hand. She said she'd heard so much about me, and then she told Conklin she'd be in the file room.

He said, "Wait, Mackie. I'm going to bring the sergeant up to speed on the Faye Farmer case. Stick around for that."

"Sure," I said. "Stay."

It's rare to meet someone you like immediately, but I felt good about Mackie Morales. She had an open smile, a good handshake, and apparently Conklin approved of her.

"Thanks," she said. She pulled a spare chair up to our desks, and I asked Conklin what he had on Faye Farmer.

"I was just on my way to notify her parents. Ask them about my list of her friends, her devotees, and her detractors," Conklin said. "CSIU is down in the ME's office now, going over the premises for trace after the body went missing."

"The *Chronicle* just broke the story online," Morales told me. "We've got phone calls, tweets, e-mail, and our website is swamped."

Conklin said, "While Mackie runs down the phone leads—"

He never got to finish his sentence. Brady came out of his office, strode toward us, and then loomed over our desks. He said to Conklin, "Remember that weirdo professor, dreamed about a murder?"

"Dr. Perry Judd," said Morales.

"The woman he described yesterday was gunned down in Whole Foods an hour ago. Same woman, down to the greenbead necklace and the roots growing out of her blond hair. Conklin, you and Boxer check out the scene. Then go pick up the professor. Talk to him again."

Morales leaned over my shoulder and pulled up the professor's contact info on my computer while I called Joe.

I didn't like the sound of his voice when he answered.

"Joe, what's wrong?"

"It's going to be okay, honey, but Julie has a little fever."

My stomach clenched and the blood left my head. I thought I might be sick all over my desk.

"How little is little?"

"It's a hundred and three. It's not unusual for a baby to have a fever, so I'm just letting you know. Don't worry about this. I'll see you later."

"Joe, you'll see me in twenty minutes. I'm leaving now."

"Lindsay, no. I've got her. Everything is under control."

"How do you know that?"

Conklin said, "Boxer, you okay?"

Joe said, "I've seen this before. I looked it up online, and I also put in a call to Dr. Gordon. Please, Lindsay. Let me handle this. I'll call you if we need you."

I had to say, "Okay," and I did. I hung up, and the blood returned to my head. I told Conklin that I was ready, and the two of us headed downstairs to the parking lot behind the ME's office.

I got into the passenger seat of the squad car and tried to get my mind on my two cases.

But I kept hearing my little girl cry.

Chapter 26

BY THE TIME Conklin and I arrived on 4th Street, the CSIU van and half a dozen squad cars had blocked a lane of traffic and run up on the hundred-foot stretch of sidewalk in front of Whole Foods. Morning commuters beat on their horns and shouted out their car windows, but no amount of yelling moved the stalled traffic.

Conklin double-parked and we exited the car into the wall of bystanders who were packed behind the barrier tape, sending a gale of tweets and snapshots out to the Web.

Officer Tom Forcaretta was at the front door. He was new on the force, but appeared to be coping well with the chaos. I signed the log and asked him to tell me what he knew about the crime.

"The shooting happened between seven thirty and seven thirty-five," he said. "The vic is Harriet Adams, white female, thirty-eight, looks like she took three bullets—right arm, neck, right chest. She was alive, but barely conscious when I got here. She told me her name. That was all. Ambulance took her to Metropolitan but she was DOA."

"How many witnesses?" I asked.

"Two semiwitnesses. A stock boy and a customer, but neither of them got a look at the shooter. They heard breaking glass and saw the victim go down. Both of them were interviewed and released."

"And where are the other customers?"

"The ones we could stop from leaving are in the stockroom. A team from Robbery is interviewing them, then releasing them through the rear door."

"How many customers are we talking about?"

"Too many to count, Sergeant. Over a hundred, prob'ly."

"And the people who work here? Could be an employee went postal."

"Yes, ma'am. Employees are in the manager's office. Bambi Simmons, that's the manager, said our vic was a regular customer and maybe a pain in the butt. She returned opened cans and so forth."

"I take it the weapon hasn't been recovered."

"No, ma'am."

"And the surveillance tape?"

"Yes, ma'am. We've got it, such as it is."

Automatic doors slid open and Conklin and I stepped into the thirty-thousand-square-foot crime scene. It wasn't Columbine, but it was freaking overwhelming, anyway. Crime techs were all over the place, putting down markers, snapping photos. If they didn't turn up two million unique fingerprints, it would be amazing.

Conklin and I were directed to the far right-hand side of the store, where Charlie Clapper, head of our crime lab, was shooting pictures. He did a double take when he saw me.

"Good God, Lindsay. Aren't you on leave?"

"I was. This is my welcome-back party."

"Good to see you, kiddo," he said. "And here's what we've got for you: a violent death in a humongous haystack. No idea if there's a needle in here or even what a needle would look like. Did you hear? No witnesses, no weapon, no robbery. Just 'bang, bang, bang.' It's a real who-freakin'-dunit."

Chapter 27

THE DAPPER CHARLIE Clapper was a homicide cop before he became director of forensics, and we were lucky to have him. He was thorough, insightful, and after he pointed out the evidence, he got out of the way.

Now he led us to the frozen-foods section, and Conklin and I got our first look at the primary scene.

Blood spatter, mostly of the arterial kind, had sprayed the contents of the freezer and the doors on both sides of the shattered glass. There was a long smear of blood on the unbroken bottom half of one door, showing where Harriet Adams had slid down after taking those shots.

An open handbag lay at the edge of a puddle

made up of water, blood, and ice cream. The pool had been entirely corrupted by the EMTs' attempt to save Harriet Adams's life.

Conklin and I gaped at the number and assortment of footprints, drag marks, handprints, and gurney-wheel tracks running in and out of the pool.

"Textbook example of EMTs—evidence-mangling technicians—at work," Clapper said. "Unless there's a signed death threat in the victim's handbag, we'll never solve the case out of this."

Conklin said to Clapper, "You have a picture of the victim?"

"The hospital just sent it," he said. He pulled up a photo on his mobile phone. I took a look.

Harriet Adams was on a metal table with a sheet pulled up to her chin.

Conklin asked Clapper, "Can you make a call? Find out what she was wearing? Find out if she wore toenail polish?"

"I'll be back," I said.

I called Joe from the soup-and-nuts aisle. He said Julie was sleeping. He didn't want to wake her to take her temperature. I asked him a lot of questions: Was she hot? How did she look? Did he think maybe a run to the hospital was in order? Joe talked me down, and then I called Brady.

"You need a senior team on this," I told him. "We'll take over again after we interview our person of interest."

Once again, Conklin and I bucked the crowd outside the food store on our way to the squad car.

"What are your thoughts?" I asked my partner as we pulled out and headed east toward Brannan Street.

"It's crazy, Lindsay. The scene is exactly what the professor said he dreamed—except for one thing. He dreamed that the victim was shot dead in the store.

"He didn't get that right, but he nailed everything else, down to the green glass beads and the blue paint on her toenails. What the hell are we dealing with? A guy reports that he's going to kill someone—and then he does it?

"He's crazy or he's messing with us, one or the other," Conklin said. "Right?"

He leaned on the horn, then switched on the siren. It was as if the traffic were welded into one piece.

"Right," I said.

Chapter 28

I'D LEFT THE house this morning whistling heigh-ho, heigh-ho. Three hours, a sick baby, and one bad crime scene later, Conklin and I were sitting across the table from the squirrelly Professor Judd.

My mind was only half in the moment. I opened my phone and put it on the table, staring at it as if staring would make it ring. While we waited for coffee, Conklin warmed up our person of interest with softball small talk.

Judd was at ease, blathering to Conklin about a book he was reading. He didn't seem surprised or alarmed or even aware that he was in our interrogation room because he had predicted a murder twenty-four hours before it had happened.

I tried to picture this neat and bookish man as a killer, and it didn't quite compute. Mackie brought coffee and left the room, stationing herself behind the one-way glass.

"We need to go over a couple of things, Professor," Conklin said. Have I said that Conklin has mastered the art of being the "good cop"? Most of the time, being sweet and a good listener gets suspects to tell him the truth. If sweetness doesn't do the trick, he's got me.

"Sure," said Perry Judd. "How can I help you?"

"Can you tell us where you were at seven thirty this morning?"

"Sure. Absolutely. I was in my office. Three of my students missed the second semester final and I was giving them a makeup exam before class. Why do you ask?"

"And how long did it take them to do the test?" Conklin asked. He sugared his coffee. Gave it a stir.

"I can tell you exactly because it was a timed test. Forty-five minutes."

"Were you in the room the entire time?"

"Oh, sure. Not that I don't trust the kids, but if you leave them alone, they're bound to converse. Another way of saying, 'They'll cheat.'"

"And all three of them will say you were in the room from seven thirty to eight fifteen?" asked Inspector Rich Conklin, the good cop to my bull in the china shop.

"You bet they will."

I butted in, not because my partner wasn't doing a perfect interrogation. He was. I did it so I could keep my mind in the room, and maybe get this a-hole to confess to premeditated murder.

"Professor. The woman you described from your dream was shot and killed this morning in the frozen-foods section of Whole Foods. Just like you said. How did you know about the shooting? Or did you make a plan, report it, and then execute it?"

"She was really shot?"

Perry Judd seemed to be very pleasantly surprised. In fact, as I watched him, his face brightened from his goatee up to his hairline.

"Really? You're saying it actually did happen?"

I scowled. "Middle-aged white woman, blond hair with dark roots, green beads, sandals, and blue toenail polish. Just the way you described her to my partner yesterday."

"Good God. It's true; it's really true."

"What's true?"

"It's in literature going back to *Macbeth*. No, going back to the Greeks. The *Iliad*. Cassandra, who prophesied doom, but no one would believe her. It's like schizophrenia, to have foresight and at the same time to be powerless to prevent tragedy."

I was worried about my baby. I snapped.

"Professor, what the hell are you talking about?"

"I have precognition," he said. "I'm clairvoyant. I can see the future."

Chapter 29

I HUDDLED WITH Brady in the break room and relayed the few facts we had about the late Harriet Adams, who'd picked a bad day to buy ice cream. She was divorced, had no children, had worked at Union Bank as a teller for the last seven years, and lived three blocks from Whole Foods in a one-room apartment on Zoe Street with her live-in boyfriend. The boyfriend was not a beneficiary of her five-thousand-dollar life insurance policy and he had a solid alibi for the time of the shooting.

Harriet Adams didn't have a rap sheet. She'd never disturbed the peace, jaywalked, or tossed a candy wrapper on the sidewalk. She was clean.

I said, "Conklin is looking at the surveillance tapes taken from the two cameras in Whole Foods.

One was trained on the manager's office, the other on the bank of cash registers. Neither would have picked up the shooting, so if the shooter didn't go through the checkout line with his gun in hand . . ."

"And the professor?"

"His alibi checks out. Three kids said he was breathing down their necks at the time of the shooting. Professor Judd says he's clairvoyant. Maybe he is. But I've assigned a team to tail him, anyway."

I left Brady, went down the fire stairs and out the back of the Hall, then took the breezeway to the ME's office. The receptionist's voice came over Claire's intercom as I passed through her open office door.

"Dr. Washburn? Sergeant Boxer just bulled her way past me."

Claire was stuffing files into a cardboard box. She had another box on her desk already full of personal items—doodads and her diploma, awards certificates and framed photos.

A picture of the Women's Murder Club was on top of one of the boxes—Claire, Yuki, and Cindy looking bright and cheery; me, the tallest one in the group, brooding about something or other. As usual.

"What is this?" I said, indicating the packing. "What's going on?"

"I've been benched," Claire said. "Haven't you heard?"

She looked awful—scared and mad and like she'd been kicked in the gut. I stretched out my arms and she came from around her desk and we hugged. A long minute later, I dropped into the side chair and Claire went back behind her desk. She put her feet up next to the phone.

All eight buttons on the phone console were blinking.

Claire drew a long sigh, then told me, "The city administrator said, and I quote, 'You may occupy your office for now, but I'm relieving you of your command.'"

"I didn't know Carter was in the military."

"He's a World War Two buff. That jerk. My access to my computer is blocked. Sheila is taking my calls out front, and it's just as well. Ninety-nine out of a hundred calls are from the tabloids. And then there are the calls from next of kin wanting to check that their loved ones hadn't been sold to body shops for spare parts."

"This is so wrong."

"When Dr. Morse arrives, I'm supposed to give him administrative assistance until—"

"Dr. Morse?"

"Retired ME from Orange County. Last time he held a scalpel was in 2003. I don't know if he can even manage the paperwork, let alone the actual job. Anyway. He can have my desk," Claire said with a sigh, "until we find Faye Farmer's body."

"What's your gut say happened to her?"

"My guts are, like, taking Lombard Street at ninety miles per hour, at night, without headlights —and no brakes, either. So I'm not consulting my gut.

"But listen, Lindsay. I do have an idea who could have had something to do with it."

Chapter 30

"TAKE A LOOK at this."

Claire handed me a manila folder with a name printed on the tab: Tracey Pendleton.

There was a photo stapled to the top sheet of Tracey Pendleton's employment records. She had short gray hair and her face was plain, without a single distinguishing feature. Her DOB said that she was in her late thirties, but she looked fifty. She probably smoked and drank, might have had drugs in her past.

The word *Hired* was stamped on the first page, as was the date—August 23, 2009. Reading further, I learned that Ms. Pendleton had a license to carry a weapon, owned a registered 9mm Glock semiauto, and was employed as a security guard for the ME's office.

I flipped through her time sheets.

Tracey Pendleton worked nights—including last night.

Claire was watching me, and when I looked up, she said, "Tracey clocked in at twelve oh two. She didn't punch out."

"You've called her?"

"Every ten minutes. No answer. I also texted her and sent her a bunch of e-mails. No answer to those, either."

"Tell me what you know about her," I said.

I teed up the question, but my mind was already racing ahead. Had Tracey Pendleton stolen Faye Farmer's body? If so, what was her motive?

"I don't know her at all," Claire said. "Our schedules only overlap if I come in way early or I'm working way late. And even then, it's 'Hey, how ya doing?'"

"When was the last time you saw Pendleton?"

"A couple of weeks ago. She seemed okay to me, Lindsay. But when I look at her, I'm just looking to see if she's sober. She failed to show up for work a couple of times and was on warning. But not showing up and not punching out are two different things entirely."

I asked, "She just forgot to punch out?"

Claire shrugged.

"It would be the first time. The time clock is right there at the back door."

"Okay. Could she have taken the surveillance disk, switched the John Doe for Faye Farmer, and gotten Farmer's body into her car? Is she strong enough to do that?"

"I think it's physically possible."

"You think someone could've paid Pendleton for the body?" I asked.

"They say everyone has a price," said Claire. "Tracey Pendleton makes fifteen dollars an hour. I guess her tipping point wouldn't be too high."

Chapter 31

FLOYD MESERVE WAS clean-shaven, neatly dressed, his hair in a ponytail short enough to reveal the tattoo of a naked woman just above his collar.

Yuki approached her witness and said, "Lieutenant Meserve, what is your job title?"

"Lieutenant, Crimes Against Persons Division, Northern District, SFPD."

"Do you know the defendant?"

"Yes. I met with him on February twentieth of last year."

"What were the circumstances of your meeting?"

The jurors were attentive, some of them leaning forward in their seats. The gallery was still. Yuki was absolutely sure there would be no surprises with Floyd Meserve.

"I was working undercover at the time," said Meserve. "One of my CIs told me that a lawyer was looking for a hit man. I told him that I could pose as such."

"Did this confidential informant give your contact number to the defendant?"

"Yes."

"And did the defendant contact you?"

"Yes, the same day. We set up a meeting."

"When did you meet the defendant?"

"I met the defendant in a parking lot outside the Westlake Shopping Center on Southgate Avenue at five in the evening. We each drove there in our own vehicle. The defendant wanted me to talk to him inside his car, but I told him I don't do that. He had to get into my vehicle."

"And why did you want him to get into your vehicle?"

"I had a video recorder set up."

"I see. So did Mr. Herman get into your car?"

"Yes. He got straight to the point."

"What did he say?" Yuki asked.

"He said he wanted me to dispose of his wife

because she was abusing their daughter. And he said he wanted me to kill his daughter, too, because he said his wife had ruined her."

"He wanted you to kill a seven-year-old?"

"That's what he said."

"And what did you say to this proposition?"

"I asked him if he was sure. He said he had thought about it for a long time. So I told him it would cost him a lot to take out a woman and a child."

"Was a dollar amount discussed?" Yuki asked.

"We negotiated the price of one hundred thousand for both people. Half down, half after proof of the hits."

"Did your recording equipment capture this conversation?"

"Yes, it did."

Yuki said, "Your Honor, I'd like to show the video to the jury."

"You have the transcript?" the judge asked.

"Right here, Your Honor."

"I'll take that, and if you would give a copy to the defense, you may roll the video."

Chapter 32

NICKY GAINES TAPPED on his keyboard and, after a couple of fumbles, the video projected onto the monitor in the courtroom. Yuki watched along with the jury as the time- and date-stamped recording started with Keith Herman getting into the undercover cop's car.

Oh, man, Yuki thought. *No way Kinsela could discredit this.*

The images were black-and-white, medium quality, shot from the window on the driver's side. The angle was across Meserve's lap, and it took in Keith Herman's face and upper torso. Herman had been bearded when the film was shot, and he had worn a blue baseball cap.

On video, Floyd Meserve told Keith Herman

that his name was Chester, then he listened as Keith Herman said, "My wife is mentally ill—schizophrenic, you know? She's sweet as pie, then she turns on a dime. She beats our little girl for no reason, and abuses her in other ways you don't need to know, but my little girl has also turned mental. I mean psycho. I don't want her to go through the hell of being a mental case for her whole life. Or being drugged to the gills, either. It's a crying shame."

Meserve said, "You thought of getting a divorce? Filing for custody of the child?"

"Many times, but my wife is foxy. She'll take everything, including the kid, and leave me broken and ruined. No. This is the best way. I want it to be quick, you know? Shots to their heads. No fear, no pain. Make it look like a robbery. Take my wife's ring. It's worth a ton. It cost thirty grand. I don't know what you can get for it, but it's a good bonus, anyways."

Meserve, a.k.a. Chester, said that he needed pictures of the wife and child, and a down payment, and that the client had to furnish the gun.

Keith Herman agreed to the terms and agreed to meet Chester in twenty-four hours—"same time and place, and I'll bring the stuff."

The video brightened as Herman opened the door and got out of the car. When he was alone, Meserve spoke through his microphone to the cops in the surveillance van. "Did everything come in clear?"

The screen went dark and the lights came up in the courtroom. Yuki stood beside her witness and said, "Lieutenant Meserve, did you meet with this man again to receive the down payment and photos?"

"I was there, but he failed to show," Meserve said. "Later that day, my snitch informed me that someone had ratted me out. The deal was blown and so was my cover."

"Did you have enough to charge the suspect?"

"I didn't have his full name, so I couldn't do anything but sweat. Even if I'd known him, no money changed hands, which woulda made an indictment impossible."

"Did you believe that he intended to have his wife and child murdered?"

"Without a doubt."

"That's all I have, Your Honor," Yuki said.

John Kinsela's expression was unreadable, but he revealed his agitation by jingling the coins in his pockets.

He said, "Lieutenant Meserve, you didn't know the defendant's name. He didn't give you any money or pictures of the targets, and he didn't give you a gun?"

"No."

"So he hadn't committed any crime?"

"That's correct."

"And you don't know if he was looking for a hit man or if he was trying on an idea he never intended to go through with, or even if the man in your vehicle was my client."

"Objection. What is counsel doing, Your Honor? He seems to be arguing his case, not questioning the witness."

"Sustained. Stop doing that, Mr. Kinsela, or you will be fined."

"I'm sorry, Your Honor. I don't have any other questions. This witness has completely satisfied my curiosity."

"Ms. Castellano. Redirect?"

Yuki stood and addressed the witness from her table.

"Lieutenant Meserve, when did you learn the full name of the man who tried to hire you to kill his wife and daughter?"

"On March first of last year, when Jennifer Herman's dismembered body was discovered."

"The man who contacted you about two weeks earlier, on February twentieth, and ordered a hit on his wife and child: Is he sitting in this courtroom?"

"Yes."

"Will you point him out?" Keith Herman showed no emotion as Meserve pointed a finger at him as if it were a loaded gun.

"The defendant. That's him. I'm positive."

"Thank you, Lieutenant. You may step down."

Chapter 33

AFTER THE UNDERCOVER cop stood down, Yuki introduced Lesley Rohan, a strikingly attractive and wealthy friend of Jennifer Herman's, who told the court that Jennifer had been afraid of her husband.

"Jennifer was sitting at my dining table, shaking her head and crying. She told me that if anything happened to her, I should call the police and tell them that Keith did it," said Rohan. "Jennifer's arms were bruised and she had a black eye. I suspected for a long time that Keith was abusing both Jennifer and Lily."

"Objection," said Kinsela. "Speculation, Your Honor."

The judge said to the court reporter, "Ms. Gray,

please strike the witness's last sentence. Thank you. Just tell what you know, Ms. Rohan. Not what you think."

"I'm sorry, Judge Nussbaum."

"Please go on, Ms. Castellano."

Yuki said, "Ms. Rohan, did Jennifer ask you to do something for her?"

"Yes. She asked me to take pictures of her and keep them safe."

"Your Honor, I'd like to introduce these photos of Jennifer Herman, dated February fourth of last year."

After the pictures were entered into evidence and Yuki was sitting at the prosecution table, Kinsela addressed Ms. Rohan.

"Do you know for a fact that those bruises were put there by Keith Herman?"

"Jennifer told me he did it."

"But do you *know* that Mr. Herman inflicted those bruises on Jennifer? You didn't see him do it, did you?"

The witness squinted. She looked like she'd been struck across the face.

"No. But why would Jennifer lie?"

Kinsela said, "We just don't know. Do we?"

Yuki called Ty Crandall from the sanitation department, who told the jury about finding the bags of human remains and that ever since he found them he no longer could sleep through the night. Although he was healthy, he had resigned from the city at half pension.

Kinsela had no questions for the sanitation man.

Forensic pathologist Dr. Roy Barclay testified that he had examined the body parts that had been parceled into the eight construction-grade garbage bags. He said that the parts were conclusively from the body of Jennifer Herman.

Barclay told the jury that he had determined the cause of death to be a bullet fired through the left eye at close range, the manner of death to be homicide, and that the time of death would have been within eight hours of the discovery of the parts. He sent the bullet to his ballistics department.

Kinsela asked, "Did the bullet match a gun in the national ballistics database?"

"No. It's consistent with four or five firearms."

Kinsela thanked the witness and had no other questions.

After the forensic pathologist stepped down, Judge Nussbaum called for a lunch recess. Nicky and Yuki had sandwiches at her desk, buttoned up every detail, and when they returned to the courtroom one hour and twenty minutes later, Yuki called her star witness, Lynnette Lagrande.

Lagrande was critical to the prosecution's case. And because she had been photographed by the press, and because Mr. Herman had a reputation for having witnesses threatened, terrified, and possibly killed, Yuki had kept her witness in a safe house with 24-7 security for the last two months.

Now the bailiff called her name.

As if they were at a church wedding, as if the organ music had just begun, the jurors, the attorneys, and the audience in the gallery turned as one to watch Lynnette Lagrande come up the aisle.

Chapter 34

YUKI, LIKE EVERYONE else in Arthur R. Nussbaum's courtroom, watched Lynnette Lagrande come through the wooden gate in the bar, which separated the gallery from the judge, jury, and prosecution and defense tables. She was wearing a black-and-white print dress with a high collar and a hem that hit midcalf. The thirty-year-old woman was so stunning that the simple dress only enhanced her spectacular figure.

Lagrande swore to tell the truth, then took her seat and crossed her legs at the ankles. When she moved her wavy black hair away from her eyes, she revealed her beautiful, heart-shaped face.

Yuki walked up to the witness and asked, "Ms. Lagrande, what kind of work do you do?"

"I teach first graders at John Muir Elementary School. I've had this job for four years and I love it."

"Are you acquainted with the defendant?"

"Yes, I am."

Lagrande didn't look at Keith Herman, but he fixed his sharklike eyes on her.

"How did you come to meet Mr. Herman?" Yuki asked.

"Two years ago, Lily Herman, Mr. Herman's daughter, was in my class. I met him one day when he came to pick her up after school."

Under Yuki's questioning, Lagrande described the course of her relationship with the defendant: parent-teacher conferences, accidental meetings in town, then a lunch with Mr. Herman that turned romantic and was the start of a liaison that had continued for more than a year.

"How would you characterize your feelings for Mr. Herman at this time last year?"

"I loved him."

"And did he ever tell you how he felt about you?"

"He claimed to love me."

Yuki brought a packet of letters and e-mails from the prosecution table to the witness stand and showed them to the witness.

"Do these cards and printouts of e-mails belong to you?"

"Yes. They're mine."

"Your Honor, I'd like Ms. Lagrande to read some passages from this correspondence and then I'll introduce all of it into evidence."

Kinsela said, "Your Honor, the defense concedes that the defendant expressed feelings of love for the witness."

"The tenor of the correspondence goes to motive, Your Honor," said Yuki.

The judge was attacked by a fit of sneezing. Everyone in the courtroom waited him out. A few people, including Yuki Castellano and John Kinsela, blessed him.

The judge blew his nose. He thanked everyone, then he said, "I'm not going to deprive the jury of the opportunity to hear these communications, Mr. Kinsela. Ms. Castellano, please proceed."

Chapter 35

YUKI SAID, "MS. LAGRANDE, will you please read these e-mails aloud, including the dates?"

Kinsela leaned in and whispered to his client, but Keith Herman didn't acknowledge his lawyer or seem to be aware of him at all. He seemed transfixed by the sight of his former lover.

Lynnette Lagrande bent her head and read from the pages in front of her.

"December twenty-fourth. Lynnie, I know I promised to be with you on Christmas and I am so sorry that I have to let you down. There is no place I'd rather be than in your arms and in your—"

The witness looked up and said to Yuki, "He goes on to say how it makes him feel to have sexual relations with me, and if you don't mind, I'd rather not read this out loud."

Yuki said, "You can skip that passage and just read the last paragraph."

"Okay.

"When you open your present in the morning, I hope you will know how much I love you. With all my love, the K-guy."

"Please read your response, Ms. Lagrande."
The witness sighed.

"December twenty-fourth. Keith—I don't want presents. This is hurting me too much. It's really unfair to all of us. Fondly, Lynnette."

"Please read the next e-mail."
The witness read e-mails for the next fifteen minutes. But the correspondence consisted, emotionally, of a two-step dance.

The defendant wrote that he loved Lynnie

without reservation and that he would do anything to be with her.

Ms. Lagrande wrote back that she was suffering from his attentions, not because she didn't return his feelings, but because she did.

Yuki asked the witness to read the e-mail dated February 27, two days before Jennifer Herman's dismembered body was recovered. The beautiful woman dabbed at her eyes, sipped from her water bottle, then read:

> "Lynnie, I know you don't believe anything I say anymore, but actions speak louder than e-mail. We will be together by this time next week. I promise you that. All my love, Keith."

Lynnette Lagrande put the papers in her lap and put her hands to her eyes. Her sobs were soft but her shoulders shook.

Yuki said, "Do you need to take a minute?"

After a moment, the witness said, "I'm okay."

Yuki waited until Lynnette Lagrande seemed composed, keeping her own face composed as well. This entire day was going perfectly. Couldn't be better.

She asked, "Did you see Mr. Herman on February twenty-eighth, the day before his wife's body was discovered?"

"No, I did not."

"Did he write to you?"

"I don't know. I changed my e-mail address and my phone number. I left my apartment and moved in with my sister."

"To be clear, did you see the defendant at any time after he wrote to you on February twenty-seventh, saying that the two of you would soon be together?"

"No. He wants me to give him an alibi, but, I can't lie for him anymore. I didn't see him in February at all."

"Thank you very much, Ms. Lagrande."

Chapter 36

NICKY GAINES TYPED on his tablet, "Red Dog was standing in back. Caught yer *amazing* direct."

Yuki smiled at Gaines, deleted the message, and turned her attention to Kinsela, who, to date, hadn't been worth the two grand an hour Keith Herman was paying him.

Kinsela approached Lynnette Lagrande and put his hand on the witness stand, as if he were gently touching the witness herself.

"Ms. Lagrande, what was the Christmas gift that Mr. Herman gave you?"

"A diamond necklace."

"Do you know the value of that necklace?"

"Not really. Maybe twenty-five thousand dollars."

"And do I understand correctly that you kept the necklace?"

"I kept it. It was for pain and suffering."

"Really? A legal term. Well. Ms. Lagrande, did you also accept a new Lexus sedan from the defendant in January of last year?"

"Yes. Keith gave me a car. It was a birthday present."

"I believe the going rate for that car is in excess of sixty thousand dollars, is that correct?"

"I don't know."

"You kept the car."

"Yes."

"It's worth more than your annual salary, isn't that right, Ms. Lagrande?"

"Yes. I suppose it is."

Kinsela walked to the witness stand, then asked loudly, "Did the defendant ever give you money?"

The witness tossed her hair defiantly. Yuki leaned forward. Lynnette knew Kinsela was going to go after her, and Yuki had coached her to remain calm and matter-of-fact—take a moment to think before answering if she were attacked.

But the witness answered angrily, "I'm not a

whore, Mr. Kinsela. Do *not* call me a whore."

"Your Honor?"

"Ms. Lagrande, you must answer the question or I will be forced to find you in contempt. Mr. Kinsela. Please ask the question again."

"Did you receive cash from the defendant? Yes or no."

"Yes. And so what?"

"Did you tell him that you liked nice things?"

"I don't remember."

"Ms. Lagrande, were the expensive gifts and cash the reason you dated the defendant, who was, after all, a married man?"

Yuki stood, said, "Your Honor, objection. Opposing counsel is badgering the witness."

"Overruled, but get to the point, Mr. Kinsela."

"Okay, Your Honor. Ms. Lagrande, were you looking for a big payday when Mr. Herman finally left his family? Is that why you accepted expensive gifts even though you plainly didn't return the defendant's feelings?"

"I *did* return his feelings. I *did* love him. I still *do*."

"I believe that you do love Mr. Herman. That's why you spent the weekend with him at the time someone else was murdering his wife and child. In fact, weren't you making love with the defendant that entire weekend, Lynnette?"

"No, no, no. I was not with him that weekend. No."

"When the murders were discovered, and Mr. Herman was arrested, and this whole sordid affair was coming to light, you decided to finally cut him loose so that your reputation wasn't trashed, isn't that right? You'd rather betray your lover than tell the truth about your actions, right, Lynnie? You say you're not a whore, but exactly what kind of woman would you say you are? Would you say that you're fickle? Or disloyal? Or would you just call yourself a user? Which is it?

"What kind of woman are you?"

John Kinsela continued to glare at Lynnette Lagrande even though Yuki objected loudly, even though the judge repeatedly slammed his gavel against the block and found Kinsela in contempt. Even though Kinsela's questions were stricken.

Kinsela looked triumphant and Yuki felt his triumph like an ax through her star witness's credibility. Kinsela had bullied the first grade schoolteacher with the heart-shaped face, painted her as a gold digger, muddied her character, cast doubt on her testimony, and threw a bright light on the legal concept of reasonable doubt.

Yuki felt blindsided.

Nussbaum said, "Redirect, Ms. Castellano?"

Lynnette had her head down and was sobbing into her crossed arms.

Yuki didn't know what she could do to rehabilitate the woman who had taken great big gobs of money from the man she said she loved.

Chapter 37

YUKI BROUGHT A box of tissues to the stand and let Lynnette take a couple of seconds to pull herself together. Yuki had made a mistake not to have realized that Kinsela was going to use Keith Herman's gifts against Lynnette.

It was a sickening oversight. But was it fatal?

As Lynnette dabbed her eyes, Yuki thought out her redirect with the speed of a supercomputer, and when the witness seemed more or less composed, Yuki said, "Lynnette, did you ever try to hide the fact that you received gifts from Keith Herman?"

"No, of course not."

"Did these gifts always come on holidays?"

"Yes."

"Did Keith ever tell you why he bought you such expensive presents?"

Yuki took a slow turn away from the witness stand, headed toward the lectern, and stole a look at the jurors. They were attentive. For the moment, that was all she could hope for.

"Could you repeat the question?" Lynnette said.

She was still looking shaky, Yuki thought, but shaky was vulnerable and vulnerability was better than defiance any day.

"Lynnette, did Keith ever tell you why he bought you such expensive gifts?"

"He said different things at different times."

"Go on," Yuki said.

"He said that until he was free, this was the only way he could show me how much he cared."

"Anything else?"

"He said that he felt guilty for my pain and suffering."

"Pain and suffering. Those were his words?"

"Yes."

"The money that Keith gave you—what was it for?"

"He gave me twenty-two thousand dollars to

pay off my student loan. I appreciated the help. I don't make a large salary."

"Did you expect to cash in—that is, get rich—from marrying Keith Herman?"

"I knew he had money. But the only thing that was important to me was that we had a real relationship, with holidays together, and that I could be with Lily. I wanted to be able to go out into the open, to stop feeling bad because I loved someone else's husband. And when I saw that I couldn't have that, I tried to break it off with Keith many, many times."

"And Keith pursued you, isn't that right?"

"Yes."

"You testified that you changed your phone number. You moved out of your home."

"Yes."

"On the weekend of February twenty-eighth through March first, were you with the defendant?"

"No. I was not. I was alone in the hunting cabin my father left me in Oroville. I don't have a TV there. I don't even get a cell phone signal. I just wanted to be by myself."

"So when the defense tells the court that Keith Herman was with you the weekend his wife and daughter were murdered, that's a lie, isn't it?"

The witness winced ever so slightly. Yuki took it to mean that Lynnette still loved Keith Herman.

"Yes," she said. "That's a lie."

"Thank you, Ms. Lagrande. I have nothing more for this witness, Your Honor."

Kinsela had nothing to add, a good move on his part, Yuki thought. If one juror believed that Lynnette Lagrande was a money-grubber and a liar, Kinsela had done his job.

Yuki watched Lynnette Lagrande step down from the stand. She had recovered much of her poise. Looking neither left nor right, she walked up the aisle and back out through the front door of the courtroom.

Had the jury believed her?

All of them?

Honest to God, Yuki didn't know.

Chapter 38

CONKLIN AND I stood outside Tracey Pendleton's front door. Her house was small and nearly identical to the surrounding cheap wooden houses, which had been built in the fifties.

School was out. Kids called out to each other as they biked along the patched asphalt on the poor residential street. Cars with loud radios and old mufflers sped past.

We had knocked on the door, peered through the dirty windows, and looked up and down to see if Pendleton's Camaro was parked anywhere on Flora Street. It wasn't.

It didn't appear that the ME's night-shift security guard was at home.

Conklin and I had our weapons out and were

ready to execute the warrant that gave us the legal right to break down Pendleton's door.

I stood back, looked under the cushion of the porch rocker, and found it just as Conklin kicked open the door.

"Oops," I said, holding up the key.

Conklin called out, "Miss Pendleton, this is the police. Please come out with your hands over your head. We just want to talk to you."

There was no response and no sound coming from the house at all.

The house had two and a half rooms—about four hundred square feet altogether—and I could see almost every inch of it from the doorway.

We were standing in the living room, which was furnished with a worn brown sofa and a sagging armchair. The TV was off, and the only movement was the upward spiral of dust motes in the dim ray of sunlight coming through the window.

Conklin went ahead of me and toed open the bedroom door. A moment later, he called, "Clear."

I went ahead to the kitchenette, checked the broom closet, then called out to Conklin that the room was empty.

There was a pot of old food on the stove, one

dirty dish, one glass in the sink. The refrigerator was empty, except for the bottle of vodka in the freezer. The garbage pail held two beer bottles and an empty can of Beefaroni.

Conklin came in and said, "Her suitcase is in the closet. I couldn't find a weapon."

He checked under the sink and found more vodka standing among the containers of Mr. Clean, Easy-Off, and Windex.

We went through the house again. There was no computer, no sign of pets. No purse. No keys. We searched the hamper, the cabinets, and drawers, but found nothing but the residue of a life lived on the night shift and boozy days spent passed out on a single bed.

Conklin used a dish towel to pick up the phone. He tapped the redial button, then let me hear the ringing. The call was answered by a recorded woman's mechanical voice announcing the time and temperature.

Conklin said, "It's like she checked the time, went to work, then vanished along with Faye Farmer's body. Where'd she go? Who is she, anyway?"

I called the squad room.

"Lieutenant, we need a warrant to dump Pendleton's phone records and see her bank activity. Yeah, there's no sign she's been home in the last twenty-four hours. There's hardly any sign of life here at all."

Chapter 39

WE WERE SEATED at the polished stone conference table at Fenn & Tarbox. Brady, Conklin, and I sat along one side. Five lawyers and their thirteen-million-bucks-a-year client held down the swivel chairs across from us, the backs of their heads reflected in the floor-to-ceiling windows. Beyond the glass was a wide waterfront view of the Ferry Building and the Bay Bridge, sparkling against a dusky sky.

We'd been introduced to the senior partner, the silver-haired George Fenn, who now took his place at the head of the table. I forgot the names of his younger associates because I was riveted by their client, Jeffrey Kennedy, superstar linebacker for the San Francisco 49ers and also the former reputed fiancé of the late celebrity designer Faye Farmer.

Fenn was friendly, even affable, when he said, "I've heard a lot about you, Sergeant Boxer. All good. I'm glad you're working this case."

Maybe he was glad that I was working the case. Or maybe the big-time lawyer was working *me* so that we didn't bring his client down to the Hall for questioning.

Jeff Kennedy was twiddling his BlackBerry, giving me a chance to look him over without being rude about it. I'd seen him on TV, of course, and from high up in the bleachers. I'd watched him wrestle down tailbacks with his 4.4 speed, sack quarterbacks as though they were rag dolls, then shake off goal-line pileups like a cocker spaniel after a bath.

But now I was getting the up-close-and-personal view of this human tank.

Kennedy was strikingly handsome, with a strong jawline, an off-center nose, gray eyes, and plenty of dark hair. He hadn't shaved and his clothing was rumpled, as though he hadn't cleaned up in a day or two. Even though the air-conditioning was blowing, Jeff Kennedy was sweating.

George Fenn said, "Just so you know, we're taping this meeting. Standard procedure."

Brady said, "Mr. Fenn, this isn't a deposition. We just want Mr. Kennedy to tell us about Ms. Farmer."

"Of course," Fenn said. "But still, we always tape for the protection of our clients."

Brady flipped his hand as if to say, "Fine," and then asked Kennedy, "When did you last see Ms. Farmer?"

Brady was a first-class interrogator. It was going to be a pleasure to watch him question the man who was quite possibly the last person to see Faye Farmer alive.

Chapter 40

KENNEDY PUT HIS BlackBerry on the table and said to Brady, "Last night. Well, it started in the afternoon. We had a party. Me and Faye. A bunch of our friends came over. Different people at different times drifted in and out."

He spoke haltingly. Was he remembering the event? Had he been coached? Or was he in shock? Brady asked for the names of his friends and Kennedy listed six ballplayers and eight women, including Faye Farmer.

"What was the occasion?" Brady asked.

"No occasion. Just hanging out. Drinking. Watching videos of old games. And then Faye got worked up about nothing. She'd do that if she wasn't getting enough attention. Or if I was getting too much. I told her to chill, and she told me to eff myself."

His cheek muscles twitched. His hands clenched on the table, as if he were having a bad dream or an angry thought.

"You're saying you fought," Brady said.

"I ran after her," said Kennedy, "but she drove off. The next thing I know, it's morning and a friend is calling to say, 'Turn on the TV.'"

Kennedy shook his head as if he still couldn't believe it.

Brady said, "Which was it this time? She didn't get enough attention? Or you got too much?"

"There was an extra girl. Friend of one of the other girls. She was showing a little too much skin. Kept flouncing around me. Touched me a few times."

Kennedy named the girl and the girl's friend, and then Brady asked, "Did you see or speak to Faye after she left your house?"

"No. I didn't call her. I was still pissed that she went all diva in front of my guys. If only I'd stopped her. Taken her for a walk or a smoke or something. What the hell am I supposed to do with myself now? We were supposed to get married."

Conklin asked Kennedy what time Faye left the party, and Kennedy said he didn't know.

"It was late," he said. "I'd had a few. Now I gotta live with the fact that we had a fight and I never saw her again. Christ. We were in love. We were really in love."

Tears fell from Kennedy's eyes. He used his forearm to dry his face. Fenn put a hand on his back, said, "Take it easy, Jeff."

Brady said, "Mr. Kennedy, do you know of anyone who wanted to hurt your fiancée?"

"You cannot know what people think about people they see on TV," said Kennedy. "People are crazy. They stalk celebrities. Sometimes they shoot them. But do I know any specific person who hated Faye enough to kill her? No. And now I have a couple of questions for you."

I looked up from my notepad. Kennedy had his massive forearms on the table and was leaning in, looking menacing.

"Where is Faye's body? How could someone have stolen her out of the ME's office? How are you going to find her killer if you don't have her body?"

"Forensics is processing her car," I said. "Do you own a gun, Mr. Kennedy?"

"Hell, no. Are you seriously asking me that?"

I said, "Does the name Tracey Pendleton mean anything to you?"

"Who?"

I repeated the security guard's name. Kennedy grunted, "Never heard of him." Then he shot up from his seat and, crying, stumbled out of the conference room.

Fenn was saying, "He's understandably upset."

Kennedy seemed appropriately devastated and clueless. But I wasn't buying that his breakdown meant that he was innocent. He had graduated from Stanford with honors. He was 230 pounds of muscle and he'd had a fight with his girlfriend.

Kennedy was a smart jock with a cultivated violent streak.

That could be a lethal combination.

Chapter 41

I OPENED THE front door to our apartment at just about 8:00 p.m. I was desperate to hold our baby, have a bath, a glass of wine, and a bowl of pasta with red sauce. I wanted to get out of my clothes and hug my husband and sleep until morning, not necessarily all at the same time.

I called out, "Helloooo. Sergeant Mommy is home."

Martha careened around the corner, jumped up against me, and would've knocked me down but for my baby weight keeping me anchored.

Girly laughter came from the living room.

What was this?

I followed Martha around the bend and saw that the Women's Murder Club was loosely arrayed around the room. Claire danced Julie on her thighs and held her up for me to see. Couldn't help but notice that the baby had a pink gift bow stuck to the top of her head.

"Heyyy," Claire said. "Look who I've got."

"Heyyy," I said back. "Give her to me."

I grinned at my baby and at the same time noted Claire's slurred greeting and lazy laughter, the open bottles of wine and empty glasses on the coffee table. A party had started without me.

Joe was on his feet and coming toward me with open arms. He kissed me and asked, "What can I get you?"

I tipped my chin toward Claire, said, "I want what she's having."

Yuki's laughter is one of the most adorable sounds I've ever heard. If laughter were a flower, Yuki's laugh would have to be called merry bells.

Julie was laughing, too, as Claire flew her over to me. I said, "Hang on a sec."

I removed my jacket and gun, then took Julie into my arms. And still she didn't cry.

"Aren't you the little party girl?" I said.

I sat down, kicked off my shoes, and smooched my pretty baby as Cindy brought over cheese and crackers and Joe put a glass of Merlot on the lamp table.

"So," Cindy said, sitting so close to me on the sofa she was almost in my lap. "How was your first day back at work?"

My reporter girlfriend was interviewing *me*. We all just cracked up, Cindy saying, "What? *What?*"

I said, "It was a long twelve hours."

"We brought presents," said Yuki.

Gifts were on the coffee table and Joe took Julie so that I could open the sixteen-flavor margarita kit from Yuki, a stack of Monster Proof pajamas from Cindy, and a pair of Giants tickets from Claire. Front-row seats!

My postpartum party was great, but after I slugged down my wine, I began to fade.

Claire clapped her hands and said, "Time to go, girlfriends. Lindsay, we're making Morales an honorary member of the club, summer pass only. Come with us to Susie's?"

"Me? Thanks, but I'm a dead mom walking."

Everyone laughed and I hugged them good-bye at the door, shouting after them, "Claire, let Cindy drive." I took Julie back from Joe, and what do you know? As soon as the girls were gone, Party Girl started to cry.

"Aww, sweetie."

I sank into Joe's armchair and patted Julie's back as Joe cooked dinner and then put the baby to bed.

He kissed me, sweaty as I was, and he said, "Why don't you hit the rain box?"

When I returned from my shower smelling like lavender, wearing blue pj's, barefoot, and with my hair up in a ponytail, linguine marinara was on the table and Louie Armstrong was on the Bose.

"Tell me about your day," said my wonderful Joe.

Chapter 42

AFTER THE MEETING at Fenn & Tarbox, Rich Conklin had stood on Battery Street with Brady and Lindsay, their collars up against a misty rain.

Brady had said what they'd all been thinking—that if Kennedy had motive and a gun, he could have gotten into the car with Faye Farmer, shot her, then walked home. He would never have been missed at his free-floating party.

If he had a motive. *If* he had a gun.

They still had no idea how Faye Farmer's body had left the morgue and if the theft had anything to do with her murder.

The three had parted, driving away in separate cars.

There was almost no traffic downtown, and

Rich drove from the Embarcadero Center through North Beach and Pacific Heights without catching a single light. From the Richmond he crossed the Panhandle on his way to the apartment he shared with Cindy on Kirkham.

As he drove, he thought about Jeff Kennedy's story about his last fight with Faye Farmer, and understood how frustrated the man had been with the woman he loved.

He and Cindy had also been fighting. He said she was inconsiderate. She said that *he* was. He thought she'd changed. She shrugged, said, "Maybe I have."

He wanted comfort and affection when he came home. And maybe some good sex once in a while.

She said, "I'm busy," and "I'm tired."

Rich grabbed his cell from the passenger seat, speed-dialed Cindy, and when she didn't answer their home phone, he called her cell.

"It's me," he said when she answered. "Where are you?"

He could hear background noise, dishes clattering, and the muffled roar of shouted conversation.

"Susie's," she said.

Susie's. Where the "girls" meet to eat. Also blow off steam, commiserate, and do some problem solving, too. Maybe they could solve his problem.

He said to Cindy, "We've got a bad connection," then clicked off.

He reversed his direction, headed east on Oak to Van Ness, and then turned onto Broadway. He was steaming the entire time. Cindy hadn't told him she was going out. He'd had a day he would've liked to have told her about. He would have enjoyed seeing her face across the dinner table.

Ten minutes after he hung up with Cindy, Rich parked the car on Sansome and walked a couple of blocks to the corner of Jackson. The light coming through the windows of Susie's brightened the sidewalk and made him think of food.

He pushed open the front door and walked into the Caribbean-style café and its welcoming ambience—steel drums, the pungent smell of spicy food, and the good feel of conversation bouncing off the walls.

The hostess had her back to him and he didn't wait for her to turn around. He broke through the bar crowd in the front room, made his way along the narrow passageway, and walked past the pickup window, where he sidestepped a waitress with a loaded tray.

When he got to the back room, he saw Cindy, Claire, and Yuki at their favorite booth. Cindy's blond hair was curled tight from the rain. It looked like a halo around her sweet face.

He said, "What's today's special?"

Cindy looked up and he kissed her.

She didn't look happy to see him.

Chapter 43

CINDY COULDN'T BELIEVE that Richie had appeared without warning and was looming over her. He leaned down and kissed her and Cindy accepted his kiss, but she was pissed, giving him the eye that clearly told him so.

"What's going on?" she asked.

"Hey, Claire. Yuki. I haven't eaten. Cindy, I'm starving. What's good here?"

Rich swung into the banquette, squeezed in next to Cindy.

"The pulled pork is tasty," Yuki said.

"This seat is taken," Cindy said, pointing to the half-full beer mug at Rich's right hand.

"Not a problem."

Rich signaled to the waitress, asked her for a

chair, then ordered an Anchor Steam and pulled pork with plantains.

Claire said, "Richie, you're looking pale, buddy. You sure you're okay?"

"No, I'm *not* okay," he said. "Here's the thing, Claire. And I really want you to be honest. Cindy and I are engaged. I proposed, she said yes, jumped into my arms. We moved in together and now, a year later, no wedding date. She says, 'What's the rush?'"

Cindy said, "Rich. Not here."

"I'm taking this rare opportunity," he said, "to get advice from our friends. They know us. Let me talk, Cindy."

"You're being ridiculous and you're embarrassing me. But I guess you know that."

"When I actually see her," Rich said to Claire and Yuki, as if Cindy hadn't spoken, "I want to cook dinner with her, watch a movie. But she says, 'Not now, hon, I'm writing.' She writes in her head, you understand," Rich went on. "Then, when she starts typing, she might as well be in an underground bunker."

The waitress put Richie's beer down on the table, then dragged a chair to the head of the booth. She sat in it and said to Rich, "Hi—I'm Lorraine."

"I'm Rich Conklin. Cindy's fiancé. Nice to meet you."

"We just ran out of the pork," Lorraine said. "Want to try the pulled chicken?"

"Okay. Fine."

"I'll be back in a minute."

Yuki said, "We're all obsessed with our careers, Richie. Women have to work harder—"

"Do you talk to Brady?" Rich asked Yuki.

"Talk to him? Sure."

"You go out to dinner with him?"

"Uh-huh. Couple times a week."

Cindy looked up as Mackie Morales came back from the ladies' room. She looked cute, seemed smart, had been working in the squad room for the last couple of months. Richie thought she was a good assistant. Very helpful.

Mackie tapped Rich on the shoulder, said, "I believe you're in my seat, Inspector."

Rich jumped up and said, "Morales. I didn't know you were here."

"Don't let me interrupt."

Morales took the chair at the head of the table

and sipped from her mug. Cindy thought that Rich didn't look so pale anymore. In fact, his ears were red.

"So I feel very bad," Rich continued. "Cindy won't talk about what's bothering her. This is a bad situation for both of us. What do you think we should do?"

Cindy felt like something had exploded between her ears. She couldn't take it for another second. It was outrageous. *He* was outrageous.

"Rich, are you *high*?" she shouted. "I make breakfast for you every morning. I do your laundry. I have to work all hours. You do, too. You do the same thing as I do."

"I need more than breakfast," he said. "I need devotion."

"Oops," said Morales. "Well, my babysitter likes to go home about now. Thanks, everyone," she said, putting a twenty on the table and grabbing her purse from the floor. "This was fun."

"Yeah, me, too," said Yuki. "Well, I don't have a babysitter, but I've got a conference call. Play nice, you two."

She kissed Claire's cheek, did the same but more awkwardly with Cindy, who had gone stiff and was staring at Richie as if her eyes were the business end of a double-barreled shotgun.

"I'm staying right here," said Claire. "Let's talk it out with Mama."

Chapter 44

CINDY SAID, "NO offense, Claire, but I don't want to talk this out with anyone. Not you, not Dr. Freud, not anyone. This is personal between Rich and me."

Claire said, "Dr. Freud?"

"Rich wants us to go into therapy, and I'm not going. I refuse, and I've tried to explain it to you, Rich. I don't have a mental disorder. Newspapers are folding worldwide. Writers are creating free content on blogs and are competing for the chance to work for no pay at all.

"I have to nail down my niche so that when the music stops, I have a chair."

"I'm not getting enough out of this relationship," Rich said. "You have to decide what's more important to you—"

Cindy bolted from the booth, pushed past the tables in the center of the room, threaded her way through the passageway, and went out into the bar. There was a limbo competition in progress and a skinny woman in hot pink was shimmying under the bamboo pole.

Cindy bumped into the stick and it clattered to the ground, which was followed by loud and very vocal disapproval from the crowd.

Cindy said, "Sorry," and kept going through the doorway, into the misty night. She began running up the street to where she had parked her car, on Jackson and Battery.

Rich was calling her name, but she didn't stop. She had her key fob in hand, and when she was within range, she disarmed the car alarm.

Rich was saying, "Stop running, Cindy. Just stop."

When she got to the car, it chirped as the alarm reset itself. What the hell? She pressed the button and the car chirped again, then again.

Rich had a duplicate of her fob. Every time she turned off the alarm, he turned it on again. This was insane.

She spun around to confront him.

"Leave me alone, Rich."

"First we talk."

"Do not go cop on me."

He smiled.

She said, "And do not try to humor me, either."

"Answer me this, Cindy. When was the last time you kissed me like you meant it?"

Everything seemed to stop but the rain.

Chapter 45

CINDY STARED AT Rich as he rested his butt against the left front fender of her car, crossed his arms over his chest. He looked seriously angry. She was pretty mad herself. When was the last time she'd kissed him with feeling?

He said, "You're ambitious to a fault."

"Oh, really?"

"Other women would be planning a wedding. They'd be designing their wedding dress and so forth. Picking out a honeymoon spot. You don't want to set a date. You make a little sound in your throat when you see a baby."

"What sound, Rich? I don't know what you're talking about."

"It's like you're disgusted."

Cindy felt the sting of truth. Tears welled up and spilled over. Rich came to her and tried to put his arms around her, but she shook him off, said, "Don't touch me. Please don't."

"Let's go home," he said. "I'll drive your car. I'll get a ride in the morning."

The truth was opening her up, but the price of the truth was the loss of Richie.

"Rich. I'm sorry that I can't be . . . I'm sorry that I'm not like other women. But I'm not. I didn't want to face it, but you're completely right. I've been keeping walls up because I knew that if I admitted that we want different things, this would be over."

She had been wearing Rich's mother's ring for almost a year. She pulled at it until it came off, and then she pushed it at Richie. He grunted as if he'd been punched in the belly. But he took the ring, closed his hand around it, then put it into his pocket.

Cindy felt light-headed. Had she meant to break up with him? Her face was wet from the rain. Oh, my God. Richie.

"It's not that I don't love you," she said. "I do."

"And now you're going to say that love isn't

enough?" His voice was cracking. He was crying, too.

Cindy reached up, took Richie's dear face in her hands, and kissed him. Then she released him and turned toward the car.

"I'll pick up my clothes in the morning," Rich said. "I'm going to make sure you get home okay."

"You don't have to do that."

"I want to."

"Where will you go?"

"Don't worry about it, Cindy. I can always find a place to sleep."

This was happening too fast, but it felt inevitable. Cindy opened her car door, got inside, and waited for several minutes as Rich got to his car, then pulled up behind her. His headlight beams filled the interior of her car with a cold and lifeless illumination.

Cindy released the brakes and turned the wheel, astounded at what she had done and that Rich had let her do it.

As she drove along Jackson, she had a flash of understanding.

Rich had gotten *her* to break up with him. He'd been loaded with determination when he arrived at Susie's. She should have known it from the look on his face.

Rich had already met someone else.

Chapter 46

I SAT WITH Claire on the fire stairs between the third and fourth floors of the Hall. Claire looked hungover and depressed.

"So the mayor says to me, 'Claire, I gotta cut your pay.' 'Okay,' I say. 'Why?' And he says, 'We're not budgeted for two medical examiners.'

"You getting this, Lindsay? He's installing a hack in my office and he's cutting me back to half pay. What a freaking insult. You know how many dead people came through my doors last year? I'll tell you. Two thousand three hundred and nine. It only cost the city about a thousand bucks a person. I'm already doing the work of *two* medical examiners."

It was true. Along with running her

department, supervising her staff, and overseeing the processing of thousands of deceased human beings, Claire also managed Dr. Clapper and the entire forensic lab at Hunters Point.

"And by the way," she said, "I didn't actually lose Faye Farmer's body. I was robbed."

Claire lit another cigarette. She had stopped smoking about five years ago.

"How did you leave things with the mayor?"

"I said, 'Yes, sir. I live to serve, sir.' I've got a kid in college. I can't afford to tell him to shove it."

"It really sucks, Butterfly, but it's not forever."

"What did you get from Jeff Kennedy?"

I told her about the interview at his lawyers' office, the party at his house, and that we had a list of names to check out.

"How many names?"

"Twelve. If your two investigators can check out the party guests, Conklin and I can stay on Kennedy."

"Deal," said Claire. "You can have Kain and Dedrick. If they're still letting me assign anyone to anything."

She was jiggling her knees as though she were still dancing Julie on her thighs. From my phone, I sent her the list of party guests, then asked, "Find anything in Faye Farmer's car?"

"Gunpowder on the dash. Faye's blood on the seat back. I know. Shocker."

My best friend inhaled, let out a plume of smoke.

She went on to say, "Clapper thinks she was most likely shot from the passenger seat. We have fingerprints—hers and Kennedy's and a lot of prints that aren't in the database. Nothing useful on the door handles. You have anything on Tracey Pendleton?"

"She hasn't used her credit card or her phone."

Claire said, "So she bought a no-name phone for forty bucks. Or maybe pesos. She could be buying gas with cash. I can't figure it out. What does she want with that body?"

I said, "Here's a late-breaking thought. Maybe Tracey Pendleton doesn't have the body. Maybe whoever stole the body took her, too. Tracey was a witness."

My phone rang. Conklin. We exchanged a few words, then I closed the phone, told Claire that I had to go.

Claire ground her cigarette out on the cement

step. Ground it to powder. We both stood up. The look in Claire's eyes was unutterably sad.

I hugged her and said, "This case is only thirty-six hours old. We've just gotten started."

"I know. Shit."

As she went back to the morgue, I trotted a half flight down to the squad room. I was already thinking about what Conklin had said: "The nutty professor is back."

Chapter 47

PERRY JUDD LOOKED as elated as if he'd just won a million dollars and the title of Mr. America at the same time. He stood up from the chair in Interview 2 and grabbed my hand with both of his. His color was high. There was spittle in the corners of his mouth.

"I had a dream," he said.

Conklin was rocking on the back legs of his chair. Morales brought coffee for three and left the room. I was pretty sure everyone in the squad was behind the one-way glass. We had a soothsayer in the house who had accurately predicted a fatal shooting.

It was a first for all of us.

I uncapped my coffee container and glanced

at the corner of the ceiling to make sure that the camera was recording. Conklin said to the professor, "When did you have the dream?"

"It was with me upon awakening," said Judd. "It was so real, I thought I truly was on a streetcar. When I say 'real,' I mean it was as if I were actually there."

"So take us through the dream from the top," I said.

"Certainly. I was on the F line, heading toward the Ferry Building. I go to the Ferry sometimes, on the weekends. But in my dream, if that's what it was, it was a weekday. There were commuters and tourists, all of us packed in."

"Morning?" I asked him. "Afternoon?"

"I can't tell," said the professor. He squinted as if he were trying to get the scene in focus. "Daylight, anyway. And I recognized the driver. She's about your age," he said to me. "A little slimmer than you are. Her hair was blond, but not like yours. She had coarser hair."

"Have you ever seen her in real life?" Conklin asked.

"Yes. But I don't know her name. In my vision, she was taking tickets. I was looking at the advertising above the windows. A Geico ad. 'Save fifteen percent in fifteen minutes.' I told you it was that real."

"Go on," I said.

"I held out my ticket to the driver. She was looking at me—and that's when I heard a cracking sound. A shot. I saw the blood come from her forehead. I was staring at that hole in her head and her brown eyes were locked on mine. Locked.

"This was something out of this world, Inspectors. To see someone's eyes just full of life— and then go utterly blank. I couldn't have made this up. It has to be a premonition. It has to be foresight. I'm telling you, I've never had dreams like these."

"So she was shot dead," Conklin said. "You're sure."

"I'm sure."

"What did the shooter look like?" I asked.

"People panicked," said the professor. "The driver dropped and people jumped back, screaming. The streetcar was stopped and everyone rushed out onto Market."

"Professor Judd," I said. "Be there now. Look into the corners of your mind. What did the shooter look like? Male? Female? Old, young?

You should have seen someone if you were there."

"I never saw the person with the gun. I woke up. I was shocked to find myself in my own bed. I thought I had gone to sleep in my chair."

"And when is this shooting supposed to happen? Today? Tomorrow? This week?"

"I don't know," said Professor Judd.

I stepped into the hallway with Conklin and the two of us talked about the professor's dream. Then I went into the standing-room-only observation room and asked Inspector Paul Chi to join us outside.

Chi is not only smarter than all of us put together but he can also slip almost unseen into a crowd, observe minute details of behavior, put two and two together, and come up with forty-four.

"What do you make of Professor Judd?" I asked him.

"He's enjoying this too much," Chi said. "Someone should shadow him. I should go to the SFMTA, see if I can pull up the name and schedule of a thin, blond-haired conductor on the F line. And then I should be her bodyguard."

"Do it," I said.

BOOK III

103 IN THE SHADE

Chapter 48

I'VE BEEN MERE yards from the epicenter of a bus bomb. I've been a target in a shooting gallery in the 'hood, and I've taken bullets and almost died.

But nothing was as scary or as emotionally devastating as my tiny daughter having a fever of 103.

The second I got home and read the thermometer, I called Julie's pediatrician and insisted that she be paged, because I wasn't getting off the phone until I spoke with her.

Dr. Gordon was very patient. She said that Julie's fever meant that she was fighting an infection—that she could have an earache, for instance—and to give her a lukewarm bath followed by liquid Tylenol every four hours.

I made an appointment to bring Julie in to see the doctor in the morning. Then I sat in the bathtub with my baby in my lap. I desperately wanted to bathe away her fever without letting her know that I was scared out of my freaking mind.

Joe sat on the toilet seat, singing "Oh! Susanna" in the soft, slow way James Taylor recorded it. His singing was like a lullaby, but it didn't soothe the baby.

She cried. She was limp. I wanted to take her to the hospital right then, but Joe said no.

"It's too risky. She could pick up a worse infection in the hospital," he said. "Let's do what Dr. Gordon said."

I sponged Julie down with the tepid water and when we were both wrinkled, Joe helped us out of the bath and we took her with us into bed.

Her temperature had dropped to 102. It was a change in the right direction, but still outside my comfort zone. I called Dr. Gordon again and she phoned back at just before ten that night.

"It's probably nothing. Try not to worry," she said.

"Right," I said into the phone.

"If her temperature goes to a hundred and four,

take her straight to the emergency room."

"Okay."

"I'll see you in the morning. Try to get some sleep."

"Thanks, Doctor," I said.

No one slept at our house except Martha, and we were at the doctor's office as soon as the doors opened.

Dr. Gordon weighed Julie, examined her, made notes on her chart. The doctor's expression was so neutral I couldn't read it, not even between the lines.

"I wish she'd put on a little more weight," she said.

"She's been fussy from the beginning," I said.

"I'm going to draw some blood. Standard procedure," said the doctor. "Just to get a baseline."

Joe held Julie as the stick pricked my daughter's tiny pink heel. Julie howled, of course, and I just hid my face until it was over.

I asked the doctor to tell us everything. "Don't hold anything back."

Finally, Dr. Gordon cracked a smile.

"She's got a fever, but it's not abnormal. I'll call you when I get back her blood work. Meanwhile, you should all get some sleep."

As soon as I hit the sheets, my cell phone rang. I read the caller ID and then told Brady, "Whatever it is has got to wait. I need four hours of sleep. Just four."

Brady ignored me.

"Boxer, that streetcar driver on the F line?"

"What? Who?"

"Your professor said a streetcar driver was going to be shot, remember?"

"Oh. No. Don't tell me."

"We've got a female streetcar driver who took a bullet about an hour ago. Right between the eyes. Just like the professor said."

Chapter 49

BY THE TIME I dragged myself to the Ferry Building, at the Embarcadero and Market Street, the perimeter was in place and the building was the backdrop for a messy crime scene made worse by the stationary streetcar and the throttled morning rush.

Of the three lanes of traffic running in each direction, four were stopped cold and the other two were stalled. There is a wide median strip adjacent to the streetcar tracks, a strip of plaza between the northbound and southbound lanes. On any other day, this strip would have been busy with buskers, mimes, cyclists, and skateboarders. Now, in place of all the activity, there were black-and-white cruisers, ambulances, the crime scene mobile unit, and traffic cops.

I parked the Explorer at the edge of the pack of law enforcement vehicles and headed toward the evidence tent that had been set up on the median. I picked out Conklin and Morales, who were talking to Clapper and a stocky guy I didn't know. He had an authoritative air and tiny little eyes.

He had to be our temporary medical examiner.

Conklin introduced me to Dr. Morse, and I said, "Pleased to meet you." Then I asked Conklin to give me the details.

"That's the primary crime scene," he said, pointing to the 1940s-style green-and-cream-colored trolley.

Conklin said, "The victim is still in there. Her name is Janet Rice, thirty-four, African American, married with two children. She's been working as a driver for sixteen years."

"She's black?"

"She was on her usual route," Conklin said. "There was a shot fired. She was killed instantly."

"Tell me we've got some witnesses," I said.

"Someone pulled the door lever and everyone

who could get out did. A bystander called nine-one-one. Units are canvassing now."

I heard my name and turned to see Paul Chi and his partner, Cappy McNeil, coming toward me.

Chi had been bodyguarding a blond streetcar driver and McNeil had been shadowing Professor Judd.

Chi said, "Sergeant, the driver we identified with the blond hair is Tara Moffett. Always works the F line. I've been her constant companion for the last week, and Lemke took the second shifts. Ms. Moffett is a hundred percent fine. I'd say she wasn't the target."

The sun was beating down. There were sailboats out on the bay. This should have been a beautiful sight, but there were also helicopters overhead, news choppers. If there was anything worse than a shooting, it was a shooting that affected the city's tourist business.

The video guys in the helicopters were getting phenomenal photos that would play brilliantly on national television. The San Francisco Bay. The bridges. The sailboats on the sun-flecked waves. The streetcar in front of the monumental Ferry Building and the buglike cruisers around the evidence tent.

McNeil said, "I watched the professor night and day. Samuels watched him when I was off duty. Professor Judd couldn't have taken a shit without our knowing it."

To my left, Brady was lifting the barrier tape for the mayor, then both of them came toward us.

"Brief the lieutenant, will you?" I said to Conklin. "I've got to call home."

Chapter 50

THE INSIDE OF the streetcar was crawling with crime techs in bunny suits and booties, shooting pictures, capturing prints, trying not to fall over one another or step in potential evidence.

I stood on the street, looking through the open folding doors at the front part of the streetcar, especially at the driver's seat, where Janet Rice had been sitting before she stopped at Market to take on passengers.

A dozen feet away from me, Conklin and Morales were at the doors in the middle of the car, Conklin explaining crime scene procedure even as Claire's stand-in, Dr. Morse, stood impatiently behind him.

Janet Rice's body was lying across from

Conklin, her head and shoulders wedged between two seats, legs in the aisle, blood pooling under her head and running under the seat behind her.

As Judd described his dream, he had been about to hand his ticket to the driver when she took a shot between the eyes. So if the dream matched reality, the shooter would have been standing behind the professor and would have fired the gun from over his shoulder.

If that was true, Rice's killer had likely waited for the streetcar to stop. He had climbed aboard, or maybe just stood on the top step. From there, he had a fleeting clear shot at the driver and had taken it. Then, as all eyes went to the victim, he'd stepped back down onto the street and blended into the crowd.

As the ME's techs struggled to remove the victim, I heard Morales say to Conklin, "I'm going to do my dissertation on this psychic angle. Whether the professor is clairvoyant or not, this case has all the elements of a classic serial killing."

Conklin nodded and said, "Oh, absolutely."

I noticed something of a frisky nature in their body language. They were standing hip to hip. Making lots of eye contact. What was going on between those two, exactly? Was this your typical workplace flirtation? Or was it something more?

I didn't have a chance to chase down this train of thought because to my left, coming from the direction of the Ferry Building, a female voice shouted out, "No, no, nooo."

I picked her out of the crowd.

A teenage girl in a Catholic school uniform was making a run for the streetcar. Cops grabbed her by the arms before she breached the tape, but they were having a hard time restraining her. She was determined and desperate and she was breaking my heart.

"Mom-ma," she screamed. "Mom-maaaa."

Chapter 51

ONCE AGAIN, CONKLIN and I were closeted in an interview room with the little professor and his gigantic ego. Professor Judd had predicted a second murder and he could not be happier with himself.

Right then, he was drawing a diagram on a pad of paper.

"Clairvoyance means 'clear seeing,'" Judd said. "There are several forms of clairvoyance—for instance, telepathy. With telepathy, a person reads another person's thoughts. Remote viewing is when you can see what someone else sees, as they are seeing it."

Judd drew circles and arrows to illustrate what he knew about extrasensory perception. If he really was clairvoyant, I had to say it was an impressive talent. Still, he didn't seem to care that another person had died. And that his "talent" was useless unless it led to catching a killer.

"I have precognition," Judd said. "I see events before they happen. Frankly, I don't yet understand how I suddenly came to have this gift."

The professor was musing. He'd gone into his head—a scary, mysterious, and also tedious place to be.

A good interrogator befriends the subject, flatters him, encourages him to talk, hoping he'll trap himself in a lie or make a confession.

But patience was my partner's forte, not mine.

I was overtired and in a bad mood. Also, I couldn't stand this guy.

I slapped Janet Rice's photo ID down on the table and said, "Do you know this woman?"

"Is this the driver who was shot?"

"Yes. This is our victim. Janet Rice. Married. Two children. Churchgoer. Taxpayer. Home owner. Employee of the city of San Francisco. Friend to many, enemy to none. Do you recognize her?"

"She's not the person I envisioned. So . . . what could this mean?"

"Have you seen her before?" I asked for the third time.

"No. Never."

"Where were you this morning between eleven and twelve noon?"

"I told you, Sergeant Boxer. I was in class with thirty students," Judd said. "We're reading *Anna Karenina*."

Conklin said, "Why do you suppose you saw a blond driver in your dream? I mean, this woman isn't blond and she has never been blond. You think she was a victim of circumstance? She was just in the wrong place at the wrong time?"

"I am wondering the same thing, Inspector. But I have absolutely no idea."

His sappy voice made my last nerve snap like an old guitar string.

"What happened inside that streetcar?" I said to the professor. I grabbed the pad and pencil away from him and drew an arrow off the word *clairvoyance*, encircled a bunch of question marks.

"Give us an educated guess. Maybe you have an idea that doesn't involve extrasensory malarkey."

Judd looked shocked. Then he got pissed.

"Don't talk to me that way, Sergeant. I came

here at your request and of my own volition. I've told you everything I know. Where's the thanks I deserve?"

"You know about lucid dreaming?" I asked him.

"Well, yes. Lucid dreaming occurs when a person is conscious that he is having a dream. He's lucid. According to the literature, if the dreamer is aware that he's dreaming, he can change the direction, even the outcome of the dream."

"Exactly."

"Oh. I see."

"Try lucid dreaming, would you, Professor Judd? Next time you're in a dream, get your head on straight. Grab the gun. And then remember who the killer is and tell us. Thank you for coming in. Always a pleasure seeing you. Please don't leave town."

I flipped the pencil into the middle of the table, said to Conklin, "My baby is sick. I'm going home."

Chapter 52

YUKI AND HER associate, Nicky Gaines, returned from the lunch recess a few minutes before court reconvened and took their seats.

Yuki had rested her case, and now it was the defense's turn to present theirs. She hoped like mad that her case was strong enough to hold up no matter what Kinsela said to convince the jury that Keith Herman, a subhuman piece of garbage, was not guilty.

Yuki thought about Patricia Reeves, a woman who was tried for the murder of her two-year-old daughter. Reeves's lawyer had stated that his client had been sexually abused by her father and that the father had been complicit in covering up the child's accidental death.

In Yuki's opinion, the defendant had lied, the lawyer had lied, too, and Patricia Reeves had gotten away with murder.

Like Reeves's attorney, Kinsela was a master of the ad hominem attack. He'd assaulted Lynnette Lagrande's character to discredit her. And he would certainly come up with a load of random bullcrap in his client's defense.

Thinking over Kinsela's case, looking for holes in her own, Yuki didn't see any quicksand.

Come to think of it, she also didn't see the defense.

Yuki poked Gaines with her elbow and angled her chin toward the defense table. No one was there; not the lawyers, not Keith Herman. Where were they?

Just then, Judge Arthur R. Nussbaum came through his private door and the bailiff called the court to order. Nussbaum saw the void at the defense table, called the bailiff over to the bench, leaned down, and whispered loud enough for Yuki to hear, "Have the clerk call Kinsela. Find out where the hell he is."

Worst-case scenarios were now rising in Yuki's mind. Had Keith Herman escaped from jail? Had he hanged himself? Had her wish that John Kinsela would eat shit and die actually come true?

The judge apologized to the jury for the delay, saying, "If the defense and the defendant aren't here in five minutes, I'm going to adjourn court for the day." Then he muttered, "And there will be hell to pay."

Five minutes passed. Very. Very. Slowly.

The bailiff returned to the bench and had another whispered conversation with the judge, which was interrupted by a young lawyer in a severe charcoal-gray suit and high heels coming up the aisle in a great clacking hurry.

"Your Honor, I'm Linda Gregory from Mr. Kinsela's office."

"What's going on, Ms. Gregory?"

"May I approach?"

As the attorney came toward the judge, the doors at the end of the aisle opened again. Nicky said to Yuki, "Lookit this, will you?"

Yuki turned and saw Keith Herman, handcuffed and flanked by two armed guards, walking toward the bar. He was smiling as if he'd just gotten a free pass to the good seats in heaven.

A woman in the gallery said loudly, "Oh, my God."

Two more people had come through the double doors; John Kinsela was holding the hand of a cute little girl with honey-blond hair. The child was about eight, wearing jeans, a floral print shirt, and a pink hoodie. She looked neat and clean.

Yuki's heartbeat sped over the legal limit. She recognized that little girl. From the rustle and gasps in the gallery, everyone did. This child's picture had been on the news and had circumnavigated the Internet a million times since she'd gone missing.

Kinsela stopped in the aisle beside his table and said to the judge, "I apologize for being late, Your Honor, but I received an urgent call just an hour ago. Then I needed my client to confirm this little girl's identity."

"Explain yourself, Mr. Kinsela."

"Judge, I'd like to introduce you to my client's daughter, Lily Herman. She was found alive and well, sitting on the front steps of her former home.

"We respectfully request that you dismiss the charges against Mr. Herman."

Chapter 53

YUKI THOUGHT SOMETHING was very wrong with Lily Herman. The child seemed distracted, as if she were seeing things from a distance or through a filter. She had to have been traumatized, or maybe she was drugged. Where had she been for the last year? What had happened to her?

The judge sat behind the desk in his chambers, opened his drawer, and said, "Lily, I'm a bit of a chocolate nut. How about you? Do you like M&M's?"

"I like Jell-O," Lily said. "The purple kind."

Nussbaum said, "I'm sorry, Lily. I'm out of Jell-O. We'll be able to get you some after we talk. Do you mind if I ask you some questions?"

Lily kicked her feet under the judge's side chair,

looked around, blinked at Yuki, then slid her gaze over Kinsela, who was sitting in a chair against the wall. Kinsela smiled, but the child turned away and brought her attention back to the judge. He asked her if she knew the difference between a lie and the truth.

"Yeppers. I know the difference."

"It's very important, so important that you have to swear to God to tell the truth."

"No problem," said the eight-year-old. "I swear to God."

"What's your full name, dear?" Nussbaum asked.

"Lily Baines Herman."

"And how old are you, Lily?"

"I don't know."

"Do you know what month this is?"

"Is it summer yet?"

"Not yet, but soon," said the judge. "You've been missing for a long time. Everyone has been worried. Where have you been?"

"In a room. In a house," she said. "I had a TV and a little tiny tabby kitten. Pokey."

Lily's gaze wandered again as she took in the rows of law books, the many-paned windows, the heavy furnishings, and the landscape paintings. Yuki would have given a million bucks to know what she was thinking.

"Who else lived in this house?"

"Marcia and Alan."

"Do you know their last names?"

"Nopey-nope-nope."

"Are you related to them? Are they family members?"

"No way!"

"So help me out, Lily. Tell me all about these people and how you came to be living with them. Okay?"

"Okay."

Yuki, Kinsela, and Judge Nussbaum waited for the little girl to elaborate on her one-word answer. Finally, she stopped swinging her legs and began to speak as if she were reading or playing a part.

"They had masks. Different ones on different days. Like devil masks. Like pig masks. They told me their names but I never saw their faces. I had my own room and a bathroom and I had a computer for games. I had three meals a day and a snack before bedtime."

"Could you use a phone?"

"Nopey-nope-nope."

"You were kidnapped," the judge said.

Lily shrugged. "They didn't hurt me." Then, "I miss Pokey."

"Did your father have anything to do with this, Lily? For instance, was he keeping you safe? Is that what he told you?"

"My daddy didn't know where I was or he would have come to get me. He loves me. He would have given Marcia and Alan a beating."

"Did Marcia and Alan take you home this morning, Lily?"

"When can I see my mommy?"

Chapter 54

I PARKED THE Explorer three feet away from the curb on Lake Street, but I was so dirty-dog-tired that I didn't have the strength to park it again.

I opened the apartment door, and when Martha didn't throw herself at me, I tiptoed around the entranceway to the living room. Joe was in his big leather recliner, Julie in his arms with her head on his shoulder, both of them sound asleep. Martha lifted her head, flapped her tail, then put her face back down on Joe's slipper.

I couldn't imagine a warmer welcome.

I ditched my gun, phone, jacket, and shoes— just dropped all of it on a chair. Then I hit the soft leather sofa with the puffy cushions, drew up the chenille throw, and settled in.

I was dreaming about Julie wearing a big-girl party dress and blowing out birthday candles when I heard Joe speaking. I opened my eyes a crack, saw that lamps were lit, and that it was dark outside. I must have gotten about four hours of sleep.

Joe was saying into the phone, "Okay. Tomorrow morning, nine a.m. We'll be there."

He hung up looking grim and walked with the baby to the kitchen, where he heated up a bottle in the microwave. When the oven beeped, he tested the milk, then started back across the room with the baby.

"Honey, who was that on the phone?" I asked.

"Hey, you were really out. Do you feel better?"

"Was that Dr. Gordon?"

"Uh-huh. We have an appointment tomorrow morning."

"Did she get the tests back?"

"I think so. But she would have told me if anything was wrong. The baby is warm," he said.

"How warm?"

"She keeps fluctuating between normal and a hundred and three. She goes up. She goes down. Our roller-coaster baby."

"Joe. This can't be right. I'm really getting scared. Actually, I'm way past scared. I'm terrified."

I rolled Julie's crib into our bedroom, next to my side of the bed. It was another night when supposedly nothing was really wrong with Julie, but I didn't believe it. I'd been told that babies get fevers, that all new mothers worry this way, but I felt alarmed every time I touched her skin.

I was hovering uselessly over Julie's crib when my phone rang. I didn't answer, and then I didn't answer it when it rang again. It had been a long time since a phone call had brought me good news.

If I didn't pick up the phone, maybe the caller would go away.

Chapter 55

AFTER THE PHONE had rung three times in five minutes, I gave in and dug it out from under the pile of clothes on the chair. I looked at the caller ID.

"For God's sake. Whose life is this, anyway?"

Joe said, "Who is it?"

"The bad news bear."

I said, "Boxer," into the mouthpiece and he said, "You're not going to believe this."

Julie set up a wail from her crib. Her voice was pitched at extra loud. I could hardly hear Brady's voice.

"I'm a little busy right now, boss," I said.

"Remember Randolph Fish?"

"Did he die?"

"No, he woke up."

Randolph Fish was a brutal, clever, truly diabolical killer who had been linked to nine dead or missing college girls over a three-year span, all on the West Coast.

The remains of five of the young women had been found in wooded areas and remote industrial locations. The victims had been tortured and mutilated, each dying by different means. Bludgeoning. Strangulation. Stabbing.

The other three girls had never been found or heard from again, but they matched the killer's type—petite, darkhaired, and very trusting. Because of the different locations and manners of death, it had taken years to connect the dead and missing girls to one killer.

And then the killer made a mistake.

A fingerprint found on a car belonging to one of the dead girls matched that of Randolph Fish, an itinerant bartender who had been arrested in San Francisco a month before for assault and then released.

After victim number nine, Sandra Brody, was abducted from the campus of the University of San Francisco three years ago and taken to whereabouts unknown, Jacobi and I were asked to work with the FBI. Jacobi and I joined the stakeout in the Mission.

It was about nine at night, windy and cold. We were watching two bars and a movie theater on 16th when Fish came out of the theater.

He saw an FBI vehicle and, like a praying mantis nabbing a bug, Fish snatched a woman at random who was also leaving the theater. He held a knife under her throat and shouted to the agents in the black SUV, "I'll kill her. Believe me, I will."

I was on the theater side of the street, crouched between two cars, and I had a clear shot at the back of Randolph Fish's head. I couldn't see the hostage's face, only the line of her throat and the blade pressing against it.

I stood up, held my gun with both hands, and shouted, "Fish! Let her go or I'll blow your brains to the moon."

I hoped like hell that he would obey because I didn't know if my aim was good enough to take him out before he killed his hostage. Luckily, I didn't have to find out.

The human shield broke free. Fish bolted into the street toward oncoming traffic. I ran, too, yelling, "Stop or I'll shoot."

He must've heard the conviction in my voice.

He stopped running, and when I told him to drop to the ground and interlace his hands behind his neck, he did it. He laughed at me when I kicked the knife into the gutter. When Jacobi cuffed him, Fish told Jacobi he was so fat he was headed for a heart attack.

Frankly, I couldn't believe what Fish looked like in person. I had to shake my head and reorder my thoughts. But never mind his appearance—he was down. The FBI took him into custody and we were all jubilant.

It was frigid and I was shaking from the cold. It was one of the best moments of my life.

Chapter 56

THE NIGHT WE captured Randolph Fish, Ronald Parker, special agent in charge of the FBI's San Francisco field office, said that Fish would be more responsive to a female interviewer than to the men working the case.

"He's all about control," Parker said. "He's like a drug addict, and his drug of choice is dominating women. He'll try to get under your skin, Lindsay. If there's any chance of getting Sandra Brody back, you'll have to get under his."

I interrogated Randolph Fish for fifteen hours on each of three consecutive days. I used every interview technique I knew. I threatened him. I negotiated with him. When these methods failed, I shut off the camera and I threw the man to the floor. I kicked him nine times, once for each of his victims.

Fish laughed and told me what a cute piece I was when I was mad. He had gotten under my skin after all, and he never told me or anyone else what happened to Sandra Brody.

Fish was tried, convicted on five counts of homicide in the first degree, and sent to the federal prison at Atwater, where he was locked in a nice private cell.

A year later, he was on the way to the infirmary for shooting pains in his chest when a riot broke out and a guard was shot. Fish made a break for an exit—and was clubbed across the back of the head.

He slipped into a persistent coma and was handcuffed to a bed in the prison wing of a nearby hospital, where he had been for the last two years.

I'd long hoped that Randolph Fish would wake up with his memory intact. There were four families who wanted to know where their daughters were buried, and nine families who wanted to watch Randolph Fish die in the chair.

Now I gripped the phone and said to Brady, "What's his condition?"

"He spoke in full sentences," Brady said. "He

told the warden he'll take the feds to the missing bodies if he gets a deal, and if he gets to talk to you. Do you want in on this, Boxer? Ron Parker asked for your assistance."

I didn't want to say no to Ron Parker.

"I'll do it," I told Brady, "but I can't make it tomorrow. I just can't."

"Fish could go back into a coma. It happens, you know. Parker's not going to wait," he said.

"That's okay."

"Are you all right, Lindsay?"

"I'm absolutely terrific. Joe and I were just saying that these are the best days of our lives."

"Uh-huh. Go feed your baby. I'll ask Jacobi to call Parker. See what he can do."

Chapter 57

JOE, JULIE, AND I were in Dr. Gordon's office promptly at nine the next morning. I looked down into my baby's sweet face, hoping for a smile, some little sign that would make me say, "She's fine."

"I'm not so happy with the results of the blood test," Dr. Gordon said.

I tried to read her inscrutable face. I realized that Dr. Gordon was younger than I am. And for the first time, that really worried me. Did she have enough experience to help Julie? Was she the best doctor in the world?

"What about her blood tests? What's wrong?"

"Her white blood cells are abnormal in shape."

Abnormal? I grabbed the desk with both hands, as if to stop myself from lifting off and rocketing away from the planet. I had never heard more terrifying words in my life.

"What do you mean by 'abnormal'?" I said.

Joe shielded the baby from me and from what the doctor was saying. He said, softly, "What's the worst-case scenario?"

Dr. Gordon said, "Let's not go to worst cases. We're not at that point, not even close. I want to check Julie into the hospital and get a full clinical workup," the doctor said. "I think she may have an infection, but I want a second opinion."

"An infection like the flu? Is that what you mean?" I said, my grip on the desk relaxing a tad.

"I think so, but I want other doctors to look at her. Look, Lindsay, she's not gaining weight. She's running intermittent fevers. It could be just how Julie is, or maybe she picked up something from one of the firemen who delivered her. But I'm guessing.

"I want to test for everything, aggressively. We should do X-rays, biopsies, the works."

I shouted, "Oh, my God. You don't think she has the flu. What is this? What do you think she has?"

Joe shushed me and put his hand on Julie's head.

Dr. Gordon said, "I'm going to make sure that next time you ask me what's wrong, I can give you an unqualified answer. California Women's has a wonderful pediatric facility. I'd like you to bring her over—now."

I had been worried for weeks, and now I thought those weeks had been wasted, that we should have pushed harder for answers.

I blamed myself for not overriding Joe and taking Julie to the hospital the first time she had a fever. I should have followed my instincts. I should have done it.

"I'll meet you at admitting," Dr. Gordon said.

I held the baby as Joe drove. He looked drained. Gray. "We'll get to the bottom of this, Linds. We won't have to wonder anymore, and Julie will get better."

Yeah? And how did Joe know that?

We found a spot in the outpatient parking, carried the baby through the pale stone lobby, and took the elevator to pediatrics.

We got through the check-in procedure without either one of us blowing up or going crazy. We met the radiologist, who handed Julie to a nurse, who snapped a bracelet around her tiny wrist—and took her away.

Dr. Gordon said, "She's in very good hands. I'll call you as soon as I have something to tell you."

"We'll be right here, in the waiting room," I said.

"This will take a couple of days," Dr. Gordon told us. "Please go home. There's nothing you can do for your daughter by waiting here when you live ten blocks away. You can look in on her tonight."

I had a good hard cry in the hospital lobby. Joe held me tight, and then he drove us home.

Chapter 58

AT SIX THIRTY the next morning, my former partner, chief of police Warren Jacobi, swooped down on Lake Street in his shiny black sedan. He pulled up to where I was waiting for him outside our apartment building, leaned across the seat, and opened the passenger-side door for me.

He took a look at my face and said, "Good morning, sunshine."

"Don't start with me, Jacobi. I haven't slept."

"You worried about our meeting with Fish?"

"I meant I haven't slept since Julie was born."

"Well, you do look like hell." He laughed. "On you, it looks good."

I pulled a face, got into the car, took a container out of the cup holder, and pried off the lid with my shaking hands. Jacobi was a worn-looking fifty-five, white-haired, jowly, and, to my eyes, beautiful.

"Julie is in the hospital," I said.

"Shit. What for? What's wrong with her?"

The coffee was black, two sugars. Jacobi knew how I like it. I strapped in, then told my former partner everything I knew about what was wrong with Julie.

I didn't know much.

Jacobi listened as we cruised up Lake Street, the nose of the car pointed east toward Modesto and then south to the U.S. penitentiary in Atwater.

Jacobi said how sorry he was that the baby was sick, and he also told me that I always worry too much and that everything would be fine.

"Of course, when you stop worrying, that's when things really turn to shit."

"I've really missed you, Jacobi. Like a migraine."

He laughed and got me to do it, too.

It was almost like old times.

During the ten years I worked with Jacobi, we logged innumerable twenty-hour days in a squad car, arrested a few dozen killers and unrepentant dirtbags, and we both took bullets one bad night in an unlit alley in the Tenderloin.

We could have died and almost did.

A year later, Jacobi stood in for my dead father and gave me away to Joe Molinari. I tripped down the petal-strewn path, fumbled the wedding ring, and Jacobi laughed out loud on the best day of my life. We've had hilarious times and horrific ones, but we've never doubted that we're friends forever.

As Jacobi drove, I told him, "I've never been so scared, and I mean never. You don't know what love is until you have a sick baby."

Joe had insisted that I go to work and he'd promised he'd sit at the hospital all day, all night, never leave Julie alone. I'd left the house only a half hour before, but I called Joe anyway.

"Just—call me if you learn anything, anything at all."

"I will, sweetie. You know I will."

After I hung up, Jacobi and I talked about the Faye Farmer case and the ugly shootings foreseen by the so-called clairvoyant professor.

And we talked about Randy Fish.

Jacobi said, "I'm glad that sack of crap is alive and can still use his shit for brains. Doubly glad he's back in maximum security."

In another couple of hours, we were going

to be talking to that sack of crap. I hoped that, having almost died, Randy Fish would feel some compassion for the parents of the missing girls. He was on death row. He had nothing to lose by telling us where he'd disposed of their bodies.

Chapter 59

THE LANDSCAPE SURROUNDING the penitentiary is remarkable for its emptiness. If you stand in one spot and turn a full 360 degrees, you'll see the stark prison buildings, a few distant farmhouses, and dusty flatlands out to the horizon.

We met Ron Parker at the front gate. He told us that Fish would speak only with me and there was a condition. I had to apologize for the way I treated him.

"Really? He comes out of a coma after two years and that's what he wants?"

"That's what he said, Lindsay. He wants to make a deal, but you know, he's a manipulative prick. I think you should apologize, see if you can get some kind of rapport going. This might be our best and only chance to find out where he put those girls."

One hour and many checkpoints later, I entered a small room with one glass wall. On the other side of the glass was a maximum-security hospital room. Randy Fish was wearing a hospital gown, sitting up in bed, reading a book.

I felt like Clarice Starling meeting Hannibal Lecter in *The Silence of the Lambs*.

But Randolph Fish was no Anthony Hopkins. He wasn't a David Berkowitz or a Ted Bundy, either. At close to thirty years old, Randolph Fish looked like a teenage movie star.

I pulled out the straight-backed chair and Fish looked up, recognized me, and gave me an endearing smile.

I said, "Hello, Randy."

"Well look at you, Lindsay," he said. "You've put on, I'm going to say, twenty-two pounds since I saw you last. You look healthy."

At five five, Randy Fish might have weighed 135 pounds when I'd kicked him around three years ago, but he weighed less now. His brown hair was clean. He had large brown eyes and bow-shaped lips. He looked unbelievably sweet and vulnerable and frail.

It was easy to see how women had fallen for him, done what he'd asked of them, without having the slightest sense that he was a sexually deviant psychopath with an insatiable desire to maim and kill.

"How're you feeling?" I asked him.

"Rested," he said, smiling again.

"I'm glad to see that you're okay," I said truthfully. "I still have some questions for you."

"Don't you have something to tell me?" asked the killer.

"What are you reading?" I asked.

"*The Poet* by Michael Connelly. I'm not going to beg you, Lindsay. You know what I want."

I felt literally sick. I'd seen the morgue pictures of the five women we knew Fish had killed. One had had her fingers and toes cut off while she was alive. Another had hundreds of knife slits all over her body. All of them had been brutally raped, bitten, hanged. I knew too much about what this psycho had done and I didn't want to give him anything.

But if I wanted to find Sandra Brody's body and those of the three other missing young women, I was going to have to give in.

I quashed my gag reflex, but I still tasted bile at the back of my throat when I said, "I'm sorry I had to be so rough with you, Randy. But you know, you had threatened to kill a hostage. And Sandra Brody was still missing."

"You call that an apology?"

"You remember Sandra," I said. "She's a pretty girl, brunette, size four, has a bit of an overbite. She was a biology major. I might be able to help you if you tell me where she is."

"I don't remember a Sandra Brody," he said. "In fact, I can't even remember why I was locked up. But I do remember you, Lindsay Boxer. I wish we'd met under different circumstances. You're very dear to me."

He showed me the book he'd been reading and said, "This is pretty good. Have you read it? Do you read?"

He was back into his book, turning the pages, seemingly absorbed. As far as Randy Fish was concerned, the interview was over.

I had apologized.

He'd given me nothing in return. And I was absolutely sure he was messing with me. If I had gotten down on my knees and given him an unconditional apology, he would still have messed with me.

He liked the game. He loved it.

I tapped on the glass.

Fish looked up.

I smiled and said, "Go to hell, okay?"

He shouted as I left the room, "I'm crazy about you, Lindsay Boxer. I really am."

Chapter 60

YUKI HAD JUST about gotten a grip on the astounding fact of Lily Herman's reappearance when John Kinsela called his first witness.

"The defense calls Gary Goodfriend."

Yuki said, "What?" just loud enough for Nicky to hear. Her associate shrugged and looked at her with big eyes, as surprised as she was that their witness had been called by the opposition.

Yuki watched as the gun dealer who had sold Keith Herman a gun passed her chair on his way to the witness stand. He was wearing the same fringed buckskin jacket he'd worn when he was a witness for the prosecution, but the swagger was gone now that he'd gone over to the other side.

Goodfriend swore on the Bible and took his

seat. Yuki looked directly at him, but he avoided her eyes.

Kinsela jingled coins in his pocket as he asked his witness, "Mr. Goodfriend, did you call my office yesterday afternoon?"

"Yes. I did."

"And why did you call me?"

"Because I was having a whatchamacallit—guilty conscience."

"Will you please tell the court what you told me?"

"I told you that I don't really remember if it was Keith Herman who made that comment about having a rug rat problem, or if it was some other customer."

"But you testified that it was Keith Herman."

"I misremembered," Goodfriend said now. "I definitely sold Keith Herman a gun. I've got the yellow copy of the sales slip. But like I said, I sold thirty guns that weekend. There was a lot of talking all around. It was noisy. It was a trade show, you know. And, what I'm thinking now is that I got confused."

Kinsela said, "So to be clear, you're retracting your earlier testimony. You no longer believe that

Mr. Herman wanted to kill his daughter."

"That's right."

"Thank you for coming forward, Mr. Goodfriend. That was an act of good citizenry."

The judge said to Yuki, "You've got some questions, Ms. Castellano?"

"Just a few, Your Honor." Yuki struggled for composure. No good to let Kinsela see that he'd rattled her. She relaxed her face and smiled.

"Mr. Goodfriend, I want to understand the timeline of your memory reversal."

"Okay. Sure."

"Last week you swore on the Bible that Mr. Herman had made a comment that you took to mean that he wanted to shoot his child."

"Uh-huh. But that was then."

"You realize that either that statement or the one you just made is a lie. Do you know that perjury is a felony?"

"I wasn't intentionally telling a lie. I just remembered it one way and then, yesterday, I remembered it a different way."

Yuki sighed. "You also stated that you believe that Mr. Herman is a violent person. Have you been threatened?"

"Mr. Herman is in jail."

"I understand that, Mr. Goodfriend. Did anyone put pressure on you to retract your testimony?"

"The only one that put pressure on me is you."

"Me?"

Yuki was dumbfounded. What was this guy saying? She hadn't been sure of him when he contacted her, but he had checked out as a legitimate gun dealer, with no record of any kind. His testimony had been good for her case because he had described the defendant's violent personality for the jury.

Goodfriend said now, "When I came to you and said I thought the defendant had made a threat, you said, 'Are you sure?'"

"Yes, and you said you were."

"Well, I *wanted* to be sure because of you putting pressure on me to get it right. I thought I was sure. Now I'm not sure anymore."

"So maybe your original memory was wrong. Or maybe your original memory was correct?"

"Huh?"

"Your Honor, I'm done with this witness. I reserve the right to charge him with perjury once

I determine if he has even the most basic grasp of the truth."

Kinsela snorted from across the room.

The judge said to Yuki, "Duly noted," and told Gary Goodfriend that he could step down.

Nussbaum looked at the big white-faced clock over the exit door, then said, "Seems like an appropriate place to adjourn for the weekend."

Chapter 61

IT WAS 7:40 on Monday morning when Claire saw Rich Conklin's truck parked off by itself in the open lot on Harriet Street. When she got closer, she saw that Richie's head was tipped back and his mouth was open. Looked like he'd passed out.

She called out to him a couple of times and when he didn't come to, she rapped on the window, said, "Richie. Yoo-hoo. Wakey-wakey."

He sat up, said, "Huh?" and then, "Oh, hi, Claire. Am I late?" He ran his hands through his hair, tucked his shirt into his pants.

Claire went around to the passenger side and climbed up into the truck. The cab smelled of beer. There was a crumpled hamburger bag in the foot well, dirty laundry lying loose on the backseat. Richie hadn't shaved.

She said, "Actually, you're early, my friend. How long you been sleeping here?"

Rich leaned across her, opened the glove compartment, and took out his cell phone. He checked it for messages, then put it in his shirt pocket.

Since he hadn't answered her question, Claire had a few more for him.

"What's up, Richie? I suppose you've got a good reason to be camping out in the parking lot. When was the last time you took a shower?"

He laughed, then said, "Hold on, Claire. That was a good idea. May I use your shower?"

Claire had a private shower at the morgue. Problem was, it wasn't exactly hers at the moment. Her stand-in, Dr. Herbert Morse, would be arriving in a few minutes, if he wasn't already there in her office, boning up on how to be a medical examiner.

"Honestly, if it was mine to give you, I'd tell you to shave, shower, and take your time on the potty. But I'm on the sidelines, as you know. Working out of a cubicle."

"Ah, I'm sorry, Claire. Well. I'll think of something."

"Cindy kicked you out?"

"We broke up after I crashed your dinner at Susie's."

"So that's what happened. I haven't spoken with Cindy since then."

Rich sighed. "I don't know what I'm doing. Should I rent a place? Should I live in my truck for a while until I know what to do with myself?"

Claire said, "I didn't see this coming, Richie. Cindy's always been crazy in love with you—and I thought vice versa."

He sighed again. "She's changed."

"Uh-huh. You seeing that girl with the curly black hair?"

"Morales?"

"That's the one."

"What makes you think I'm seeing her?"

"She looks at you like you poop rainbows."

"Yeah. Well, it's complicated."

"Oh. How's that?"

"She's got a little boy. And she's still in school. I don't know. There was a spark that took hold and you know, it just feels good to have someone look at me like I'm special. Especially when Cindy is always in her own world, by herself."

"You sleeping with Morales?"

No answer from Richie.

"Look at me," Claire said.

Rich did what she asked. His eyes were bleary. He didn't even look happy.

"People go through stages. It's hard to find someone like Cindy, someone you love and trust. No one gets to have a relationship all their way all the time."

"I like kids," Richie said. "I like kids a lot. It's not a phase I'm going through."

There was a tap on Richie's window. Lindsay was right there and Claire could see she was feeling crabby. Rich buzzed down the window.

"Let's go, okay?" Lindsay said. "I want to get back to the hospital as soon as possible."

Chapter 62

THE COOLER WAS packed, what with everyone in there. Conklin, Claire, her two investigators, and I were grouped around a stainless steel table between stacks of drawers full of dead people. No coffee allowed. I needed coffee.

The investigators were used to the walls of dead people, and to having no caffeine. They were eager to prove themselves.

Jessica Kain was young and trim, and wore black tights, a baby-doll dress under a thin cotton jacket, and sunglasses pushed up in her streaked blond hair. Jay Dedrick was dark-haired, wiry, and had a tattoo of his wife's name on his wrist —Jackie.

The two were friends, but definitely competitive.

Dedrick took the lead.

"We went through every inch of Kennedy's house. Faye Farmer lived there, too, but it was his house and most of the stuff was his. We went through his closets, his garage, the crawl spaces.

"He left his computer on and we went through that. He said he didn't care what we looked at; he had nothing to do with Faye's death and didn't know who did. We selected some of his DVDs at random. All of them were football games.

"Bottom line on the search of Kennedy's house: we found nothing indicating that he was planning to kill his girlfriend."

Kain pushed up the sleeves of her jacket, even though it was about forty-six degrees Fahrenheit in the cold storage. She said, "We dumped their phones. There was a call from Kennedy to Farmer at two forty-five on the morning of the shooting. She answered the call. Took fourteen seconds."

I said, "Long enough for him to say, 'Don't be a bitch' and for her to say, 'Screw you.'"

Kain said, "That was the last call either one of them made or received that night. Kennedy got a call at seven sixteen a.m. from his sister in Seattle. Then he got calls from everyone in the world. Same for Faye, but she wasn't taking calls by then. She was here."

Dedrick looked at notes on his tablet and read out names of the male partygoers they had interviewed, some of whom I knew from watching them play ball. Dedrick said he spent a few hours with Niners' quarterback Calvin Sandler. Whenever Kennedy was spotted in a club or a restaurant, he was either with his fiancée or Cal Sandler or both.

Dedrick told us, "Sandler said, and I quote, 'This whole effing thing is effed up. Jeff was at his effing party the whole effing day and night and he never effing left.'

"Sandler corroborates Kennedy's story and says that he was with Kennedy when Faye Farmer stomped off," Dedrick said.

Kain listed the women guests, including Linda Banks, the "extra woman" whose flirting had detonated the Faye Farmer explosion. Banks, too, corroborated that Farmer had left in a huff.

"Did Faye have any enemies?" I asked. "Did anyone want to kill her?"

"Both Farmer and Kennedy had haters," said Kain. "They each had thousands of followers on

Facebook and Twitter. Also, there was a rumor that Faye might have been seeing some guy in the movie business. He's a mystery man, if he even exists. I couldn't find out his name."

I said, "So maybe Faye had an unknown admirer and she and Kennedy had at least a billion virtual fans. This just keeps getting better."

Claire spoke up. "What about Tracey Pendleton? Find out anything on my former security guard?"

Dedrick said, "Pendleton has vanished. She has not used her credit card. She has not taken out any of the hundred and forty-five dollars she has in her checking account, and she has not used her phone. There's no sign of her car, either."

Claire said, "Is she afraid to call in because she let the body snatcher into the morgue? Or is she drinking off a big paycheck for letting someone steal Faye Farmer's body?"

I was pretty sure that Tracey Pendleton knew who killed Faye Farmer because she opened the door and let someone in. That someone was either the killer, or a fixer who'd come to clean up for the killer.

I was saying, "Tracey was likely collateral

damage," when the door behind me opened and FBI honcho Ron Parker poked his head in.

"'Scuse me, Lindsay. May I have a word?"

Ah, nuts. What did he want now?

Chapter 63

I EXCUSED MYSELF, went out of the room, and asked Ron Parker what was up.

He said, "There's been a development."

Parker was wearing his weekend clothes—chinos, pink polo shirt, sunglasses hanging on the placket. He was looking at me as though he were about to open a trapdoor under my feet.

I said, "You bring good news, I'm sure."

"It could be good."

I didn't believe it for a second. I said, "Please don't ask me to see Fish again."

"You've cast some kind of spell on him, Lindsay. He loves you, or maybe that beat-down you gave him turned him on. He says he's willing to help us—meaning you—locate the bodies in this neck of the woods. Those are his words."

"I already went to see him, Ron. He got over on us, and now I'm done with Randolph Fish."

"He says he'll give up names of girls we didn't know we were missing. This is important. It's an opportunity to close out some ugly cold cases. I don't see how we can turn him down."

"Ron, c'mon. He's jerking us around."

"I don't think so."

"Really?"

"I told him that if he fucked us over, I'd have him transferred to the Q."

San Quentin is the oldest prison in California, with a death row that is the most decrepit, over-populated hellhole imaginable. Originally built to hold forty-five prisoners, it now has a population of 725 convicted killers and more condemned dirtbags on the way every week.

Fish wouldn't like it there. No one ever did.

"So the Q is the stick," I said.

"Yup. And here's the carrot. If he helps, he gets one of those electronic book readers. Depending on how many of his victims he leads us to, we'll talk about taking the needle off the table."

"I still say he's conning us."

"You could be right. Still a good bet that Fish may have had an attack of conscience."

I said, "Fish has the conscience of a fish."

Ron laughed.

We made a plan.

Then I drove to the hospital to see my baby girl.

Chapter 64

I KNEW HOW to get to the neonatal ICU by heart. My baby was there. I could have found her in a blackout. Without a flashlight. With both hands cuffed behind my back.

I took the first elevator in the bank and rode it to the fourth floor, a place that had been furnished in vanilla and soft lights, designed for the newly opened eyes of the preemies who were housed there most often.

When the elevator opened, I stopped at the desk, exchanged pleasantries with the receptionist as I signed in, then I headed toward the waiting room. The walls, carpeting, and the furnishings throughout followed a vanilla color scheme.

I found Joe slumped in a pale armchair,

newspapers falling off his lap, his eyes closed. I called out to him.

He smiled, said, "Hey, sweetie." He stood and I went into his arms.

"How is she?" I asked.

"She's sleeping quietly."

"Any news?"

"I don't think we'll hear anything today—"

The woman in the seat next to me was in her early twenties, wearing a red tracksuit and running shoes.

She said, "I made this for Scotty. Want to see?"

I said that I did and she took out a little knitted outfit, blue and white, with a pom-pom on the top of the hat. Her husband was sitting next to her. He said that he was going outside to use the phone.

Just then, pandemonium cut loose.

There was a loud beeping, like a truck's backing-up alert, and simultaneously a voice came over the intercom: "Code blue in NICU. Code blue."

I screamed, "Oh, God." I bolted out of my chair and pitched myself toward the NICU's swinging double doors. Joe ran along with me as I rounded the bend and headed to the windowed room at the end of the hall. I pulled up short, saw only the infant incubators lined up in four rows of four— when a nurse closed curtains across the window.

I hadn't been able to pick out my baby. I hadn't been able to see Julie.

Three doctors pushing a crash cart blew through the doorway. I tried to see around them, but the door closed in my face.

I clutched at Joe and said, "It's Julie, I just feel it, Joe."

He shushed me and held me and walked me back to the waiting room, where we sat with three other sets of parents who were nearly paralyzed with fear.

We were all strangers to each other, yet drawn together like people in a lifeboat, watching as the ocean liner goes down.

And then a doctor left the NICU and came toward us.

He stood in the alcove, pulled down his mask, and looked around. I didn't know him.

But still, his eyes locked on mine.

Chapter 65

THE ICU DOCTOR was looking straight at me when he said, "Are Scott Riley's parents here?"

The young woman sitting next to me, the mom who had knitted the outfit for her son, stood up and said, "I'm Scotty's mom. Is there a problem, Doctor?"

"Let's walk a little," he said.

I watched them go out into the hallway. I was afraid for Scott's mother, hoping that the doctor would tell her that her baby was out of danger. But Mrs. Riley screamed, her voice echoing in the hallway.

"Nooo, no, no. It can't be. I just saw him this morning and he was fine."

Mr. Riley ran toward his wife, who had dropped

to her knees and was rocking herself as she sobbed. Scott's father said to the doctor, "Who are you? I've never seen you before. Maybe you've mixed up the babies. I know Scotty is going to be fine."

Nurses swarmed into the hallway and helped Mrs. Riley to her feet, tried to walk her out of the public space.

My heart broke for the Rileys, and their fear reignited mine. It was like lighting a match in a gas-filled room. I felt that I could explode.

Maybe the babies *had* been mixed up.

Joe put his arms around me and I folded myself into his embrace. I said to Joe, "Scotty was a preemie. Julie is a big girl. She'll be okay. Won't she, Joe?"

The head nurse came out to the hallway and was walking toward the end of the corridor when Joe and I got out of our seats and boxed her in.

I said, "We're Julie Molinari's parents. Have you seen her? Do you know how she's doing?"

The nurse put her hand on my arm and told us that our baby was sleeping, that all her vital signs were normal. I thanked the nurse. I overthanked her. I just felt so damned grateful.

"I'd like to hold her now, if that's okay."

Joe said, "Honey, never wake a sleeping child."

We went back to the waiting room, held hands, and took turns pacing for another hour before Joe said, "Sweetheart, you're making yourself crazy. I'm here for Julie. I'm not going anywhere, and besides, she's sleeping soundly. Didn't you tell me there's someplace you're supposed to be?"

Chapter 66

I DROVE FOR two hours, some of that time wishing my eyes had windshield wipers. I pulled myself together about the time I saw the guard towers and the razor wire of the Atwater penitentiary. I parked in the law enforcement lot, combed my hair, and put on lipstick so that I looked like I had some game.

I showed my badge thirty times before being shown to Warden Haight's corner office overlooking the yard. FBI big cheese Ron Parker joined us, and we talked about the psycho we were taking for a day trip and how dangerous he was.

The warden took a call, then said that Fish was ready for transport to his "playground." All I had to do was say hello to Fish so he knew that I was on board.

Parker and I walked through the loud, labyrinthine prison corridors out to the lot inside the north gate. The transport vehicle was a black armored van with a steel grille between the front seat and the rear cargo area, where Pretty Boy Fish was flanked by armed guards and shackled to an iron loop in the floor.

Fish smiled when he saw me. It was a great smile, seemingly genuine. The killer was a charmer. With a different mind-set, he could have been a talk show host or a real estate broker dealing in upmarket homes.

"It's a wonderful day for a treasure hunt," said Randolph Fish. "I think I know where we might find Sandra Brody."

We pulled out of the prison yard caravan-style. A pair of motorcycle cops took the lead, then came Fish's transport van. More cops on bikes followed, then the red van with the hounds. Parker's government-issue SUV was next, and I brought up the rear in my geriatric blue Explorer.

As I drove blindly through the cloud of dust, I thought about Fish saying, "I think I know where we might find Sandra Brody," a vague but intriguing statement that was a mile short of a confession.

So far, all that connected Fish to Sandra Brody was that she fit the pattern of young women Fish had been convicted of killing. She had dark hair, was attending college, and she had vanished at three in the afternoon without a trace.

A friend of Sandra's had taken a cell phone picture of her an hour before she disappeared. Sandy had been crossing the campus on her way to her volunteer job at the Raphael House, a shelter for homeless people. Her jeans looked new, her shirt was powder blue, she was carrying a brown saddle-leather backpack, and she was wearing loafers. Her long, dark hair was shining. To me, she looked like an angel.

Sandra Brody never arrived at her destination.

Jacobi and I had interviewed Sandra's friends, her boyfriend, and her devastated parents. We had seen videos and photographs of Sandy from the time she was born to the time she was last known to walk the earth.

That cell phone picture had been flashed over the Web and was posted on her Facebook page.

HAVE YOU SEEN SANDY?

The reward for information increased from ten thousand dollars to ten times that amount as money flowed in from friends Sandra hadn't known she had. Three years after she disappeared, her page was still up. People still wrote on her wall. Her parents hadn't given up hope that the phone would ring and Sandy would be on the other end of the line.

If Randolph Fish helped us to find Sandra's body, at the very least, her family would know what had happened to her. I prayed that we were on the road to solving the mystery.

We traveled up Highway 99 north to I-580 west and from there to Redwood Regional Park. I'd been there before and knew it to be 1,829 acres of sequoia, evergreens, chaparral, and grasslands just outside the dense urban areas of Oakland and the East Bay. Wildlife abounded, and that was one of the elements that made this wilderness a good dumping ground.

If coyotes had found a dead body, they would have carried it away, along with any evidence that might lead to Sandra's killer.

That's what I was thinking when suddenly the caravan veered onto the verge. Parker nosed his car onto the weedy edge of the road and after avoiding the motorcycles spinning their wheels in loose stone, I came to a stop.

The transport van doors opened and a guard jumped down. He helped his prisoner to the ground and the second guard joined them. He unlocked Randy Fish's leg irons as the driver and another armed guard dismounted from the front of the vehicle. The cadaver dogs put their noses to the ground and their handler got a good grip on their leads.

Despite the reason we had all driven to this spot, I noticed that it was a beautiful day. The new leaves were a fresh green. The sun was blazing in a clear blue sky, and the air was a mild, pine-scented sixty-two degrees.

Randolph Fish hadn't stepped on natural earth in more than three years. He took in a deep breath, closed his eyes, and tipped his face up to the sun.

Parker advanced on him and said, "Okay, Mr. Fish. Let's get to work."

Chapter 67

I HEARD THE psycho killer say to the head of the FBI's San Francisco field office, "I'd like to have my hands free."

"I don't think so," Ron Parker said. He took a panoramic look around the steep, heavily wooded terrain.

Fish said, "I know you think I'm going to run, but really, I want to read. My paperback is in the van. It's a great story and I'm dying to find out what happens."

"Tell you what: when you get back to your cell, I'll be sure to get that book to you. That's if you show us where you buried Sandra Brody."

We were caravanning again, this time on foot. I stayed behind Fish, my hand on my gun. I could imagine that freak in the orange jumpsuit breaking free, zigzagging through the scrub, and bullets missing him, flying into the trees. It wasn't so hard to believe that Fish might want to get shot out here rather than wait twenty years for his walk to the death chamber.

But if Fish was anticipating "suicide by cop," you couldn't tell from watching him. He chatted with Ron Parker, told Ron that he was a happy person. That he had been a happy baby, and hardly ever experienced doubt or frustration.

Parker asked, "So what made you kill those girls? What made you cut off their fingers? I really want to know."

"If I told you, you'd judge me."

"Try me," said Parker.

"I might be willing to tell Lindsay."

"No. You won't," said Parker. "She's not that interested in your twisted facsimile of a mind."

"See? I knew you'd judge me," Fish said brightly.

I thought of the way Fish had tortured his victims for hours or days before finally strangling them or stabbing them to death. All those young women had been loved by their friends and their families. I thought about their mothers, and tears came into my eyes.

I clamped my lips together, using the back of my hand to dry my eyes. I was thinking of Julie. I couldn't bear to think of losing Julie.

I heard Fish say, "Hey, Ron. I recognize that rocky outcrop. I climbed past it and turned left at the top of the ravine. There's a trail up there that goes off to the east."

We crossed a brook and dug our hands into crumbling earth in order to climb up the side of the ravine. We turned left at the rocky outcropping and continued east on a deer path.

Fish, looking as pale as the underbelly of a trout, said to Parker, "It's been a while since I've been here, but see that tree limb that looks like an elbow? You'll find what you're looking for under that."

The dogs snuffled but didn't alert. The guards shoveled dirt, but only uncovered roots and stones. Fish suggested that they try just a few more yards up the trail, and they did. After some digging, a shovel hit something that caused interest.

Parker hiked up his pants cuffs and squatted near the hole. He reached in and removed a bone from the freshly turned earth. Then he pulled out a skull—with antlers.

Fish laughed.

"I don't think I had anything to do with killing that. But I can't say for sure."

He called out to me, "Lindsay, I haven't been here in a long time, you know?"

Fish had manipulated all of us to get his outing in the woods. I was mad at myself for letting Ron Parker waste my time. As we hiked back to the road, I called Joe to get an update on our baby girl, but he didn't answer the phone. I left him a message to call me, and a few minutes later I called him again. Still, Joe didn't answer.

Fish was walking backwards, talking to me, telling me he was as surprised as we were that we hadn't found Sandra. "I'm not so sure what I remember. You know, being in a coma for two years is a big deal. In fact, I'm not sure if I ever knew Sandra Brody or if I just got her name from you."

He was screwing with my head.

I thought maybe God was messing with me, too.

BOOK IV

ECLIPSE

Chapter 68

PROFESSOR PERRY JUDD tried to make sense of the enormous black hole that had opened in front of him. It was like a portal ringed with light, a tunnel of some sort, and he was being pulled through it as if he were being drawn into an eclipse of the sun.

The image was stunning, and the feeling of effortless movement was heady. At the same time, the professor knew that what he was experiencing could not be real.

Either he was dead—or he was having a dream.

A dream.

That had to be it.

He had prepared himself for the possibility of a waking dream by marking an X on the back of his left hand before going to sleep. Now he held out his hands, palms facing away from him, and spread his fingers wide. The bluish light limned each of his fingers, and he could clearly see that there were no Xs, no marks of any kind on the backs of his hands.

He was almost certainly dreaming, but to be sure, he ran another reality check. This time he pushed two fingers of his left hand into the palm of his right.

The fingers went straight through his palm.

He had *really* done it. He was lucid, aware that he was inside a dream, and that meant that he had control of the story and the ending.

But first—where was he?

He was sure he had never been in this place before, but then the location came to him. This had to be the Aquarium of the Bay. He had seen a video of it on the Web. He had planned to take his nephew there one day.

The main feature of the aquarium was a moving walkway that went through a long glass tunnel, and the fish swam above and around the walkway.

The shapes he saw bobbing in the halo of light were sharks. Perry Judd didn't feel that this was a dream about sharks. But he did sense danger.

He swung his head from side to side and took in the people who had appeared on the moving walkway with him. There was a girl traveling alone, and two young men talking to one another. Someone else had a camera and was angling for various shots of the sea creatures.

The professor was trying to memorize the sights around him when a sharp, cracking sound tore through his dream. It was a gunshot. He remembered that Sergeant Boxer had told him to look around, to grab the gun, and to remember who the shooter was.

Who had fired?

The professor was startled awake.

He blinked in the blue light of his digital clock, his heart fluttering fast against his ribs like a moth on a lightbulb. He double-checked to be sure. There was his TV. There was his painting of a church in Munich. There was the X on the back of his left hand.

Definitely, he was awake and at his own home.

Still, he was aware that something had happened—or was about to happen—in the Aquarium of the Bay. Trouble was, he had failed to see the shooter. Or had he? Maybe it was one of the people he had seen.

Judd turned on his bedside lamp and called the SFPD. It was only five thirty in the morning, but an operator answered the phone.

"I have to leave a message for Inspector Conklin," he said. "Tell him I'll be coming in to see him this morning."

"Your name, sir?"

"This is Professor Perry Judd."

"And your number, please."

Judd gave his number to the operator, who said that she didn't know what time Inspector Conklin would be coming to work, or if he was coming in at all.

"Tell him that I'll be there. It cannot wait."

Judd hung up the phone and closed his eyes. He wanted to fall asleep and find out what happened inside the aquarium. Three hours later, he took a cab to the Hall of Justice and pressed the elevator button that let him out on the third floor. He found the homicide squad assistant behind her desk and demanded to see Inspector Conklin.

"He's expecting me," said Professor Judd.

Chapter 69

THE LAST THING Judge Nussbaum had said before adjourning court for the weekend was "I can hardly wait until Monday, Mr. Kinsela, to see what you've got up your sleeve."

Kinsela had laughed through his nose, and Keith Herman had nearly grinned his face off, but Yuki hadn't been amused.

She had left the courtroom and gone directly upstairs, where she found Red Dog Parisi conferring with Chief Jacobi. She pulled a chair up to Parisi's desk and the three of them discussed Lily Herman's kidnapping, her mysterious return, and what effect the child's reappearance might have had on the jury. They also reassured each other that the gun dealer's recanting of his earlier testimony was meaningless.

The next day, Yuki, Nicky, Red Dog, and all the ADAs had gathered to pick their case apart and to critique the new structure of Yuki's closing argument. They worked on Sunday, too, and even met again this morning to evaluate the media coverage and to incorporate last-minute thoughts.

The mind meld had been productive and Yuki was glad for the team's support, but she was still uneasy.

Damage had been done. She'd told the jury in her opening statement that Keith Herman had killed two people, not one. And while the case was still about the murder of Jennifer Herman, Yuki knew that Kinsela had damaged her standing with the jury. And, by the way, he could slip another knife between her ribs before he was done.

There was only one witness on Kinsela's list. It was another of the prosecution's former witnesses—undercover cop Lieutenant Floyd Meserve.

Meserve was a good guy and a good cop.

Keith Herman had tried to hire Meserve to kill his wife and child. No question about it. Their interview had taken place in Meserve's vehicle and had been recorded on video. The video had been shown to the jury. Keith Herman had told Meserve that he wanted Jennifer and Lily killed.

Now, as Yuki sat with Nicky at the defense table, waiting for court to reconvene, Yuki muttered to her associate, "How could Kinsela possibly use Meserve against us? How?"

The minute hand on the big clock moved. The bailiff announced that court was in session. The judge entered the courtroom and so did the jury. The judge banged the gavel, made some general remarks, then asked Kinsela if he was ready to begin.

Kinsela said, "Your Honor, we call Lieutenant Floyd Meserve."

Meserve came through the front doors of the courtroom. He wore a cheap plaid sport jacket, a starched shirt, and a wide blue tie. His pants were shiny and so were his shoes. His ponytail had been hacked off—an amateur job, as if he had done it himself.

The lieutenant in charge of Crimes Against Persons looked pissed off as he was sworn in. He took his seat in the witness box and John Kinsela, appearing fresh and invigorated in a light gray suit and yellow tie, came toward him.

Yuki thought Kinsela definitely had something up his sleeve, but she couldn't fathom what kind of something it could be.

Chapter 70

JOHN KINSELA GREETED his witness, Lieutenant Meserve, then asked him, "Are you familiar with Lynnette Lagrande?"

Meserve sat back in his chair and looked genuinely puzzled before he said, "I don't understand what you mean by 'familiar.'"

"Let me put it this way. Do you know Lynnette Lagrande?"

"Yes, I know her," said the former undercover cop.

"How would you characterize your relationship with her?"

"Social. I go out with her. Dinner and such."

Yuki felt a chill at the back of her neck. What the hell was this?

297

"That's what we call in this country dating, isn't that right?"

"Your generation calls it dating."

"Well, humor me and the jury and let's both call it dating, okay? So how long have you been dating Ms. Lagrande?"

"I really don't remember."

"Long enough to become familiar with her?"

Kinsela snorted at his own joke. Someone in the gallery let out a high-pitched giggle, which caught on and became a wave of tentative laughter.

Yuki stood up and said, "Your Honor, I object in the strongest possible terms to the way Mr. Kinsela is fooling around at the expense of this court and the jury's time. And in the process, he's taking liberties with Ms. Lagrande's reputation."

Nussbaum said, "Sustained. Mr. Kinsela, this is a murder trial. Don't do that again. This is your last warning."

Yuki sat down hard in her seat and tried to comprehend the bombshell that had just landed in Judge Nussbaum's courtroom.

Had she heard it right?

Floyd Meserve was currently a lieutenant in the police force. A year ago, he had been an undercover cop. He had put a video setup inside his vehicle and interviewed Keith Herman, a thug of a lawyer with a reputation for child abuse and jury tampering and maybe far worse. Herman had sought out Meserve, thinking he was a hit man, a contract killer. And Herman had said he wanted to have his family killed.

Now this good lieutenant was telling the court that he was dating Lynnette Lagrande, Keith Herman's former girlfriend.

How had he met Lynnette?

And why was John Kinsela asking Meserve about dating Lynnette, anyway? What could that have to do with the case against Keith Herman?

There was more to come, Yuki could feel it.

Something big was about to blow.

Chapter 71

KINSELA STOOD SIX FEET from the witness box with his hands clasped behind his back.

"I'm sorry, Your Honor," he said. "I didn't mean to make light of the proceedings."

From the smile in Kinsela's pale blue eyes, it was clear to Yuki and everyone else in the courtroom that Kinsela was enjoying himself enormously.

The judge said, "Watch yourself, Mr. Kinsela. Don't make me angry."

Kinsela apologized again, and then he continued his examination of the witness.

"Lieutenant, were you dating Ms. Lagrande at the time you met with Keith Herman?"

"You mean at the time when Keith Herman asked me to kill his wife and kid?"

300

"If that's what he actually did. But let me be more precise. Were you dating Ms. Lagrande before February of last year?"

"I guess so."

"Please answer yes or no."

"I don't keep a date book, for Christ's sake. What do you think I am? A fifteen-year-old girl?"

Kinsela said, "Your Honor. Please tell the witness to answer the question."

The judge spoke to the witness. "Lieutenant Meserve, you will either answer Mr. Kinsela's questions truthfully or you will be held in contempt of court. You will be fined and jailed. Do you understand?"

"Yes, sir, Your Honor."

"Go ahead, Mr. Kinsela."

Kinsela let the moment drag out for a second or two, then said, "Who was the informant who referred Keith Herman to you, Lieutenant?"

"I can't reveal my sources."

Kinsela put his hand on the witness stand and leaned toward the witness. "Let me help you, Lieutenant. Lynnette Lagrande sent Keith Herman to you for the purpose of arranging the murder

301

of Jennifer and Lily Herman, isn't that right? Lynnette Lagrande was your so-called confidential informant."

"I—I—I refuse to answer on the grounds of the Fifth Amendment."

"You're afraid you'll incriminate yourself, Lieutenant? Is that because Lynnette Lagrande conspired with you to put Keith Herman up to contracting hits on his family? Isn't it true that it was *Lynnette* who wanted Jennifer and Lily Herman dead? She wanted to marry Keith Herman for his money, and then Keith would have an accident. The fatal kind."

"I take the Fifth. Didn't you hear me—"

Kinsela kept going, ran right over what Meserve was saying. "And then, after Keith Herman was in the ground, and Lynnette was a wealthy widow, she could share her life and her new fortune with you. Isn't that the way it was supposed to go? Isn't that why you refuse to answer my questions?"

Meserve's face was florid and yet the skin around his eyes had gone white. He shouted, "Killing Lily was *Keith's* idea."

"Is that so?" Kinsela said. "You're saying Mr.

Herman wanted his daughter killed, and yet Lily is alive, isn't she? And Jennifer Herman is quite definitely dead."

Chapter 72

JOHN KINSELA WAS in his glory and he was basking in it.

Yuki shot to her feet, saying, "Objection, Your Honor."

"On what grounds, Ms. Castellano?"

She made sure to modulate her voice so that she didn't sound as furious as she felt. "On the grounds that Mr. Kinsela brought in this so-called rebuttal witness for one reason—to discredit him and to confuse the jury. He's confused *me*. It's absurd. It's insane. It's total bull."

The judge said, "He's entitled to question the witness, and you're entitled to cross-examine the witness—"

"I'm turning state's evidence," Meserve

shouted. "I'll testify that Lynnette Lagrande was behind everything. Judge, I haven't perjured myself. I didn't kill anyone. Lynnette wanted Keith dead, that's true, and I was seeing her, but that's not important because I did nothing wrong—"

Meserve's speech was cut off by the word "Liar," screamed from the back row of the courtroom. Lynnette Lagrande was on her feet, shouting at Meserve, "You liar. You bastard. You weak, lying murderer!"

It was as if someone had shouted "Fire" inside a circus tent.

Yuki saw Jacobi stand up in the back of the gallery. He edged out to the aisle, then walked rapidly toward Lynnette Lagrande. He said her name and she whipped her head around, her face still twisted in anger.

"Ms. Lagrande, we're gonna hold you on suspicion of conspiracy to commit murder. You, too, Lieutenant Meserve," Jacobi said loudly. "We're going to have some questions for both of you."

The judge looked stunned. His eyes darted around the courtroom as outbursts flared like fireworks going off on all sides. People in the gallery panicked and rushed for the aisle and the exit even as police poured through the courtroom doors.

Kinsela stood at the defense table with his client and shouted, "Judge Nussbaum, I move to dismiss. There is no case against my client. Lily Herman is alive. There is no evidence tying Keith Herman to the death of Jennifer Herman. Lynnette Lagrande is the responsible party—"

Lynnette Lagrande had become a wild woman. She screamed at Jacobi, "Get away from me," and lashed out at him with her nails. Jacobi was almost thirty years older and weighed a hundred pounds more.

He put his hand on her shoulder so that she couldn't touch him, then said in a booming voice, "Now you're also under arrest for assaulting a police officer. Put your hands behind your back."

Kinsela shouted to the judge, "Your Honor, I strongly urge you to dismiss the charges and release Mr. Herman—"

A juror sitting in the front row of the jury box, a woman in her sixties named Nina Tancho, stood up abruptly and shouted, "I can't take this anymore. You people are all insane."

The judge slammed down his gavel again, *bam, bam, bam.*

"Everyone freeze."

There was a moment of relative silence into which Judge Nussbaum said, "I'm declaring a mistrial. Mr. Herman, you will be returned to your cell for now. Bailiff, please take the jury back to their room. Sheriff Calhoun, clear the courtroom.

"Mr. Kinsela, Ms. Castellano, please stay where you are."

Cops pushed and pulled a handcuffed Lynnette Lagrande toward the exit. Her pretty face was unrecognizable as she screamed, "I did nothing wrong. This is slander. I'm going to sue you, Mr. Kinsela. I'm going to sue—everyone. I'm *innocent.*"

Floyd Meserve called out to Kinsela, "I need representation, Mr. Kinsela. I need you right now."

Kinsela said, "You can't afford me, Mr. Meserve. But here's some free advice. Shut the hell up."

The golden-haired little girl who had been sitting in the courtroom beside Lynnette Lagrande darted through the crowd and ran to her father. She was bawling as she grabbed him around his waist and cried out, "Daddy, let's go home."

Nicky Gaines went to the little girl and peeled her away from Keith Herman. "Lily, you'll see your dad again soon. You just have to stay with your grandma for another few days."

Yuki stood in one place and stared inward.

What had just happened?

Had Lynnette Lagrande, the beautiful and prim schoolteacher, just sprouted hair on her palms? Was Floyd Meserve, the good cop, a simpleminded dick who had in fact killed Jennifer Herman because he loved Lynnette Lagrande? Who had kidnapped the child—and why? And what did Keith Herman have to do with all of the above?

All that Yuki knew for sure was that if the judge hadn't declared a mistrial, Keith Herman would have gotten off. Because reasonable doubt of this magnitude hadn't been seen in San Francisco in the last fifty years.

Chapter 73

RICH CONKLIN WAS shaving in the men's room when Brenda, the squad assistant, pushed open the door and stuck her face in.

"Hey. Could you knock, maybe?" Conklin said. He pulled paper towels out of the collar of his shirt, dried his face.

"Here you go," Brenda said. She knocked on the open door.

Conklin laughed. "What is it, Brenda? What do you need?"

"There's been a shooting at the aquarium."

"You don't mean the Aquarium of the Bay?"

"That's the one."

"*Shit*," Richie said. "Tell Brady about this."

"He's the one called me, told me to find you and tell you to get down there."

"Is Morales in?"

"She'll be in later. Sergeant Boxer is taking the day off. It's all on you and about a hundred uniformed cops until the day shift comes in."

Conklin went to his desk, collected his weapon, and put on his jacket. Then he jogged downstairs and checked out an unmarked car from the lot outside the ME's office.

He drove north through the morning rush on the Embarcadero. It was a twenty-minute drive to the Wharf even with the siren on and a clear lane. Which he didn't have.

As he wove through traffic, Conklin thought about Professor Judd, how he'd come in yesterday morning wearing a cashmere overcoat on top of his pajamas, how he'd bulled his way into the squad room, then demanded that Conklin listen to his dream.

Conklin had said, "Let's hear it, Professor. Did someone get whacked? Or should I say, is someone about to get whacked?"

Judd had dragged out the story, talking about the arc of light, the watery eclipse, the moving walkway, and the gradual realization that he was dreaming, until Conklin had shouted, "Will you get to the fucking *point*?"

"There was a shooting," Judd had said.

"Who got shot?" Conklin asked.

"I don't know."

"Don't know? How is that? Weren't you there?"

"I didn't see a person go down, and I didn't see the shooter."

"So let me get this straight. You had a dream. You essentially left your body, materialized at the aquarium, and that's where you heard a shot."

"That's right."

The little professor had stuck out his jaw, daring Conklin to argue with him. He had crumbs on his chin and on the collar of his pin-striped pj's.

Conklin said, "Nobody has called in a shooting. So you didn't see a victim in your dream, and there's no victim in real life, either. I can't do anything with this, Professor."

Judd had said, "I guess I'm going to have to be my own detective." He patted his hip, as though he were packing a gun. "I've got a license to carry."

Conklin had said, "Thanks for coming in, Professor."

Now there had been a shooting at the aquarium. Had the professor's dream been another fulfilled prophecy? Or had the professor gone and shot someone?

Conklin called Inspector Paul Chi.

"Chi, it's Conklin. Do me a favor. You and Cappy go pick up Professor Judd and bring him to the Hall. Just hold him for questioning. You don't have to tell him anything. Just nail him down. I'll be back in a couple of hours."

Chapter 74

CONKLIN PULLED HIS car up to the command post—three black-and-whites and a clump of cops standing in front of barricades blocking the entrance to Pier 39. Conklin leaned out of his window, signed the log, and asked the sergeant what was up.

The sergeant told him, "One victim, shot through the head. It's a mess in there. Put your waders on."

Conklin drove straight ahead to the turnaround in front of the Aquarium of the Bay, a tacky-looking white building with peaked roofs, awnings, flags, and a large blue cutout of a shark on the wall.

He parked his vehicle, then called Brenda to say that he had arrived at the scene. He sat behind the wheel for a moment, feeling that whatever had happened inside the aquarium was his fault. That he should have paid more attention to that twerpy professor. That instead of posting a team at the aquarium, which he could have done, he'd told Professor Judd that there was nothing he could do.

Now someone was dead, and Conklin was 99 percent sure that the professor had done the shooting and that he would have an alibi. Not just an alibi, but a rock-solid, airtight, unimpeachable alibi.

Conklin rummaged in the glove compartment and located half of a packaged brownie. He gobbled it down, then got out of the car and headed to the staircase outside the aquarium building. He climbed the stairs, taking them two at a time.

He entered the building on the second floor, badged the cop at the door, and took a left past some exhibits, including a cylindrical tank full of shiny, swirling fish. Another cop was guarding the elevator.

"You've got to take the fire stairs, Inspector. The elevator is out."

Christ.

Conklin took the fire stairs down, opened the

fire door, and stepped into eight inches of cold seawater. He passed the 725 gallons of illuminated moon jellies, then slogged along the dimly lit corridor, following signs to the three-hundred-foot-long moving walkway that had been tunneled under the bay.

Conklin stopped at the head of the walkway, which was no longer moving, and tried to get his bearings. The aquarium arced overhead. Sharks and other large fish, schools of anchovies, and various slimy creatures from the deep swam over and around him. It was like surround sound for the eyes—and it wasn't comfortable.

Halfway down the tunnel, a stream of water poured onto the walkway through a hole about six feet up the wall. At best, the spray was destroying evidence. At worst, the entire exhibit was in danger of becoming like a submarine with a breached hull.

Feeling suddenly sick from the underwater effect, Conklin held on to the railing. He really didn't want to puke in the crime scene. He steadied himself, took some deep breaths, then he pushed off and sloshed over to where the CSIU team was processing the scene.

The victim's body was facedown on the walkway, and the rising water was almost to the point where it would cover the hole in the back of his head.

Charlie Clapper, longtime head of the CSIU, was stooped over the body, lifting a pocket flap with his gloved hand.

Conklin said, "Hey, Charlie. What's the story here?"

"Well, Rich, we've got a white male, fifty or so, shot through the back of the head, as you can see. Hold on, I've got his wallet. Crystal, can you shine a light on this?"

A young tech in high rubber boots came over to them and flashed her light on the dead man's driver's license.

Clapper said, "Here we go. Our victim is in fact a white male, fifty-two, five foot six, hundred and forty pounds, hazel eyes. Name of Mr. Perry Judd. FYI, Mr. Judd never knew what hit him."

"Damn it," Conklin said. "This man is Perry Judd? You're sure?"

"I'm only sure that I'm holding Perry Judd's driver's license."

"Can you turn his head so I can see his face?" Conklin asked.

"Not until the ME gets here," said Clapper. "You know that, Richie. Until then, we gotta cool our heels."

Chapter 75

JOE AND I spent the night inside a cozily furnished hospital room, holding Julie, bottle-feeding her, and telling her that she was a good strong baby and that we loved her so much.

When we weren't with Party Girl, we slumped in chairs in the waiting room, where we counted holes in the acoustic tiles and sometimes caught a few, very fractured z's.

As long as the night had been, the hours between 8:00 and 9:00 a.m. had been longer. We drank vending machine coffee as we waited for Dr. Erwin Dwy, Julie's hematologist, to see us. And then, finally, he came to the waiting room and brought us back to his office.

Dr. Dwy was 6 feet 9 inches tall, going gray at

the temples, and had a long, smiling face and sad eyes. He offered us chairs at his desk and we sat across from him, watching him take phone calls from parents of sick children. Between calls, he apologized, then took another call, until at last he gave us his attention.

"Let me be candid with you," said Dr. Dwy, folding his hands on his desk. "I don't have wonderful news."

I was already terrified; I had been in that state since we'd last seen Dr. Gordon and she had said Julie should have an aggressive workup at the hospital. But now, looking into Dr. Dwy's eyes, I reached a new high in terror.

I went rigid. I gripped Joe's hand hard, and I flashed on the night I gave birth to Julie in a blackout with an electrical storm crackling around me. I remembered screaming like a wounded mountain lion—and I wanted to scream like that now.

I don't have wonderful news.

Joe said, "Tell us what you know, Dr. Dwy."

"Of course," he said. "Of course. Well, we gave Julie every test in the book—blood tests, CAT scans, we even did a bone marrow biopsy. She took it very well.

"But this is what it all comes down to," said the sad-eyed man. "Julie's white blood cells are abnormally large."

I blurted, "She has an infection. Dr. Gordon said she had an infection."

"We believe she has malignant lymphoma. It's in the leukemic stage."

Everything went white.

The blood left my head and although I was staring at Dr. Dwy's face, I saw nothing. I heard a buzzing, then someone was calling my name. I was on the floor, my chair tipped over beside me. I heaved and someone placed a garbage bag right beside my mouth. I heaved again, then there was something cold on my chest.

My blouse was open. Dr. Dwy had a stethoscope on my chest and was listening to my heart. I pushed him away, saying, "I'm fine. I'm fine."

I tried to sit up, but when I did, everything began to fade again. The doctor told me to just stay down and I tried that, but after a minute or two, I asked Joe to help me up.

When I was standing, Dr. Dwy righted my chair and I buttoned my shirt.

Dr. Dwy said, "Your blood pressure is very

low. Have you ever passed out before?"

"No. Because this is the first time someone told me that my daughter has cancer."

Joe put his arm around me. Tears were sheeting down my face, but I wasn't sobbing. I was in the present and I was listening hard. I had to keep myself together for Julie.

Chapter 76

AFTER I ASSURED Dr. Dwy that I wasn't going to black out again, he told me and Joe about Julie's medical condition in a language that seemed to be English, but definitely wasn't English as I knew it. I just couldn't grasp what he was telling us; I could only apprehend that Julie's situation was dire.

I said to the doctor, "Please. Just tell us in simple terms."

He said, "All you really have to understand right now is that acute leukemias move rather quickly. I don't like to give statistics, but in this case, I have to tell you that Julie has a fifty percent chance of survival. It's fifty percent now.

"I advise chemotherapy, the sooner the better. I'd start her on chemo today."

I wanted to howl, "Nooo," but I clamped the arm of the chair with one hand, squeezed the life out of Joe's hand with the other.

My thoughts went to my tiny, helpless child, so recently born, so fiercely loved. She had only been with us for a few weeks, but I had envisioned her life extending out to the horizon. I wanted for Julie what all parents want for their children—that she would have a long and happy life.

I tuned in to Joe saying, "Doctor, what are the side effects of chemotherapy?"

Dwy said, "What you'd expect. She'll feel sick. She'll lose her hair. There may be some long-term effects. She could become infertile. And of course, the chemotherapy is not a guarantee that she will successfully beat the cancer. It's a hard decision, but I know what I would do in your situation."

Joe said, "My wife and I need a moment to talk this over."

"Of course," said Dr. Dwy. "Take your time. But just be aware that if we're to go ahead with the chemo, I have to organize things for Julie."

Dr. Dwy stood, ducked his head under the door frame, and left the room. It was unbearably bright in his office once we were no longer in the doctor's shadow. The overhead fluorescent strip glared, and so did the reflection of light on the blond wood and the white paint. The wall of windows made me feel transparent, and I wanted to be in the dark.

I wanted to grab my baby and run, disappear down a rabbit hole or hide at the back of a cave. I wanted to put Julie back inside my body so that I could protect her, so that nothing bad could ever happen to her. How could I change the devastating fifty–fifty odds Dr. Dwy had given her?

Joe looked drained and grave. He said, "Lindsay, are you feeling okay—physically?"

"Yes."

"What do you want to do?" he asked me.

"We don't have a choice. We have to let them shoot her up with chemicals. And we just have to be strong for her when she gets sick. I went through chemo with my mom—"

"I'm not so sure this is the way to go."

"*What? You aren't?*"

I was sputtering, still dumbfounded by what Joe had said, when a nurse opened the door and told us, "I have a little girl here who wants to be held."

Joe and I both put out our arms.

"You two, flip a coin," the nurse said with a smile.

Joe stood up, took Julie from the nurse, thanked her, and handed our baby to me.

Oh, my God. I almost swooned again at the smell of her, at the sight of her sweet face.

Julie *couldn't* die. She just couldn't die.

Chapter 77

I HELD JULIE and tried not to crush her with my maternal love. She fussed, and so I cooed and cradled her, pushed her dark curls back from her face. Her skin was warm but not overheated. She opened her beautiful dark eyes and looked at me.

I don't know how much a four-week-old baby can sense, but I didn't want her to know how scared I was. How scared we were.

I said, "Hi, sweetie. How's my girl?"

"I want a second opinion," said Joe.

"What do you mean, Joe? We shouldn't do the chemo?"

"I want someone else to see her, to do the tests again, see if we get the same results."

"But that could waste valuable time. Maybe that

loss of time would just tilt the odds from fifty-fifty to sixty-forty against her. I *like* Dr. Dwy. I *like* this hospital."

Joe said, "May I hold her?"

I gave the baby to my husband and he held her against his shoulder the way he likes to. He walked around the small room with her, rubbed her back. She closed her eyes and started to breathe rhythmically until she was in a deep sleep.

I thought about my mother's cancer, what a tenacious bitch it was, and how, despite the chemotherapy, the radiation, the surgery, and my mother's strong will to live, she had died.

I heard Dr. Dwy in my mind saying, "These acute leukemias move very quickly."

"I want to take her to Saint Francis," Joe said. "I've done a lot of research. There's a very highly regarded hem-onc there."

"A what did you say?"

"Hematologist-oncologist. I want to bring Julie to Mark Sebetic. He's busy. He's famous. He's well guarded by his staff. I'm going to knock down whatever doors I have to. I won't accept 'no' for an answer. I'll sleep outside his office if that's what it takes."

I was torn right down the middle of my heart. I didn't want Julie to go through the sickness and discomfort of chemotherapy, but I also didn't want to delay treatment that could save her life.

My husband is older than me, has been uncle to more than a dozen children, and has made life-and-death decisions for other people his entire professional life. But we loved Julie equally. We had to agree on the best course of treatment for our baby.

We had to decide together what was best for her.

Chapter 78

CONKLIN TURNED AWAY from the dead man's partially submerged body and saw Claire Washburn coming toward him in the watery gloom. Her scene kit was in hand and three techs trailed in her wake.

"Hey, cowboy," she called out. "Where's your partner?"

Conklin said, "You got me. She's a mom first these days. I keep getting her voice mail. So what happened, Claire? You ducked out the back door and Dr. Morse doesn't know you're missing?"

"If we didn't have a ten-car smashup on the freeway, he'd be here instead of me. Hey, Charlie," she said. "How goes it?"

"What I love about this job is that it's always

different. Take a look at that." Charlie Clapper pointed to the hole in the wall, six feet off the ground, water flowing through it as though it were a fire hose. He said, "Could be that the shot went wild, or could be it was deliberate, so that everyone's mind would go to the six hundred million gallons of water coming into the tunnel, not to the vic or the shooter."

"I hope someone's going to put their finger in the dike," Claire said, looking at the stream. "Meanwhile, I need to get a look at the DB."

Conklin stood beside Claire as she photographed the body and the wound. He said, "I think I know this guy."

"You do? Tell me about it," she said.

"This English professor came in to see us a couple of weeks ago. He said he's been having these dreams."

Claire moved around the body, got another angle on the head wound. "What do you mean, 'dreams'? I've been a little out of the loop since Faye Farmer was boosted from my freezer."

"This professor had dreams of people being murdered. First time, it was a woman who liked to shop at his local grocery store. He described her down to her toenail polish. Bang, she takes a hit in the ice cream section. Just what he dreamed."

"So you're saying this professor sees dead people? But he sees them when they're alive?"

"Something like that. So a few days after the supermarket hit, the professor comes in again. This time he's dreamed that a female streetcar driver on the F line took one through the forehead. He described her as blond-haired. Even described advertising inside the car."

Claire said, "Richie, if you're waiting to ID this man, let me put your mind at rest. I'm not turning the body in this swamp. Lyle, call Henry, tell him to hurry up with that stretcher."

"Just turn his face," Conklin said. "I've got to see if this man is the professor."

"You'll get your chance later. I'm gonna process this body by the book, and that means back at the office."

"I'll come with you."

"If you must. So the blond-haired streetcar driver was murdered like the professor dreamed?"

"Well, that's the weird thing. The victim was a streetcar driver. She did take a shot right between the eyes, but she wasn't blond. She was a black woman, had black hair."

"So he got it wrong, but at the same time not that wrong," Claire said.

"Correct," said Conklin. "Then he came in yesterday with another dream; this time his dream takes place right here. He's moving along the walkway, then he hears a gunshot. But he tells me he didn't see anyone get hit. So I say, 'This isn't a murder case.' And he said that if I wasn't going to help him, he was going to come to the aquarium and see if he could pick the shooter out of the crowd before he pulled the trigger."

"Maybe he did see the shooter, huh? And that's why he got shot."

"From behind?"

"Well, maybe the killer recognized *him*."

Clapper trudged through the water, past the guys on a tall ladder and under the divers who were inside the tank, pressing something that looked like a piece of neoprene against the hole in the glass.

Charlie held the butt of a gun with his gloved fingertips.

He said, "Inspector, look at this. We found it at

the far end of the walkway. It's drenched, but I can still smell that it's been fired. This is going to be our murder weapon."

"Excellent," said Richie. "Good job."

"Unless, of course," Clapper said with a wink, "I'm dreaming."

Chapter 79

CONKLIN SPOKE TO Sheila, who was answering phones at the front desk at the medical examiner's office.

"I'm expecting Mackie Morales from Homicide. You can send her in when she gets here."

"If Dr. Washburn says okay."

"She already did."

And then Morales appeared at the glass door.

"And here she is," Conklin said.

He opened the door for Morales, who was looking terrific in tight jeans, a man-tailored shirt, and a fitted camel-hair jacket. Her dark hair was loose and bouncy. She had a very fresh and inviting look about her. An all-American girl by way of Scotland and Mexico. She smelled good, too.

"Did the victim turn out to be Professor Judd?" Morales asked Conklin. She stood close enough for Conklin to see down into her cleavage.

"It's him," Conklin said. "If you believe this psychic stuff, then Perry Judd dreamed his own death. He didn't see the shooter in his dream, because he was shot from behind."

"I'm on the fence about precognition," Morales said. "But I believe that Professor Judd believed it."

"I'm open to other ideas," Conklin said.

He held the door to the autopsy suite for Morales, then followed her in. Claire was weighing Perry Judd's liver when they got there.

Once again, Conklin felt the cold shock of guilt. A day ago he had been sitting with Perry Judd upstairs in Interview 2. Now the little guy's chest was open like a book and his guts were overlapping the rim of a stainless steel bowl.

Morales said, "Dr. Washburn, I'll run that bullet out to the lab for you. Save some time."

"It's in the envelope on the table over there," Claire said. "Thanks for helping out."

"Happy to do it," said Morales. "See you later, Rich."

Morales left with the semimangled round

Claire had taken out of Perry Judd's skull. Claire said to Conklin, "The shooter was standing three to five feet behind the victim when he fired. There was no stippling around the wound."

"Can you confirm that the cause of death was the gunshot wound to the back of the head?"

"Yes. I can say that—conditionally," said Claire. "It's still off the record until I finish here, in about six hours."

Conklin nodded at Claire, then went back upstairs to the squad room. He was transferring his notes to the case file when Charlie Clapper called him on his cell phone.

"Here's something that will make your ears stand up," Clapper said. "The round fired from the gun matches the one Claire took from Perry Judd's head, so we definitely have the murder weapon. And I'm not done yet."

"Go ahead," Conklin said. Brady appeared out of nowhere and was standing over him, looking frayed and impatient.

"The murder weapon is registered to the victim," Clapper said.

"What? You're sure about that?"

"Yes, I am sure. A hundred percent sure."

"Any prints? Please say yes."

"Wiped clean."

"Okay, thanks."

Conklin ended the call, said to the lieutenant, "Perry Judd was shot dead with his own gun. And no, he didn't shoot himself in the back of the head. The killer was three to five feet behind him. But it still makes no sense. The professor dreams his own death without knowing it. And then someone shoots him with his own gun.

"What do you make of this, boss?" Conklin said. "Because it seems way off the hook to me."

"This just came from the aquarium," Brady said, putting two disks down on Conklin's desk. "Let's go to the video."

Chapter 80

CONKLIN SAT AT his computer, screening the surveillance footage from the aquarium.

He was looking for the moment that the professor was shot, and it was hard to see very much. The surveillance camera was old and its focal point was indeterminate. The dark areas of the aquarium were lit with pin lights that burned hot spots in the video and made the unlit areas seem even darker.

Conklin skimmed the footage, running it forward and back, looking for the professor. Then he saw him.

Professor Judd was on the walkway, wearing a herringbone jacket and khakis—the same outfit Conklin had seen on the DB. Judd was gazing around in all directions, probably looking for a shooter or someone he had seen in his dream. He touched the bulge at the back of his waistband, as though he were assuring himself that his gun was there. In every way, he was doing just what he had told Rich he was planning to do.

One minute he was walking alone, then a moment later, he was eclipsed by a group of people who were walking faster than he was, and they were closing in on him. As the group encompassed him, Judd suddenly jerked, stiffened, and fell facedown on the walkway.

Some people in the crowd stopped to see the fallen body, but within a few seconds the walkway was emptied of living people.

Conklin backed up the video, pushed in on the shooting, added fill light. Then he scrutinized the people who were around Perry Judd when he dropped.

He printed out fuzzy stills of the bystanders: an elderly man and a young boy who could be his grandson, three teenage girls, hands to their mouths, probably shrieking. And there was a slim guy in jeans, a dark blue Windbreaker, and a baseball cap, walking behind the others.

Conklin backed the video up another thirty seconds, to the point where the professor entered the field of view, hands in his pants pockets, turning his head from side to side as he glided forward on the walkway. Then the group of tourists that had been moving faster than the professor surrounded him—and Rich saw the guy in the cap join the group.

Conklin stopped the video and let it feed forward a frame at a time. He watched the ball-cap guy bump into the professor and snake his hand under the back of the professor's herringbone jacket. It was a classic pickpocket maneuver called dipping. Then the guy in the cap lifted his hand and aimed the gun that he had removed from the back of Judd's pants.

Conklin saw the flare as the ball-cap guy fired on Professor Judd.

The professor jerked, fell. Then the guy in the cap raised the muzzle and fired again. This time the bullet went into the Plexiglas wall.

It was clearly a diversion.

Water spouted. People glanced at the body, turned away, sprinted up the walkway.

Conklin pressed the forward button and

watched the jerky image of the man in the cap. The assailant never looked up, never looked at the camera. After he threw his two shots, he disappeared into the shadows at the end of the walk. He had probably wiped and ditched the gun there, but that was a supposition. And while Conklin was sure that the ball-cap guy was the killer, he hadn't seen the man's face.

Conklin ejected the disk from the DVD drawer and slipped in the second disk, which had been shot by a camera at the aquarium's entrance.

This time he knew whom he was looking for.

Another hour went by as Conklin scanned the video and found the images of the guy with the cap, a guy who was starting to look familiar. He watched him go past the security guard, hold out his ticket to be punched, and enter the dark hole that was the entrance to the exhibit.

The shooter was a pro. He had kept his face hidden at all times. Conklin had no image to compare with those of known criminals.

So the questions remained. Who was the guy in the ball cap? How had he known that the professor was carrying a weapon at the back of his trousers? Why had he targeted the professor? And had he killed the two women the professor had seen in his dreams? If so, how had *that* happened?

How had the killer tapped into the professor's *dreams*?

There was something crazy wrong about the entire dream-and-execution pattern. It was a puzzle, and Conklin felt there was more to it than the images on his screen.

What was he missing?

Conklin made a cup of coffee in the break room. Then he went back to his desk and watched the video again.

Chapter 81

FBI UBERAGENT RON PARKER sat with Randolph Fish in a small cement-block room in the bowels of the prison. Two cameras were focused on them; one angled through the one-way glass, and the other was positioned in a corner of the ceiling.

Fish was shackled hand and foot by a chain that ran through a hole in the center of the table to a loop in the floor. He was so pale you could almost see through his skin. There was a fresh hand-size bruise on his jaw, and Parker had seen the photos of the larger bruises and abrasions all over his body.

The day before, a couple of guards had been escorting Fish to the yard when they were drawn into a dispute between two other prisoners and took their eyes off Fish for a moment.

The dispute was a diversion, giving another prisoner a chance to pull Fish against the bars of his cell. He twisted Fish's arm until he went to his knees. Then a second prisoner got Fish's pants down, kicked his legs apart, and did him with a sawed-off broom handle.

The assault had been over quickly, but it had turned Fish's head around entirely. After the emergency medical treatment, which involved a row of stitches in a place where the sun don't shine, Fish had asked for Ron Parker, who had driven up from L.A. to see him.

Now Parker was watching Randolph Fish, killer of at least five but possibly twice as many young women, think over what he was going to say in an effort to come up with something the G-man might go for.

"I can't stay here," Fish finally said. "I'll be killed."

"I feel for you, I really do," Parker said in a voice that conveyed that he really didn't give a crap. "I would raise a real stink if I were you. Name your attackers. That's what I would do."

Fish didn't rise to the bait.

"I'm ready to make a deal," he said.

"Yeah? Listen, you dumb shit. I can't promise anything anymore. You made me look like a moron too many times. The governor has had enough of your bull. He said, and I quote, 'Don't tell me anything about that psycho unless his last words were "I'm deeply sorry" and that he suffered before he croaked.'"

"The guards could've protected me. They didn't, and I think they set me up," Fish said.

"I've got a meeting in an hour," said Ron Parker. "What do you want and what are you going to give up? Get real or drop dead. I no longer care which."

"Move me to another prison. I'll give you the names of four girls you know nothing about. I'll tell you where they are."

"That's what you told me last time, Randy."

"Last time I hadn't been corn-holed with a broom."

"Give me the names," Parker said.

Fish squirmed. "Got a pen?"

Parker typed the names on his phone and said, "I'll see what I can do." He called for a guard, then turned before he left the room.

"Stay out of trouble," Parker said to the serial killer. "Watch your ass."

Chapter 82

THE NEW WOMEN'S jail was a few blocks away, on 7th Street. It was a model facility, but Yuki made sure that Lynnette Lagrande was held in a special unit in the grubby, outdated, and overcrowded facility on the seventh floor of the Hall of Justice.

Lynnette would be uncomfortable there and maybe terrified, which was all to the good. The first grade teacher with the diamond necklace and the sixty-thousand-dollar car needed a reality check, and Yuki planned to spell out to Lynnette exactly how much pain she was facing.

Yuki had a statement from Lieutenant Floyd Meserve in her briefcase. Meserve admitted that he had been in love with Lynnette Lagrande, but he hadn't liked her at all. He said she was as mad as a box of snakes and he hated himself for ever getting involved with her. He said he was glad to help the DA and he wanted to just walk away from the whole deal with no charges against him.

In his sworn statement, Meserve said he had no proof but he had reason to believe that Lynnette Lagrande had arranged Jennifer Herman's death.

Meserve said that Lynnette had talked with him about getting Jennifer out of the way. She had insisted that he do the hit and said she would make it worth his while. When he had refused, she had thrown a fit and stopped returning his calls. After Jennifer Herman's body was found, she'd called Meserve and told him she had nothing to do with it, which Meserve had thought showed that she felt guilty.

Meserve had an alibi for the time of Jennifer Herman's death. He said he was in Erie, Pennsylvania, staying with his brother, Morris, visiting their dying father every day. His story had checked out.

Meserve's statement was all that Yuki had on Lynnette Lagrande, but she could make the most of it. Meserve was a cop. The probability was high that after Lynnette was arraigned, she would be held without bail while the DA's office put together the murder case against her. Yuki hoped that this stark view of her future would shock Lynnette into telling the truth.

Yuki took the elevator from the DA's offices on the eighth floor to the jail one floor below. She knew the security guard at the desk, Bubbleen Waters, and told her that she wanted to see Lynnette Lagrande. Then Yuki waited in the outer area for a half hour, returning e-mail, until her name was called.

Officer Waters escorted Yuki along a dark corridor to an interrogation room the size of a typical apartment bathroom. She sat at the table, opened her briefcase, and put away her phone in time for the door to open and Officer Waters to show Lynnette Lagrande into the room.

Lynnette looked wild. Her hair was flat, her nails were bitten off, and the residue of the eye makeup she'd been wearing two days ago ringed her eyes.

"Hi, Lynnette. Bubbleen," Yuki said to the guard, "could you please remove Ms. Lagrande's handcuffs?"

"I don't advise it, Yuki. She's taken a few pokes at people."

Yuki said, "Okay. I hear you. Lynnette, have a seat. How are you doing?"

"I'm just fine," Lynnette said. "I'm rooming with three crack whores and a baby killer. I'm teaching them how to insult each other using proper grammar."

The guard left the room and Lynnette Lagrande sat down. She said to Yuki, "Who do I have to blow to get out of here?"

Chapter 83

YUKI SAID, "A woman like you really shouldn't be here, Lynnette. You need help and so do I. Tell me about Jennifer Herman's murder. And I need to know where Lily Herman has been living for the last year."

"You don't ask for much, do you?"

"I'm asking you to tell me the truth."

"If I know something and didn't tell the police about it, does that make me an accessory?"

"Maybe, but you've got me in your corner. I'd be willing to help you if you help me."

"Could you possibly be more vague?"

"Could you?"

"Okay, listen, Yuki. I had nothing to do with Jennifer's death. Actually, I liked her."

"I'm listening."

Lynnette sighed. "I met Jennifer a couple of times when she came to school to talk about Lily. Lily was a mess. Withdrawn. Evasive. We never really got into it. Jennifer was reluctant to talk about her husband, and I didn't want to talk about him, either. I liked him a lot."

She shook her head, as if it hurt to remember.

"Talk about a colossal error in judgment. But anyway. Whatever Floyd Meserve tells you, I didn't kill Jennifer. I've never killed anything or anybody."

"Floyd will testify under oath that you set up the meeting with him and Keith."

"I made the *introduction*, but for God's sake, I knew Floyd was a cop! Keith was always talking about making Jennifer disappear. So I told Keith a story. That I knew this fixer. Blah, blah. And I'm saying to Keith, 'Can you imagine?' And Keith said, 'Give me the guy's name. Hook us up.'

"I told Floyd about Keith, and Floyd said, 'I could play the part of a hit man. I know enough of them.' I thought Floyd would lock Keith up and Jennifer would be fine. Get it? And then Jennifer could parent her daughter without Keith around terrorizing them.

"So I gave Floyd's number to Keith and at the same time I told Keith I was done with him. He's a scary man, Yuki. Even scarier when he's frustrated. So like I said, I went up to my cottage to be alone. When I heard that Jennifer and Lily were missing, I thought Floyd actually took the job from Keith. Or if Floyd didn't do it, maybe Keith did it himself. I was afraid for my own *life*."

"And where was Lily at this time? Do you know?"

"Oh, I know where Lily was. That's what I'm going to trade for getting these stupid charges against me dismissed."

Yuki thought about what Lynnette had said. It sounded true, and it wasn't even at odds, really, with Floyd Meserve's statement.

"Hey," Lynnette said. "I'm talking to you, you little gook bitch. I can help you nail Keith Herman. Have we got a deal?"

Chapter 84

YUKI SAID, "*WHAT* did you say?"

Yuki had never been called a gook in her life. Her mother was Japanese but had been an American citizen for twenty-five years before her death. Her father had been Italian American, US Army, a veteran. Yuki was born in San Francisco.

She was astonished by this new version of Lynnette Lagrande, who was not only a changeling but an ugly person through and through.

Lynnette said, "I *said*, pay attention, Yuki."

Yuki considered launching a couple of stinging comebacks, but decided to take the high road. She ignored the insult and again asked Lynnette Lagrande to tell her what she knew about Lily's disappearance and whereabouts between the first of March the previous year and last week.

Lynnette spoke with her trademark good diction and grammar, and she named names. Yuki put her notebook away and slammed the lid on her briefcase. She said, "I'll get back to you."

"When? How long do I have to stay here?" Lynnette called after Yuki as she exited the interrogation room.

Yuki went out into the hallway, found people stacked three deep at the elevator bank, and headed down the fire stairs. When she got to the third floor, she opened the door leading to the homicide squad room.

Brenda greeted her with a smile and said, "The boss is in."

Yuki thanked Brenda, breezed through the gate, and crossed the bull pen to the corner office. She knocked on the glass door and Lieutenant Jackson Brady got to his feet, opened the door, and asked Yuki to come in.

"Are you okay?"

Yuki took the seat across from Brady and said, "You've got to hear this."

Brady punched all his phone lines so that no calls could come through.

"You've got my full attention," he said.

"Lynnette Lagrande just told me who was keeping Lily Herman for the last year, and I've got their full names. Marcia Kohl, née Kransky, and Alan Kohl."

Brady typed the names into a known-criminals law enforcement database.

"They're low-level jerkoffs. Insurance fraud. Petty theft. Last known address was Bolinas," he said.

"Right. Well, according to Lynnette, they did some insurance schemes with Keith Herman. They slipped in restaurants. Fell down in front of expensive cars that were slowing for traffic lights. Herman went after the insurance companies, split the take with the Kohls."

"Okay, here we go," said Brady. "Alan Kohl, insurance fraud, charges dismissed August 2007. Attorney, Keith Herman."

"That was Keith Herman working his way up to full-blown dirtbag criminal defense attorney," Yuki said.

"So how does Lily Herman fit into this?"

"Lynnette says she overheard Keith talking to the Kohls about babysitting Lily. She presumes he wanted to get the child out of the house and away from Jennifer. Then Jennifer turned up in garbage bags and Keith was arrested. Lynnette thinks the Kohls continued to babysit and charge Keith for their services."

Brady printed out the Kohls' address, then said to Yuki, "We've got probable cause."

"Yes, we do."

"Want to ask Arthur Nussbaum for a search warrant?"

Chapter 85

YUKI SAT IN the passenger seat beside Brady, who was driving the squad car, responding to radio calls, and taking quick glances in the rearview mirror at the cop cars behind him, bumping up the narrow dirt road that ran out from the town toward the far-flung farmlands beyond it.

They were just outside Bolinas, a town of 1,600 people about thirty miles north on the coast, known for its remote location and reclusive townspeople, who habitually removed highway signs to keep strangers out.

Thickets of trees lined the road, and behind the trees were private properties, separated from each other by fences and high hedges. Brady nodded his head toward a driveway coming up on the left, marked by a couple of garbage cans and a dinged-up mailbox.

He said to Yuki, "That's it." Then he took the mike and told the cars behind him to slow and prepare to turn.

Yuki leaned forward and gripped the armrest. She had never been as humiliated as when her case against Keith Herman had blown up in her face. Far worse, the charges against him had been dropped, and now Keith Herman, presumed innocent, was as free as thought.

Yuki didn't know what Keith Herman had to do with hiding his daughter, but she had an idea. Maybe Lily had witnessed or heard something that would prove her father had killed his wife. With luck, the Kohls would fill in the blanks.

Brady turned up the overgrown driveway and drove uphill to a clearing, where an old wood-shingled house clung to the side of the hill.

He said to Yuki, "Stay here."

She said, "Oh, yeah, right."

"I mean it, Yuki. I don't know what we're going to find."

She got out of the car.

"Watch me. Stay with me," Brady said.

Yuki said, "Okay," and trudged behind Brady and four cops up the weedy lawn and broken walkway to the front door.

Brady knocked and announced, repeated both actions, and then footfalls could be heard coming toward them. The door creaked open and a good-looking man of fifty said, "What do you want?"

"Alan Kohl, we have a warrant to search your premises. Is anyone else at home?" Brady asked.

"My wife, Marcia. She's in the kitchen. What's this about?"

"It's about Lily Herman," Brady said.

"Lily who? I don't know who you're talking about."

Yuki handed the warrant to Kohl. Then she and the cops entered the house.

"Don't touch anything. Don't mess the place up," Alan Kohl said. "You need something, just ask me."

The old two-bedroom house smelled of mold and was almost pathologically neat. Boxes and cartons were stacked against the walls, counters were clean, and closets were filled with folded linens and properly hung clothing. Yuki stayed with Brady until he went upstairs, but then, following a hunch, she went down a flight of wooden steps to a half basement that ran under the back of the house.

Chapter 86

THE DARK HALF BASEMENT had a low ceiling, a dirt floor, three walls lined with shelves, and a two-door metal utility cabinet backed up against the fourth wall.

Yuki opened the cabinet doors expecting to see neat shelves of tools, but the cabinet was empty. The back of the cabinet had been replaced with a rectangle of painted plywood fitted with a hook on one side and hinges on the other. Yuki unhooked the plywood board and swung it open.

There was nothing behind the board—truly nothing but air. Yuki reached into her jacket pocket and took out her keys. She had a flashlight on her key chain, a small one with a pretty bright LED beam. She flashed the light into the back of the closet and saw a tunnel, seemingly endless, that was cut into the hill.

Yuki took out her phone and called Brady.

"Come to the basement," she said. "I think I found something."

The opening was four feet high by three feet wide by too deep for the flashlight to find the end of it. Yuki stooped, pulled her elbows in tight to her sides, and stepped into the rabbit hole.

She followed her flashlight's beam, and after about twelve feet the tunnel took a soft turn to the left and joined a concrete conduit—it looked like a drainage pipe. Yuki aimed her light and saw that down at the end of the conduit was a metal door.

Her phone rang. Jackson.

"I'm in the basement. Where are you?" he said, sounding both annoyed and worried.

"There's a tunnel, Jackson. Open the utility cabinet."

Yuki knew she should wait for him, but she had to keep going. The door at the end of the conduit had a latch with an open padlock dangling from it. She lifted the padlock, put it on the floor, and opened the metal portal.

There was an immediate rush of air from a

vent overhead. Yuki put her hand on the wall and flipped a switch. Light flooded the tiny room from an overhead fixture, illuminating every square inch of it.

The cell was six feet by six feet, five feet high, with cement walls. There was a rough wool blanket and a thin uncovered pillow on a narrow cot up against the wall. Yuki saw a bucket in one corner with a toilet seat on it, a small flat-screen TV on a wooden crate, and a hook on the wall with a rag of a nightgown hanging from it. Her eyes went to a child's crayon drawing of a kitten on the opposite wall, which bore the words POKEY BY LILY.

Yuki turned. Brady stood bent in the doorway. He peered into the cell.

"What the hell?" he said.

Yuki felt shock and disbelief. "Lily lived here. This was where she lived for a year."

Chapter 87

MARCIA KOHL WAS in her forties but seemed older. It looked to Yuki as though she was both beaten down and beaten up. She wouldn't make eye contact. She had a fat lower lip and a fading yellow bruise under her left eye. She didn't ask for a lawyer, but she refused to speak to the police without her husband present. She was being seen by a psychiatrist as Brady interviewed Alan Kohl.

Alan Kohl hadn't asked for a lawyer, either.

Yuki stood behind the one-way glass and watched Brady conduct the interview with Kohl. It had been going on for an hour. Kohl was very sure of himself, overconfident, and appeared to think that if he continued to maintain that he was innocent he would leave the police station a free man.

Brady was patient and Yuki knew he didn't care how long it took. Kohl wasn't getting out of the interrogation room until he lawyered up or Brady had gotten what he wanted.

Brady's tone was casual, even friendly. He was saying to Alan Kohl, "I just want to understand why you kidnapped Lily Herman. I know you must have cared for her, but why did you take her?"

"We didn't kidnap anyone," said Alan Kohl. "And you can't prove otherwise."

"But you admit you kept Lily Herman in your house. There in the room at the end of the tunnel."

"Okay, yes, she was a guest in our home."

"Guest? So your guest room is a six-foot-square underground box? It was okay to keep a little girl in there?" .

"She was happy, didn't she tell you? She had everything she wanted."

"I don't think a jury is going to go for that, Alan."

"I have copies of checks from Keith Herman. Three hundred dollars a week."

"What does that prove?" Brady said.

"Are you trying to trick me, Lieutenant? Or are

you playing stupid? Keith Herman was paying us to keep his kid safe. She's safe, right?"

"I'm wondering if those were payments for keeping Lily safe or if you kidnapped Lily and were extorting her father. As long as he paid you and he didn't call the police, Lily was safe. You understand, there's a big difference between minding the child and kidnapping her. Kidnapping is a felony. Comes with a death penalty."

Kohl smiled at Brady.

"Is this what you think, or are you still fishing around? I told you. Keith Herman paid us to keep his daughter safe."

"Okay, Alan. I don't believe you. You're under arrest for kidnapping Lily Herman."

"Wait. I've got copies of the checks from Keith Herman."

Brady said, "You want to get anywhere with me, I need evidence that Keith Herman killed his wife."

"Why didn't you just say so?" said Alan Kohl. "Sit down. Keep the cameras rolling. I'll tell you where you might find your so-called evidence, but Marcia and I had nothing to do with any murder. I swear to God."

Kohl talked to Brady for about fifteen minutes,

told him a lot of stuff, and when he was done, Brady said, "Stand up, Alan. Put your hands behind your back."

"What? Wait a minute. What the hell are you doing?"

Brady pulled Alan Kohl to his feet, spun him around, and snapped cuffs around his wrists.

"Alan Kohl, you're under arrest for felony kidnapping and endangerment of a minor."

"You said you only wanted evidence of what Herman did to his wife. That's all I've got."

"Get a lawyer, Alan. Go crazy and hire the best one you can afford."

Chapter 88

YUKI AND BRADY were back in Bolinas, a thirty-mile drive that took more than an hour because the roads were so twisting and narrow and difficult to navigate in the dark.

Yuki had a search warrant in her briefcase, the second one of the day. Some kind of record, she thought, but Judge Nussbaum had signed it quickly, no questions asked. He was as eager to right the disaster of Keith Herman's trial as she was.

Yuki said, "I'm afraid to get my hopes up—"

"Don't jinx it, darlin'."

Yuki had one hand on Brady's thigh, the other hand on the dash as Brady wrenched the wheel and turned the squad car up the Kohls' driveway. Branches and brush slapped at the headlights as

369

the car climbed the overgrown, rutted path. They passed the ramshackle house and kept climbing another three or four hundred yards until they reached the end of the drive.

Brady braked the car and looked up the hill. He could just make out a lean-to with a corrugated tin roof, camouflaged by weeds and overgrown with kudzu.

Brady said to Yuki, "You're not going to be able to walk around here in those shoes."

"Give me a second," she said.

She opened the door, took off first one shoe and then the other, and beat them against the lower part of the door frame until the heels popped off.

She put on her newly flat shoes.

"Let's go," she said.

Brady reached over, pulled her toward him, kissed her. They looked at each other for a few moments, both of them smiling, then they set out, wading through the weeds.

The car was under the lean-to, covered with a tarp. Brady pulled on the cloth, let it drop to the ground.

Yuki said, "Oh, my God. Black is dark."

It was the Lexus that Keith Herman's neighbor

Graham Durden had seen parked at the curb outside Herman's house. Durden had witnessed Keith bringing Lily Herman's lifeless body out of the house and putting her in the backseat.

Lily hadn't been lifeless. She'd been drugged.

"It was Keith who brought Lily here," Yuki said to Brady. "It's going to be hard to call it kidnapping."

"Hang on. I'll be right back."

Yuki walked around the car and was still peering into the windows when Brady came back. He had a Slim Jim in his gloved hand. He slid the tool down into the window of the driver's-side door and unlocked it.

"Here we go," he said to Yuki.

Brady opened the car door, reached down, tugged on the latch release, and the trunk popped open. Together, he and Yuki went around to the back of the car. Brady held the flashlight. They peered in.

"You see that?" Yuki said, pointing to the spare tire. She brought her light in close.

"Human hair," he said. "Bloodstained carpeting. And right here?" He moved a section of plastic and felt from the side of the trunk. "This looks like a Beretta Px4 Storm."

Chapter 89

BRADY PARKED ON Sotelo, then walked up the street to the corner of Lopez Avenue. It was about eight in the morning and the nice upscale neighborhood of Forest Hill was just waking up.

Brady had called ahead, said he needed to clear up a few things, and Keith Herman had said, "Sure. Why don't you meet me at my office?"

And Brady had said, "I'm on the way to work. I just need three minutes of your time. It would be a big help to me."

Herman had just enough curiosity, or fear, to tip the balance from "no" to "yes."

Brady looked at his watch. He was early, which was all to the good. He ascended the front steps of the white colonial house with the pediment and black shutters, rang the doorbell, waited a moment, and then Keith Herman opened the door. Brady introduced himself and followed Herman into a study facing the street.

Herman offered Brady an armchair and he took a matching chair beside it. Herman leaned back and clasped his hands together, elbows resting on the arms of the chair.

"What can I help you with, Lieutenant?"

Lily Herman came into the room. She was wearing jeans and a striped shirt, a blue cardigan. She asked her father if she could get some juice from the refrigerator. He said that she could. To be careful. And to hurry. That the nanny would be coming soon to take her to school. He followed her with his eyes as she left him.

Herman apologized for the interruption, told Brady to go ahead with his questions.

Brady knew that Herman had been a practicing down-and-dirty lawyer for twenty years and had a foundation of twenty years of street smarts before that. He opened his coat so that his shoulder holster was exposed and said, "Mr. Herman, I came here alone because I want to have a private chat with you, see if we can get somewhere, just the two of us."

Herman's eyes narrowed. Brady saw from the lawyer's expression that he suddenly understood that this meeting wasn't going to be quick or easy. Maybe he suspected a shakedown.

Brady continued, "You remember ADA Yuki Castellano? She and I went to Bolinas last night."

"Is that right?" Herman shot a glance toward the kitchen. Lily was singing to herself.

"We went to Marcia and Alan Kohl's house with a search warrant. We found the dungeon where they kept Lily, and they've explained that you hired them to take care of her. We have them both in custody now."

"What are you charging them with?"

"Kidnapping. Endangering a minor. A few other charges as we work through their statements."

"I see," Herman said. He looked at Brady. Dropped his eyes to Brady's gun. Raised them again to Brady's steady blue eyes. Then he looked at Lily as she came back into the study.

"Daddy, I forgot to tell you. I used the electric toothbrush this morning. It was fun."

"Good girl, Lily," Herman said. "I need to talk to Mr. Brady in private, okay? Daddy will be right with you."

Chapter 90

THE CHILD TOUCHED her father's cheek, then went back to the kitchen.

Herman said, "I'll testify that the Kohls didn't abduct Lily, if that's what you want me to say."

"So you brought the child to them?"

"Well, yes. I did that. It's not a crime. It was only supposed to be an overnight stay. I was going back in the morning, but I got picked up—"

"I'm not arresting you for kidnapping."

"*Arresting* me?"

"I am arresting you for the murder of Jennifer Herman. Anything you say can be used against you. You can call your lawyer, but as I said, I want to let you know where we stand so that you can make it easy on yourself and your daughter. I'm giving you a chance to come in with me and make a statement."

"A statement about what? You have nothing on me for anything. Don't buy anything Alan Kohl says about me. He's a loser, a . . . a . . . desperado. He'll say anything—"

"Let me stop you there. We've got your car at our forensics lab. Your wife's blood and hair are in the trunk. The Beretta you bought last year was also in the trunk. It's been tested against the bullet extracted from your deceased wife's head. Alan Kohl will testify that he drove you back to this house the night you left Lily with him and Marcia.

"So you're going down, Mr. Herman. You make a full statement, including how and where you murdered your wife, you save the people the time and expense of a trial, it will count in your favor. You see that, don't you?"

"I'm not saying a word. You can talk to my lawyer, John Kinsela. See you in court."

Something fell to the floor in the kitchen. Lily said, "Uh-oh."

"If that's the way you want it, Mr. Herman. Your face will be all over the media again, every single day you're in court. Just curious. Don't you think you owe your daughter something? Don't you think that if you spent the next two hundred years in jail, you still couldn't pay her back for what you've taken from her?"

Herman looked at Brady, kept a steady gaze.

Brady stood up, took his cuffs in hand, and said to Herman, "Stand up and put your hands behind you, right now, or I'll have a half dozen cops in here in ten seconds to drag you out."

"And if I make a statement?"

"I'll make sure you're incarcerated at Folsom. There's a nice little suburb around there. Your mother could move there with Lily."

Herman stared out the window, his face expressionless, unreadable. Brady readied himself for whatever was going to happen in the next few seconds. He was watching for furtive movements. If Herman bolted for the kitchen, Brady had to get to him before he grabbed the little girl. If Herman rushed him, he'd have to take the man down.

Keith Herman stood up, turned around, and put his arms behind his back.

"Done," he said.

Chapter 91

MACKIE MORALES ASKED Richie, "Have you ever thought about getting married?"

He said, "Instead of that, why don't I tell you the funniest thing that ever happened to me on the job?"

She laughed. "I see. Okay. Tell me your funny story."

It was their first actual date, Sunday lunch in Sausalito. They were at Scoma's, a terrific old restaurant right on a pier with a first-class view of the bay, Angel Island, and, of course, the city skyline.

Mackie had pulled her thick hair into what she said was a "side pony," and her gold cross glinted in the V of her blue pullover. Rich couldn't decide where to put his eyes. She was just entirely adorable.

He said, "So four new mosques had opened in town and we were supposed to go around, get on a first-name basis with the imams, you know, facilitate community relations."

The waiter came over with their order—a chilled shellfish platter, iced tea, and freshly baked bread. Rich passed Morales the basket of rolls and she took one.

"Go on with your story," she said. He could tell that she wanted the story to be good.

"Okay. So we're at a mosque and one of the imams comes up to me and my partner and says he's got some information on a possible terrorist threat. And he wants to give us the info, but not there. He says he has to be really careful."

"Oh, my God," Morales said, eyes fixed on his.

"So we arrange to meet him at a little park after morning prayers and whatnot, and I check out a car from impound, looks nothing like a cop car."

"Like a sports car?"

"Exactly. A BMW. Red. And so me and my partner drive to the park, and there's the imam sitting on a bench, wearing his robe and his cap and reading the Koran. And my partner waves to him like to signal him, the plan being we'll park the car in the shadows and talk. But the imam doesn't see us. And so we go around the block three times, trying to signal him, and he looks right past us."

"Humph," said Morales. "That must've been frustrating."

"Now, at the same time we're going around and around, this almost retired cop drives to the park in his black-and-white, parks at the far corner under the trees. He's just running out his time before getting his pension. And so he's sitting in the car reading his fishing magazines—and I see this whole thing unfolding."

They were cracking crab legs with their hands, putting shells in a bowl.

"Hang on a sec," Morales said. She reached over, knocked a bit of crab off his chin.

Rich grabbed her wrist, kissed her palm, released her hand, and went on with his story. Mackie colored, smiled up at him, and he smiled back at her.

"So the old-timer is reading *Outdoor Life*," Richie said, "and the imam sees him and jumps off the bench and starts running toward the cruiser. Now, understand, this sergeant knows nothing about this. He hears the door open behind him, jerks his head around, sees this guy in Middle Eastern clothes dive into the backseat."

Morales was shaking her head and laughing into her napkin.

Rich said, "And we can see all this going down and there's nothing we can do. The old-timer goes flying out of the car, screaming that there's a suicide bomber in his car, and '*Everyone run.*'"

Morales was laughing with tears in her eyes. "Richie, no, please."

"Yeah, and we get the imam out of the backseat and calm the cop down and we get the info and turn it over to the FBI. And they tell us that the intel involved New York City, and we never hear another word about it.

"And that, since you asked, is the funniest thing that ever happened to me on the job."

"Good story." Morales dried her eyes, looked at him, and said, "This is nice, Rich. I'm getting a little bit crazy about you."

He couldn't stop looking at her. Was he available? He wasn't sure. It was too soon after his breakup with Cindy to get involved and yet he really, really liked Morales.

He said, "Let me see a picture of Benjamin."

She went for her purse, which was looped onto the back of her chair, opened her wallet, and pushed the photo toward him.

"Oh, man. He is a good-looking boy."

"Thank you."

"Where is his father?"

"So you want me to tell you about the funniest thing that ever happened to me on the job?"

She grinned.

He said, "Come here."

He pulled her into a hug, her hair tickling his nose, her arm going around him, both of them still sitting at the table. He kissed the top of her head and said, "We've got time to get into the deep stuff."

"Yes," she said. "I want this to take a lot of time."

Richie held her, thought how good this felt, and that he couldn't wait for more.

Chapter 92

IT WAS THE end of another torturous night in the Saint Francis pediatric oncology wing. As light slashed through the windows, Joe and I were still waiting for something good to happen. Dr. Sebetic and his colleagues had stuck pins and needles into our daughter, ran her small body through imaging machines, sent her fluids out to labs, but nothing had yet been concluded. I'm a good interrogator, but I got nothing from the medical staff.

And so two days after we checked Julie into Saint Francis, the death sentence that would not quit still hung over her precious head.

Right then, Joe was sleeping beside me in our private hospital room and Julie was dozing fitfully in her incubator, within arm's reach of the bed.

Neither of them stirred when my phone rang.

Brady said, "How're you all doing, Boxer?"

He actually said "ya'll," his voice sugared with a trace of drawl from his years in Florida.

I told him there was still no news and then asked, "You need something, Lieutenant?"

"Someone wants to talk to you. Here's a hint. He's with the FBI. A very big cheese. I've been told he's got a private line to Washington in his pocket."

Brady patched me through to Parker's phone, after which Parker and I went a few rounds. As before, Parker told me that if I didn't help him with this world-class dirtbag, Randy Fish, the case would always be half closed, half solved, and the remains of the dead girls would never be buried in their family plots.

That would be a crime, to be sure, and that's the part that always got to me.

"I ran the new names he gave me through Missing Persons and they're all Fish's type. Every one of them is a dark-haired young female going to college on the West Coast. We've got another girl from San Francisco, Debra Andie Lane, eighteen. We had never connected her to Fish until he told me he'd killed her."

"How exactly am I going to help you, Ron? You've got the FBI at your disposal. I'm a midlevel homicide cop. On leave. And all he's done is mess with me."

"The fish man asks for you. All the time. He has conversations with you when you're nowhere around. You can help with the force of your personality. By withholding and giving praise. Dial it up, cut it off; that'll work with him."

"You believe that?"

"Yes, if there's any chance in the world."

"Well, thanks for your faith in me, but I'm done with the fish man. Please. Cross me off your call list until further notice."

I told Parker that yes, I was sure, said good-bye, and flung myself back onto the bed.

Joe opened his eyes, ran his hand over his stubble. "Done with what?"

I told him.

He rolled toward me, put his arm over my waist. "Give it some thought."

"No."

What was there to think about? I had to stay near Julie. I had to be right here if a life-or-death decision had to be made.

"Julie is getting the best of care, Lindsay. I'll be here all day and we'll both be here all night. I'll call you, I promise, the second I know anything. You don't function well when you can't take action. You're driving yourself crazy and I hope you'll understand that I love you and I say this in the kindest possible way. You're driving me a little crazy, too."

"Really."

"Randy Fish is a very big deal, and whatever you can do to clear the case, that's what you should do."

We argued in whispers for several minutes, but when Joe talked about giving peace of mind to those lost girls' families, he pushed my buttons, as Ron Parker had done.

"You're going to nail him this time," Joe said. "I just know it."

"You know me, Joe. I'm sure as hell going to try."

Chapter 93

I MET CONKLIN up on Bryant, in front of the Hall. He had the keys to a squad car and also an extra coffee and a chocolate brownie, which I gladly accepted.

"Where to?" he asked, folding his lanky frame behind the steering wheel.

It was about noon when we got on the freeway. A cold front was forming, and the marine layer filled the roadbed from shoulder to shoulder. I knew every twist, turn, and lane change by heart, and so the slow drivers and the fog didn't worry me.

I just wanted to get there, let Randy Fish do his thing, and get back to my family.

Two hours later, under a dull afternoon sun, we parked in the Atwater penitentiary's north lot. Conklin and I met Ron Parker at the front gate, then a group of us trudged down cement steps, through echoing corridors, through a gauntlet of profanity-spewing prisoners, and at last confronted Randolph Fish, who was seated behind a triple layer of Plexiglas.

Fish looked bad—bruised, small, and broken. If you didn't know better, you'd think that he was as dangerous as a sparrow.

"Tell me about Debra Lane," I said.

Fish didn't look at Parker or Conklin or the menacing, muscle-bound guards.

"Debby Lane," he said to me, "was a cute girl, but she had no fight in her, Lindsay. She wouldn't talk to me. She didn't bargain. She just screamed until I couldn't take it."

I stared at him. I'm pretty sure my face was frozen in horror as Fish complained about his teenage victim.

"She just screamed and screamed," Fish said again. "I hardly touched her. I wanted to, but I just ended up cutting off her air. She was a bad choice, I have to admit."

389

Conklin was also looking at Fish, but without expression. However, out of the killer's sight, my partner was clenching his fists, punching his thighs. I knew he was flashing on the remains of Fish's victims, wanting to do something illegal to get Fish's head on straight. Knock out a few teeth. Shatter a few bones.

Well, that's what I was thinking, anyway.

Fish told me, "I locked up Debby's body in a self-storage facility out by Pier 96. I was going to dispose of her later, but you changed my plans for me, Lindsay. You remember. You caught me outside the movie theater. Where you and I met for the first time."

"Why should we believe you?" I said. "You're a good liar, Randy. First class. In fact, when have you ever told the truth?"

"It's in my best interest to help you, Lindsay. Because I want something—and telling you the truth is how I'm going to get it."

"What do you want?"

"I want to prove to *myself* that I can change."

I looked into his deep brown eyes, something a lot of women had done while begging for their lives. Despite Ron Parker's magical belief in me, I had no leverage. Fish would take us to Debra Lane's body. Or he wouldn't.

"Let's go," I said.

Chapter 94

WE WERE BRINGING up the rear of the Randy Fish motorcade, the cherubic serial killer and his armed guards bumping along ahead of us on the patchy road.

I swore as our right front wheel slammed into a pothole on Amador Street, jarring my teeth and snapping my last nerve.

Conklin muttered, "Sorry."

A thermos rolled off the front seat into the foot well, and as I bent to pick it up my partner jerked the wheel and I banged my head into the underside of the glove compartment.

"Hey!" I said.

"The road is like Swiss cheese, Linds. I'm doing my best."

"Do better."

It was getting late, sometime after five, and as the sun bled out, I felt a strong pull to be with Joe and Julie. Yesterday at this time, I'd been checking in with Martha's dogsitter, then heading down to the basement cafeteria for mac and cheese with Joe.

My heart and soul were at Saint Francis.

But I was also being pulled toward a self-storage locker down the street, on the outskirts of nowhere. We hit a good length of road and Conklin gunned the engine. We sped past a rendering plant on our right and a cement factory on our left. Straight ahead, a spotlighted American flag flew at the entrance to the USA U-Store-It facility.

On Parker's tail, we took a right turn into the asphalt-paved lot lined with rows of garage-type storage units, with their alternating red, white, and blue roll-up doors. We braked next to Parker's SUV, in front of a red unit marked with the number 23.

We got out of the car and watched as the transport van containing the prison guards and a chained and shackled Randy Fish was unlocked and unloaded.

Parker tacked a notice to the wall, then took a bolt cutter to the padlock and rolled up the door. Fish swung his head around, saw me, then grinned and said, "Hey, Lindsay. It's great that you're here. This is going to be a very big moment for you."

I looked at him, but I didn't trust myself to speak. I might tell him that he disgusted me, that the next time I saw him, I hoped he'd be strapped to a gurney, looking at the people whose daughters he had killed, parents who had come to witness his last breath.

Randy Fish didn't read my mind, or, if he did, he didn't care what I was thinking. He looked excited, but under control. Like one of those guys on the show *Storage Wars* who had just won an abandoned unit at auction for cheap, and suspected that a '64 Corvette was inside, all its original parts in mint condition.

I followed Fish's gaze, but it was getting too dark to see into the shadows.

Conklin left my side, turned on our headlights, and the storage unit brightened. Everyone turned to face the locker as if an alarm had gone off.

No one coughed or fidgeted or said a word.

12th of Never

We were all waiting for Randy Fish to produce the body of a teenage girl who wouldn't stop screaming.

Chapter 95

RANDY FISH STEPPED forward, his chained hands in front of him, sweeping his gaze from side to side as he took in the contents of the storage unit.

I saw dinged-up, mass-produced furnishings; a well-used desk; a table with a metal top; a rolled-up carpet; and stacks of cardboard cartons, about a hundred of them, each about eighteen inches long by fourteen inches high and wide. What I didn't see was a freezer, or a fifty-five-gallon drum, or anything big enough to hold a body. Even the carpet was too thin to conceal a person. I didn't smell decomp, either.

"I remember now. There's a map in one of those," Randy said, indicating the stack of boxes with his chin.

"Map?" Parker said. The anger in his voice was almost palpable. "You said you put Debra Lane in here."

"I was confused. It's like a dusty attic inside my head, Ronnie. I thought 'body.' Now I'm thinking 'map.'"

"Map to what? Where's this map?"

"Those cartons," said Fish. "My books are in the boxes and the map to where I left the girls is in one of my books."

"You've got three seconds to tell me which carton, which book," Parker said. "Or I'm gonna cancel this outing and send you back to the smallest, darkest hole in the block. No privileges, Fish, and that includes no phone calls, no access to vending machines, no mail, and especially no books—for whatever remains of your miserable life."

Fish said, "Sweet-talking me isn't going to help, Ronnie. I don't *know* which box. I was in a coma for two years, remember? I could have some brain damage. Maybe if I can look at the labels on the boxes, it'll come to me."

Parker stepped behind Fish, hoisted him by his elbows, and manhandled him into the unit.

"I need more light," Parker yelled.

Six squad cars and cruisers rolled into the storage facility. Conklin waved them in and organized them in a semicircle, with their headlights pointing toward Randy Fish's storage locker.

Car radios chattered, doors opened and closed, cops leaned against their vehicles to watch what might be an extraordinary event in the history of law enforcement.

Conklin followed Parker and Fish into the locker, swept a box of pots and pans off a table. Then he began taking down cartons, putting them on the table, and ripping each one open. I joined Conklin, took out books, turned them upside down, opened them, shook them out, dropped them to the floor.

I glanced at Fish. He looked like a guest at a wedding, wearing a nice smile as he watched the proceedings. I got the feeling that even now, he was manipulating the police, manipulating me.

"I drew the map on the back of a sales slip, put it between pages in a book," Fish said. "I think that's what I did."

I got into a good rhythm—opened a book, shook it out, dropped it, repeat. But I didn't lose sight of Fish, and every time I edged near the cheap pine desk, a muscle twitched in his temple.

Conklin reached for another carton of books.

"Hang on," I said to my partner.

I went to the desk, placed my hand on it, and said to Randy Fish, "Am I getting warm?"

"Warm doesn't cut it, Lindsay. I'll let you know when you're smokin'."

I pulled at the desk drawers, all of which opened except for the one on the lower right. That drawer was locked. I rifled through the open drawers, came up with nothing. Then Conklin went to the squad car. He brought back a short crowbar and jimmied open the locked drawer.

I went right at that file drawer. It was full of old records, songs from the fifties and sixties. I took out the records, looked at each one in the light of the high beams, peeked into the sleeves, then passed them to Conklin so that he could take another look.

Fish was watching me and he was humming a tune, one of the "oldies but goodies" that my mom used to sing when cooking dinner or driving us in the car.

Parker said, "Shut up," and gave Fish a shot to

the back of his head with the heel of his palm. Fish fell at my feet just as I put my hands on the last record in the drawer.

The old 45 was by the crooner Johnny Mathis. Fish had been humming the song—"The Twelfth of Never."

The vinyl record was inside a sleeve. I pulled it out and a piece of paper came out with it and fluttered to the ground. I reached for the paper—a U-Store-It receipt with a rough map of the West Coast inked on the back.

As I bent down, I was eye to eye with the Fish Man. I held up the map so he could see it.

"Am I smokin' now, Randy?"

"You're red-hot," said the Fish Man.

Chapter 96

FISH HADN'T GIVEN me anything, but by humming "The Twelfth of Never," he'd let me know that the map to his dump sites was inside the record sleeve.

I felt a flutter of hope, even elation. Good, Randy. Prove to yourself that you can change.

But now, Fish was laughing. Had he taken us on another flier into his twisted mind? Was he screwing with me again?

I asked him, "What's the joke, Randy?"

"I'm just enjoying myself," he said. "It's okay for me to have a few laughs, isn't it, Lindsay? You don't have to play bad cop with me. I'm your pal."

Parker hauled the killer to his feet, and he wasn't too gentle about it. Since Parker was doing

James Patterson

a perfect bad cop, he'd left me free to wonder what that 1950s love song meant to Fish. "The Twelfth of Never" was about a man's love for a woman. I remembered one of the first lines.

I need you, oh my darling, like roses need rain.

Did Fish love an actual person? Or was this psycho-killer love? Did Randy Fish "love" women so much that he had to be the last man to touch them, talk to them, own them . . .

I straightened out the map Fish had drawn on the back of the receipt. Conklin came up behind me and said, "So let's take a look at the latest bullshit."

Parker handed Fish off to one of the uniformed cops and joined us in the huddle. We scrutinized the *x*'s and tiny handwritten notations. I was pointing out previously unknown locations where bodies might have been dumped— when something inexplicable happened.

I was thrown to the ground, as if I'd been hit by a bus.

Everything went dark and silent and my brain flickered with a single thought: What had

402

happened? I got onto my hands and knees, started crawling, bumping into things, like the deaf and blind thing I was.

A couple of long minutes later, someone shook my arm. I saw a blurry uniformed cop. His name was Mooney. Or Rooney. I wasn't sure.

"Are you all right, Sergeant?"

Stars were popping behind my eyes. I could hardly breathe. I was gagging, but somehow managed to ask, "Is anyone hurt?"

"Can you see me, Sergeant?"

I fought nausea, said, "I can see you. I hear you."

Conklin and Parker were on their feet. Conklin came over to me and said, "You okay? You okay, Lindsay?"

I grabbed his arm and stood.

Officer Michael Rooney was saying, "It was a flashbang. I saw this uniform pull the pin and lob it toward the locker. I couldn't get to him in time."

"Flashbang" was a descriptive nickname for a stun grenade, a nonlethal military weapon designed to knock down the occupants of a room to give the shooter the upper hand. The effective range is a five-foot radius from the point of impact, and the stunning effect lasts only a minute or two, but you still would not want to be in a room with one.

As it was, I was still dazed, but I could see.

"Tell it again, from the beginning," I told the cop.

Rooney said, "One of ours fired that grenade. I didn't know him. He was five six or five seven, young guy."

"You didn't know him? How did you know he was a cop?"

"He was in uniform. Drove a cruiser. After he threw the grenade, he grabbed Fish and pushed him into the passenger side. Then he took off."

"It was an abduction?" Parker asked. "Or a getaway?"

"Hard to say. Fish was very wobbly."

"When did the grenade go off?" I asked.

"It's only been a couple of minutes," the cop said. "The cruiser is headed west on Amador. Two of our cars are in pursuit."

"Call dispatch and clear a channel," I said.

Parker was moving through the semicircle of headlights toward his vehicle. I started toward ours. Conklin gave me an arm to lean on.

He dangled the keys. "I'm driving," he said.

Chapter 97

BY THE TIME we blew past the American flag and turned onto Amador, I had gathered my wits, even the ones that had rolled into the far corners of my mind.

For instance, I understood what Randy Fish had thought was so funny. While we were rooting around in his book and record collections, his ride was coming to get him.

Very frickin' hilarious joke on the SFPD and the FBI.

And the punch line was that a heinous serial killer and a rogue cop were taking us on a high-speed chase through the city on a cloudy night, visibility of about ten feet in front of the headlights, precipitation coming on and slicking the road.

I was on the car radio, using the designated clear channel, talking to May Hess in dispatch, also to Sergeant Bob Nardone and Officer Gary Hoffman in the lead pursuit car.

Nardone's voice came through the speaker as he shouted over the blare of sirens: "Turning left onto Cesar Chavez at sixty. I can't read his plates."

We were gaining on Nardone and Hoffman, and other cars joined in as dispatch sent units ahead to cut off the renegade cop car. Conklin and I followed a more or less straight route over the Illinois Street Bridge, took a heart-stopping turn onto Cesar Chavez, then an equally hard right onto 3rd. We sped parallel to the streetcar tracks on 3rd and continued over the Lefty O'Doul Bridge.

On the far side of the bridge was AT&T Park, the Giants home field—and there was a game on tonight. I could see the neon marquee and the stadium lights like a row of stars blazing through the fog. If the sirens hadn't been screaming, I might have been able to hear the fans cheering as a game-winning Giants home run cleared the wall and plopped into McCovey Cove.

As it was, the sirens *were* screaming, but I knew that the Giants had won because inebriated fans, euphoric with victory, had begun wandering out onto the glistening street.

I was looking ahead as we hit King Street and Willie Mays Plaza, and that's when, in the space of an instant, Randy Fish's ride ran into trouble.

A tractor trailer was coming toward us in the opposite lane, like a freight train appearing out of nowhere in the night. Fish's car was speeding, weaving through traffic, and had almost cleared the length of the big rig when the driver turned the wheel ever so slightly to the left.

Maybe the driver miscalculated how far he was from the semi, or maybe his hand slipped on the steering wheel. But whatever the reason, the getaway car clipped the back wheel of the looming, fifty-three-foot, twin-screw tractor trailer, and the whole freaking night exploded.

Chapter 98

I SAW IT all go down, every second of it.

Time didn't freeze. There was no stop-motion, just the awful sight of the rogue squad car winging the back wheel of a monster truck and the front of the car whipping around, being dragged beneath the undercarriage, where it was mashed and mangled.

Tires exploded like gunshots.

Plumes of sparks lit the pavement, trailing behind the semi, as its brakes screeched and the truck jackknifed across two lanes, smacking into cars like a bowling ball taking down pins before it came to a halt.

At the same time as the accident was burning up King Street, Conklin was braking and turning the wheel of our car in the direction of our skid. As I braced for a crash, I saw what was happening just ahead of us.

Nardone's car had slewed into the railing alongside the Mission Creek and the following car had piled into it. Our car slid sideways. I don't know if I actually screamed, but I can tell you that I was screaming inside my mind.

I was thinking of my daughter, my baby, and that I couldn't leave her now. *My God, not now.*

Conklin was doing his best, but still our car caromed off a guardrail, sideswiped Nardone's car, and continued moving in a sickening spin, rocking from side to side. We balanced on two wheels, right at the tipping point, then, mercifully, dropped into a four-point crouch.

Richie was blanched and sweating. He asked for the second time in about ten minutes, "You okay?"

"Yes, you?"

"Fine. Holy crap."

He took my shaking, sweaty hand and squeezed it. I have never loved my partner more.

I said, "You did great, Richie," then I tuned into the screams of people and the fire blazing under the tail of the rig.

Conklin called dispatch, ordered fire engines with heavy equipment, as many ambulances as we could get, and every available cop to clear the road of pedestrians and lock down the scene.

I bolted from the car and ran to the first of the two crashed patrol cars. Nardone was panting, said that his right ankle was broken and that he couldn't move. The cop who'd been driving the second car brushed glass off his face with his right hand. His left arm was hanging at a bad angle. He asked if everyone had made it.

"Stay where you are," I told him. "Help is coming."

Baseball fans were all over Willie Mays Plaza, some injured, moaning and crying, others forming a four-deep bank of spectators on the Portwalk, still others forming a matching wall of onlookers in front of the stadium. There were hundreds of people in harm's way, a good number of them kids.

I smelled gasoline and that scared the hell out of me. The way that truck had slewed all over the street, the numbers of vehicles involved in the collisions—there could be gas everywhere.

I reached the big rig as the driver jumped down with a fire extinguisher in his hand. I followed him to the rear of the truck and he started spraying down the flames. I couldn't see much of the car underneath the fifty-three-footer, but what I could see looked like a tin can that had gone into a meat grinder.

"I didn't see him," the driver was saying to me, tears flowing down his cheeks. "I didn't know what had happened until I heard the racket. God help me. Please tell me I didn't kill anyone."

I ducked under the rig's undercarriage to see what was left of the getaway cruiser, to see if by a miracle someone had survived.

Smoke burned my eyes and made them water. I forced my lids open and saw that the skin of the car was scorched, the roof of the vehicle flattened. No one could have survived this, I thought.

But then a groan came from inside the car.

And then—unbelievable but true—another sound ripped right through me. It was the wail of a young child.

Chapter 99

THE WALKWAYS AND streets in front of the ballpark were lit up like Christmas in hell. Red and blue lights flashed and spun, fire flared, sirens wailed, car alarms went off, and injured pedestrians cried out for help.

Ambulances came and went through the hastily erected barricades, ferrying people to emergency rooms, while Richie and other law enforcement officers corralled bystanders behind barrier tape and tried to keep the scene of an escaped convict's crash intact.

But we couldn't.

Fire engines doused the truck and the streets with CO_2 and water, and even though the roads had been closed off, emergency vehicles kept coming.

I stood by anxiously as a fire engine with a hydraulic lift jacked up the big rig. Another fire truck with a heavy-duty hydraulic winch got a hook into the squashed squad car and pulled it out from under the semi with a heavy steel cable.

The child in the backseat was a toddler of about three. He screamed with everything he had and pawed the air with bloody hands. More blood streamed down the side of his head. Thank God he had been strapped into a sturdy car seat and that seat belts had been threaded through the back of it.

His survival was nothing less than a miracle.

Rescue workers applied the Jaws of Life to the back door of the squad car and three EMTs reached for the baby at the same time.

I knew Lynn Colomello, the head paramedic.

"Do you have an ID on this child?" she asked me.

"I have no idea who he is."

"I'll get him to the ER," she said, "and I'll stay with him, but I can't even guess at his condition without X-rays. Here's my number. Call me later."

Before the ambulance had left with the baby, I was on the driver's side of the car, which was relatively intact. The door had been removed, the deployed air bag flattened. And I saw that the driver was either unconscious or dead, his head facedown on the steering wheel.

I put my fingers to his neck and felt a pulse—but I didn't feel facial hair, whiskers, or stubble. The driver was young, maybe a teenager, wearing the blues of a uniformed officer. He was still alive.

How was this young man related to Fish, and whose baby was being rushed to the hospital?

Fish was in the front passenger seat, crushed against the door. The engine block had blown through the fire wall, intruded into the passenger compartment, and was lying on Fish's lap.

From what I could see, his legs were mangled. Blood was pooling in the foot well, and I saw broken ribs coming through his shirt. Fish moaned. He was conscious.

He saw me, took in a wheezing breath, and said, "Is she alive?" He spoke again. "Please, save her," he said.

Save *her*?

Chapter 100

I MOVED BLOOD-SOAKED hair away and looked more closely at the driver's profile—and for a moment, I thought I had lost my mind.

Just then, Conklin joined me beside the car. He said, "Did the driver make it?" He looked at the shock on my face, then dropped his gaze to the steering wheel. His eyes got huge when he saw her.

"No, *no*," he said. "This can't *be*."

Conklin jerked around, cupped his hands, and yelled at every uniform within earshot. "Get her *out*. Get this woman the hell out of this *car*."

A rescue worker brought over a hydraulic ram, and *bam*—the dashboard was pushed back and Mackie Morales was unpinned. Two men extricated her carefully from the vehicle, lifted her onto a stretcher, and fitted an oxygen mask to her face.

She'd been beaten up by the collision and looked like she was barely holding on to life.

I said to Conklin, "The child in the backseat. Could he be hers?"

"She has a three-year-old. Benjamin. He's alive?"

I told Conklin what I knew. My partner looked scared and confused, and he hovered around the stretcher as paramedics strapped Morales down.

"Mackie. Mackie. It's Rich."

She didn't move or acknowledge him.

Conklin spoke urgently to the EMT. "Her name is MacKenzie Morales. She works in Homicide, Southern District. How bad are her injuries? Is she going to make it?"

"Go with her," I said to my partner. "I'll stay with Fish."

Conklin didn't argue.

He climbed into the ambulance, took a seat beside the stretcher, and was looking at Morales when the doors closed. The sirens came on, and so did the rain, precipitation ringing the lights with intermittent halos of bright, flashing red.

I watched for a moment as the ambulance headed out. I didn't know what Conklin and Morales had together, but if anyone could find out why she had become the serial killer's wheelman, Rich Conklin had the means and the motive to do it.

Chapter 101

THE KALEIDOSCOPE OF blinking lights took on another dimension as helicopters landed and took off, medevac units shuttling victims to trauma centers in and out of the city. Media choppers had also arrived and were in contact with the press behind the barricades, sending live reports over the airwaves.

I leaned in to the empty frame of the crashed squad car's windshield and focused on a man I despised but who had become very important to me. Randy Fish had an IV in his arm, but he had pushed away the oxygen mask and was having a very hard time breathing. Every time he took in air, I expected him to let it out with a death rattle.

But he was *not* going to die without answering my questions. I just wouldn't accept that.

"Randy. Can you hear me?"

"Lin?"

"Yes. It's Lindsay. Who is Morales to you?"

"I love . . . her," he said. "I love . . ."

I reached into the car, shook his shoulder. Blood was coming from his forehead, his chest, his twisted legs. His body was a sieve.

"Stay with me, Randy," I said to him. "Please stay with me. We're going to get you out of here in just another minute. Hey! Randy."

Blood bubbled out of Fish's mouth. He took another breath. I turned away from the car and toward the chaos around me. A fireman was six feet away from me, talking into his phone. Rain dripped from the brim of his hat.

"We got a survivor in there," I shouted, pointing to the car.

"I know, Sergeant. We had to extract the ones who are going to make it first. But I didn't forget him. I've got the Jaws coming back now."

The firefighter came back to the car and leaned his face through the windshield as I had done. He said to Fish, "I'm Deputy Chief Robert Wilson. I'm called Robbie. Take it easy, sir. Everything is going to be okay."

I had heard those words before, spoken in just the same way. And now I remembered the man called Robbie. The last time I'd seen him, I'd been naked, lightning blazing around me across the black sky. This man had helped deliver Julie.

"Don't I know you, Sergeant?" he said to me. "Sure I do. How's your little girl?"

My chest heaved. Tears welled, spilled, unnoticed in the rain. God, I was crying a lot these days. I sucked it up and pushed down the emotion that was on the verge of disabling me.

I put my hand on Deputy Wilson's arm and said, "Mr. Fish is an important witness to several unsolved homicides. I have to talk to him."

"Ma'am, that engine crushed his thighs and his pelvis. He's got broken ribs, punctured lungs. He's lost a lot of blood, and he's either going to bleed out or the traumatic asphyxia is going to kill him.

"He's going in and out of consciousness now, you understand?" Deputy Wilson said. "He's not leaving that car. If you want to talk to him, you should tell him that he's got very little time. I'd tell him that right away."

Chapter 102

THE AMBULANCE TOOK off like a rocket. I stood in the street and stared after the taillights and flashers until they became the size of pin lights, trying to understand what made no sense to me at all.

Why had Mackie Morales, our summer intern, been driving a stolen squad car with her baby in the backseat? Had Fish gotten to her in some way? Had he threatened her or her baby?

That had to be it.

Why else would a bright young woman with a big future and a small child commit a felony? But if Fish had threatened her, how did that square with him saying that he loved her?

Fire bloomed under a car that had been beached

on the sidewalk under the marquee. The neon sign reading HOME OF THE SAN FRANCISCO GIANTS flickered madly. Hoses came out, snaked around my feet, and that's what broke the spell.

I walked back to the twisted patrol car, where Randolph Fish was pinned under the weight of the big V-8. The car interior, such as it was, was bright from the surrounding headlights and halogen lamps. I saw that Fish was still taking in air, but his breathing was shallow and labored.

I angled myself into the driver's seat, said to the dying man, "Randy, it's Lindsay. How're you doing?"

Fish opened his eyes and slowly turned his head so that he could see me.

"Mackie?"

"She's on the way to the emergency room. My partner is with her. That's all I know."

Blood oozed through his prison jumpsuit. The weight and pressure of the engine block on his lap was likely acting as a lower-torso tourniquet, keeping Fish from bleeding out.

"Ben?" he asked me.

"He's at the hospital."

Tears shot out of Fish's eyes, ran together with

the blood on his cheeks, dropped from his chin. Christ. I thought psychopaths didn't have feelings. I reached over and tugged at the oxygen mask so that it covered his nose and mouth. He took a ragged breath.

I felt his life leaving him. It didn't take an MD to see that he was going to die, right here, right now.

I spoke to him over the noises on the street; men calling to each other, winches and engines grinding and roaring, sirens near and far.

"I have to ask you some questions."

He nodded.

"Who is Mackie to you?"

I moved the mask.

"Ben is. Our. Boy." He sighed.

"Yours and Mackie's?"

He nodded.

My thoughts scattered yet again and I did my best to corral them into a cohesive pattern.

If Fish wasn't lying or fantasizing, he'd known Morales for at least four years. Mackie Morales was a college girl, then and now. She was dark-haired, slim, definitely his type.

But instead of killing her, he'd fallen in love with her? Was that right? And they'd had a child

423

together? And then, while he was in a coma, she had gotten an internship at the SFPD?

If all that was true, Mackie Morales was a plant.

She'd embedded herself in our squad, the squad that had brought Fish down.

The idea was within my grasp, but it was slippery and I thought there was more to it that I didn't get at all.

I held the mask for Fish so he could get oxygen to his brain. I wanted to know about him and Mackie, how long the escape had been planned, and why, if Fish could love a woman, he had killed so many women so viciously.

But Stone Phillips wasn't here and there was no time to do the in-depth *Dateline* interview. Shouts got louder as a lot of men and machines converged outside the car.

The rescue team had returned with power tools to extract Randolph Fish from the wreck of the Ford Crown Vicky. It was highly likely that when the engine was lifted, Fish's blood pressure would plummet and he would die.

I moved the mask away and said, "Randy? I've got something important to tell you. Are you listening to me?"

Chapter 103

RANDY FISH HAD all the starch and vigor of a sock puppet. His chin rested on his collarbone. His hands lay limp on the engine block. Could he still hear me?

"Randy? Are you with me, bud?"

I called his name several times, and then he exhaled a groan.

"Randy, listen to me. I'm sorry to have to give you some bad news. Your injuries are severe. Your lower body, your internal organs are crushed. Do you understand what I'm telling you? Your injuries are not survivable."

He took in a breath, spoke on the exhale.

"Need doc . . ."

"Doctors want me to tell you that you have very little time."

A moment passed and Fish didn't inhale. Was he still alive? Or had he wandered down the tunnel toward the light?

"I'm tough," he said.

He was making a joke as he faced death, with thoughts of loved ones who might also be dying or dead. I thought of Ben, the little boy who'd survived the horrific crash, and I felt sorry for Randy Fish.

Which pissed me off.

Fish was a sexual predator who had maimed, tortured, raped, and murdered his victims, getting off on causing as much pain as he could. He had never confessed and had never expressed remorse. He was filth, a heinous psycho, one of the worst.

But I needed him to trust me, to tell me where he'd hidden the unrecovered bodies. It wasn't easy to find the right words.

"A miracle could happen, Randy. No one is giving up. But to be honest, you probably only have a few minutes left."

He closed his eyes, then opened them.

"You want to get right with people who love

you, Randy. You want your son to know that you helped the parents of those dead girls—"

"Sonoma," he said thickly.

"What about Sonoma?"

"Dow off . . ."

Dow off? What was this? Had his mind veered to the stock market?

Fish's head dropped forward even farther. He was blacking out, but I squeezed his arm and I think the pain brought him back. He tried hard to give me answers. He spoke in broken sentences punctuated by moans, and somehow, using the GPS on my phone, asking questions that required one-word answers, I was able to get Fish to string together enough words to give me a picture and a map.

There was an abandoned typewriter factory, Dow Office Machines, in Sonoma. Fish had dumped the girls in the woods behind the machine shop.

I named the murdered girls whose bodies had not been found and he nodded at each one, but when I said "Sandra Brody," he shook his head no and then said, "Not mine."

A week ago, about eight of us had bushwhacked through the woods with cadaver dogs, dug up old deer antlers, and had our hopes raised, then shattered, so that Fish could smell fresh air.

He'd been messing with us then.

Was he screwing with me now?

"Don't lie to me. That girl is still missing. She's just your type. You told us that you had killed her. I need to find her body, Randy. Give her back to us. I'm asking you, please."

Deputy Chief Robbie Wilson appeared in the frame of the windshield. He said, "We're getting you out, Mr. Fish. This could hurt, so brace yourself."

Wilson gave me a look that seemed to say, "Sergeant, you brace *yourself*."

The hydraulic cutters chomped through the passenger-door hinges. Heavily gloved hands wrenched the door away. A hook came in from above and Wilson positioned it under the engine block.

I heard Ron Parker calling, "Wait. *Wait*."

He ran as if he were in a steeplechase, clearing hurdles of twisted metal as he galloped toward the car. The hydraulic winch whined. Metal clanked as the hook got purchase and five hundred pounds of steel began to rise.

Fish's face stretched in pain. He looked at me, said, "Love you. Mackie."

And then he died.

Parker was right outside the wreckage when it happened. He was panting, leaning forward, his hands on his knees.

"I had more questions for him."

"Sorry," I told him. "He took the express train to hell."

"Shit. I didn't get to wish him a good trip," he said.

I put my fingers on Fish's eyelids and closed them. The last person he'd seen in this life was me. I didn't want him to look at me anymore.

I was done with Randolph Fish. Done.

Chapter 104

RICH CONKLIN BRACED himself inside the rear of the ambulance as it sped over the slick streets toward Metropolitan Hospital. He kept his eyes on Mackie Morales, who looked like she'd been catapulted into a brick wall.

Air bags deploy at about a hundred miles an hour, and Mackie had gotten the full blunt force of the bag. She had also been whipsawed during and after the collision as the car was dragged along 3rd Street.

She hadn't regained consciousness, even though they were traveling in a stream of screaming sirens, the ambulance jerking and swerving around traffic.

Right now, she was immobilized by a C-Spine

collar and strapped to a long board to protect her head, neck, and spine. She could have brain damage, internal bleeding, broken bones—all of it was possible.

Conklin reached over and squeezed her hand, got no response. He wanted to hold her, tell her she was going to be okay, and somehow make that be true.

But even as he worried about Mackie, he was completely mystified as to why she had been driving the killer's getaway car. Had she fired the flashbang into the storage unit? Was she the cop who had bundled Fish into the passenger seat? Why would she do that?

What didn't he know about Morales?

The ambulance took a hard right on Valencia, a sharp left on 26th Street, then blew into Metro's ambulance bay. The EMTs had the back doors open the instant the vehicle braked to a stop. Rich jumped down, then ran with the EMTs as they transported Mackie's gurney into the emergency room.

The ER was noisy and full. Victims of the multi-car crash were being treated in curtained cubicles, and those who weren't in danger of dying had been parked in wheelchairs and on gurneys wherever space permitted.

Mackie, on the board, was lifted onto an exam table in a trauma room. Medical personnel crowded in, began assessing the damage.

The attending physician was about forty, wiry, efficient. Her name was Emily Bruno and she and Conklin had met many times in circumstances like this one.

Bruno said to Conklin, "What's the patient's name? What happened to her? Do you know anything about her medical history?"

Conklin said, "This is MacKenzie Morales, twenty-six, single mother, and I don't know her medical history. She drove the car into that semi outside the ballpark. Two fatalities so far. I've got to talk to her."

Dr. Bruno threw a loud, exasperated sigh.

"Okay, you know the drill, Conklin. Stand back. Turn off your phone. Don't get in anyone's way."

Conklin said, "Understood."

He stood about eight feet back from the table as the nurses cut off Mackie's blue cop uniform while she was still strapped to the board, checked her airway, her breathing, examined her head.

Conklin saw the great purple bruises on her torso, the angry abrasions on her arms and chest, a seat-belt bruise from shoulder to waist.

Dr. Bruno flashed a light into one of Mackie's eyes and said, "Concussion," but the rest of her words were lost as Morales batted the doctor's hand away and opened her eyes on her own.

"What happened?" she said.

"You were in a car accident," Bruno said. "Do you remember it?"

Conklin saw the memory light up Mackie's eyes. And then the impact of the thought came to her in a rush. She heaved upward and tried to sit up, totally impossible to do, strapped as she was to the board.

"Where's my *baby*?" she screamed.

Conklin went to her and said, "Mackie, Ben's okay. I saw him. He's going to be fine."

Did she recognize him?

"Mackie, it's Richie. It's me."

"Oh, fuck," she said. "What are you doing here?"

433

Chapter 105

CONKLIN TRIED TO keep the shock off his face. Mackie looked feral. She'd been severely traumatized. Maybe she actually didn't know him.

He said it again. "Mackie, it's me. Richie. Conklin."

"Where's Randy?"

Where's Randy? The sexual predator? The homicidal maniac? That Randy?

Morales was highly agitated, trying to release herself from her restraints even as the nurses tried to soothe her, listen to her heart, hook her up to air and fluids.

"Oh, *God*," she screamed out. "Everything hurts. Give me something for the pain."

Dr. Bruno was shouting, "I need CTs, stat,"

when Conklin interrupted, said, "Emily, before you take her anywhere, give her anything, I need two minutes."

"What are you asking me, Conklin? We're not wasting the golden hour."

"I'm asking for two minutes. This woman filled up your ER tonight. We've got bodies in the morgue. I need to talk to her while I can."

Dr. Bruno said, "I'm walking out of the room to call radiology. When I come back, you're done."

Conklin returned to Morales, who was crying, her voice guttural, unrecognizable. "Oh, my God, oh, my God. Put me out, please, give me something."

"Mackie," Conklin said. "Talk to me."

"You're kidding," she shouted. "I hurt like a son of a bitch. Tell them to put me out."

"Why were you driving that car?"

"Why? Because I was breaking Randy out. Don't you get that, you moron? We were running off with Ben. It was finally our time."

Conklin muzzled his outrage. He liked this girl, really liked her, but clearly he didn't know her. Whatever he'd been thinking about her was a reflection of what he wanted her to be.

She grabbed his wrist. It was like being clapped into an iron wristband.

"I don't want to die," she said.

"We don't have a lot of time, Mackie."

"Oh, no, oh, no."

"Talk to me now. What's your connection to Randy Fish?"

"Damn you. You want your dying declaration, Richie? Here's the whole enchilada. I killed that Whole Foods woman. Harriet Adams."

"Say that again?"

"Yeah, and I killed the streetcar driver, too, okay? It was *me*. It was a real fucking rush, believe me."

Conklin's bullshit meter was going off. It was impossible to pull off a murder that someone else dreamed. Mackie was delusional. She was concussed and probably had bleeding in her brain.

He glanced at the corner of the ceiling. Saw the red light on the video camera. It was recording.

Mackie gave a shrill scream of pain.

Conklin pulled up a chair so that he was sitting right near her head. "*Make* me believe you," he said. "Because what you're telling me is hard to understand."

"Then *listen*. I watched you interview the professor. I typed your notes, remember that?"

Her angry expression collapsed. She begged him, "Richie, I need drugs. I hurt so bad."

A nurse was at the exam table.

"We're going to roll you onto a stretcher, dear. We'll be very careful."

Conklin shook his head, said, "Another minute. We need one more minute."

He turned away from the nurse and back to Morales.

"Who are you protecting, Mackie?"

Her face changed again, tightened into a scowl, and then she laughed. It was like the bark of a small dog confronting a larger one—manic, hysterical, definitely no mirth in it.

She said, "You *would* think I was covering for someone, you jerk. You underestimated me, Inspector. I watched your interviews with Professor Judd, then after I made his dreams come true, I went to the aquarium and shot him.

"Look at the video. Look at the fucking video. I'm on it. In a baseball cap. We looked at that tape together and you never connected the dots. What a laugh. What? Why are you looking at me that way?

"Oh. You don't get me, right? You never did. I was playing you, Richie. I did it for Randy and he is proud of me. Now get me drugs. I want to die in peace."

Conklin stood up, attached Mackie's wrist to the stretcher with a restraint, and said, "MacKenzie Morales, you're under arrest for murder—"

She said, "You didn't read me my rights. You can't use what I said."

"You gave me your dying declaration, and it's all been recorded on disk. But I hope you don't die, Mackie. You shouldn't get off so easy. You shouldn't get off."

Chapter 106

I WAS SLEEPING in our bed in the oncology wing when a booming voice paging Dr. Sebetic ended in a feedback squeal that rudely woke me. I groaned, reached for Joe, but he wasn't there.

I rolled over and saw that the baby's incubator was no longer at our bedside. Seeing that empty spot dropped me into unadulterated, heart-stopping, blinding terror.

What had happened while I slept?

Where was my baby?

I was on my feet when Joe rounded the doorway to our room. He was wearing a T-shirt, shorts, and paper slippers, and was holding two containers of coffee.

"Hey. I've got something for you," he said. "If

you want a shower, go now. We've got a meeting with Dr. Sebetic in fifteen minutes."

"Where's Julie?"

"She's in the baby room. Go. Splash some water on yourself."

I stood in the tiny stall under the hot spray, not moving, just letting the water work on me. The baby was in her incubator. We were going to meet with Dr. Sebetic and he was going to give us a thumbs-up or a thumbs-down. And whatever he said, we were going to deal with it.

Still, I didn't like the freaking odds.

Joe rapped on the shower door.

"Let's go, Lindsay. We don't want to keep the doctor waiting."

I dried off with a towel the size of a dinner napkin, then dressed in yesterday's smoky jeans and one of Joe's clean T-shirts. If paper shoes were good enough for Joe, they were good enough for me. I opened a packet and put them on.

After brushing my teeth and hair, I went out into our room, drank down my coffee in one long gulp, then said to my husband, "Are you ready?"

"No," he said. "I'm not."

We went into each other's arms and held on

tight. I gathered strength from my husband and I asked God to please let her live. Joe dropped his head to my shoulder and I put my hand in his hair.

Then Joe released me. "We're late," he said.

Chapter 107

DR. SEBETIC WAS in his forties, stood 6 feet 3 inches tall, weighed about 170, had red hair, black-framed glasses, and wore a sporty green plaid tie with his lab coat. He had seemed distracted each time we had met with him, but he was a hematologist and oncologist of distinction, and that was all that mattered.

The doctor looked up when we entered his office, said hello, and offered us chairs across from him at his desk. He called out to the hallway, "Nurse Kathy, please bring in Baby Girl Molinari."

The nurse called back, "Coming right up, Doctor," then came into the room with our baby. Julie was swaddled in a blanket, wearing a pink stocking cap, and waving her fists.

"She had a good breakfast," Nurse Kathy said.

I stood up, took Julie from the nurse, thanked her, and sat back down. Then I held the baby up so that Joe could kiss her, took her back, kissed her cheek, wiped my tears off her face, nestled her in my arms.

"So," said Dr. Sebetic, looking at the space between me and Joe. "I have news."

He removed his glasses, polished them with a tissue, then squared them on the bridge of his nose.

"The test results are back and the blood cell appearance is returning to normal. It's what's called a polyclonal lymphocytosis, which is a benign, temporary, self-limiting disorder—"

"For God's sake, Doctor," Joe said. "In English, please."

"I'm sorry. Let me say it another way. Julie had abnormal lymphocytes, and that diagnosis is a banana peel that many an experienced specialist has slipped on.

"You see, the blood cells in mononucleosis look just like the ones that you find in lymphoma."

I didn't see.

I said, "Mononucleosis? The kissing disease?"

"Exactly. You didn't have a sterile delivery room, correct? As I was saying, you can look at two slides and one is malignant lymphoma, the other is mononucleosis, and you can't tell the two apart. Many a pathologist has made the wrong call."

I thought I was tracking him, but I was afraid to hope. I held on to my child and my wits, pictured the two slides, imagined doctors slipping on banana peels.

Dr. Sebetic said, "The bottom line is that Julie is getting better all by herself."

"She's out of danger?" I asked. "She's going to live?"

"She's perfectly healthy and as cute as ten buttons. I'm sorry, but I have to be in a tele-conference with Shanghai, uh, five minutes ago. Nurse Kathy will be happy to help you check Julie out of Saint Francis."

Chapter 108

OH, MAN, TALK about home sweet home.

A half hour after leaving the hospital, Joe, Julie, and I were safely and joyously back in our nest on Lake Street.

Joe put the camera on a five-second delay, set it on the TV console, and ran across the room to the big leather sofa, where he flung himself down and swept me and Julie into his arms.

We grinned, the two of us—nothing contrived about it. This was over-the-moon time. This was what extreme happiness felt like.

After the shutter clicked, Joe dashed back to the camera and set it again, returned to his girls, and this time, when Julie looked at the lens, she laughed.

"Did you see that?" I yelled at Joe, way too loudly. "Did you see her smile for the birdie?"

"What is this?" Joe said, pointing at her left cheek. "Is this a dimple? Who's your daddy?" he said, showing dimples of his own.

We took more pictures, laughed like crazy people, and then put the baby to bed and hit the phones.

I called my sister and the other three members of the Women's Murder Club. I called Conklin and then Brady and Jacobi, the two guys I called Boss. Last but not least, I called our dogsitter, Karen, and asked her to bring Julie's big furry sister home in time for dinner.

Joe made serial calls to people from coast to coast, all of them named Molinari. And when we were ready to stop shouting and dancing, we went to bed.

We made tender love, quietly, so we didn't wake the baby in the next room, and it was so sweet that if I had any tears left, I might have cried.

I slept hard and woke up laughing.

Joe mumbled, "Tell me the joke."

"A horse walks into a bar. The bartender says, 'Why the long face?'"

Joe laughed. "You're giddy," he said.

"Yeah? A hamburger and a french fry walk into a bar. The bartender says—"

"We don't serve food here."

"Nuts."

"You know I love you, Blondie."

He went across the hall and returned with the baby. She didn't cry, which was the most amazing thing, something I was going to love getting used to. She put her cheek on her father's shoulder and he rubbed her back.

"I know you love me, Joe," I said. "But do I hear a 'but'?"

"No flies on you, honey. I got a job offer. The job is in DC."

I wanted to explode. I shouted in a whisper, "No, you don't. No, Joe, just flat-out no effin' way."

"For a lot of money. Enough to buy a pretty good house."

"Oh, my God."

"But."

"But *what*?" I asked him.

"I turned it down."

"Really?"

"I didn't even have to think about it. I couldn't leave my sweeties, my party girls."

447

Chapter 109

CINDY THOMAS HAD been obsessed by the Faye Farmer mystery since Farmer's body disappeared from the morgue and she'd been assigned one of the best stories of her career.

Fact: Faye Farmer had been murdered.

Fact: Farmer's fiancé, 49ers star Jeff Kennedy, was the only suspect and at the same time a dead end. There was no evidence against him.

Fact: Forensic evidence that might have nailed Farmer's killer had disappeared with her body, probably forever.

Other facts: The police were nowhere on the case, but the public and the press still wanted to know the identity of the killer.

Cindy had used every waking moment to

chase rumors, interview Faye Farmer's friends and enemies, and in so doing had become the *Chronicle*'s featured headliner in print and on the Web.

This opportunity was priceless, but in the dark and lonely night, Cindy was not at peace. She replayed her conversations with Richie over and over again, and when she stopped rationalizing, she knew that Richie was right and that she had blown it.

She had neglected him, had put her work first, and even now was using work to cover up the pain of losing the very excellent man she loved.

Cindy had expected him to call her, and when it was clear that he wasn't going to do it, she'd called him.

And now here she was.

Richie was staying at the Marina Motel, a cluster of old, two-story, Mediterranean-style structures with red tile roofs and iron railings around the balconies. At 8:15 p.m., Cindy pulled into the motel's parking lot, nosed her car into a spot between a pickup truck and a station wagon, and turned off the ignition.

She looked up at the second floor, picked out

the room, saw Richie's silhouette against the curtains. She got out of her car and walked up the outdoor steps, her heart hammering as she walked along the pathway to room 208 and knocked on the door.

Richie called out, "Hey," came to the door, and opened it. He had a towel around his waist and his hair was wet. He was backlit by the yellow light coming from the bathroom.

He looked good.

He said, "Come in, come in."

He pointed the remote control at the TV, switched off the sound.

"Hi, Rich," she said.

She thought he might kiss her hello, but he said, "Have a seat. Give me a second, okay?"

Cindy looked around at the plain, clean furnishings and at Richie's familiar clothes draped over the desk chair. He pulled his clothes off the chair, disappeared into the bathroom, and closed the door. That reminded Cindy of the many days, weeks, and months they'd lived together, dressed and undressed in front of each other, feeling neither modest nor inhibited.

Now all that had changed.

Cindy swept the remote off the table and boosted the volume, watched the rehash of the crash outside the ballpark, then muted the volume again when Richie came back into the room. He was dressed, barefoot.

He sat down on the end of the bed. She thought she saw tenderness in his face. She knew that he must miss her as much as she missed him. They'd had the real thing. And she knew that it wasn't over.

He said, "You saw reports on this crash, huh? It was brutal."

"I miss you, Richie."

He looked at her, his eyes soft, and she thought he was going to say, "I miss you, too."

But he got up, took some socks out of the dresser, brought them back to the bed, and sat down. He was still mad at her. That's what it was.

"I started therapy, Richie. I thought I should get some help, you know? My therapist's name is Mary. She's very good. And I was wondering if you'd come and see her, too. With me."

There was a pause; maybe it lasted only a couple of seconds, but it felt eternal.

Rich said, "Ah. I don't think so, Cindy."

451

Cindy felt sick. Cold and sick. "You don't want to see if we could work this out?"

Richie stood up, reached out his hand and pulled her to her feet, took her into his arms and held her.

He said, "Cindy, it's not that I didn't love you."

"Don't say 'didn't.' Don't say that."

"Cin, what's wrong with us can't be fixed in therapy. I don't want to force you to sacrifice what you want. And I don't want to give up my dreams for a family.

"I'm sorry," he said as she shoved him away, turned from him, and started to cry. "I'm sorry it turned out this way."

Chapter 110

WE WERE AT Susie's Café in the back room, the booth by the window. It was happy hour on a Friday night and "our place" was packed tight to the walls. Conversation was almost impossible, but Cindy, Claire, Yuki, and I really needed to connect with one another, and so we shouted over the noise and gestured wildly with our hands.

An old dude at the bar had sent over a pitcher of tap, so I guess we looked good enough to go out in public, but Cindy was devastated, Claire was depressed, I still smelled like a fire pit, and I hadn't slept in twenty-four hours.

Yuki, however, looked as though she'd been granted three wishes: world peace, eternal youth, and everlasting love. The girl was happy. And she does love her fruity margaritas.

At the moment, Cindy had the talking stick.

"Just tell me that Richie isn't showing up here, okay? Promise me that," she said.

Last time the girls had been to Susie's, Rich had crashed the party, after which he and Cindy had broken up. Since then, Cindy had been nursing regret and hope. Now she took us through her horrible encounter with Richie at the Marina Motel, reporting the dialogue between them verbatim.

I felt like I was in the room with her, watching Richie pull on his socks, then hug her and tell her it was over. The entire time she'd been wishing that he was in their bed, telling her that he was sorry, too, and not to worry anymore.

Claire put her arm around Cindy and Cindy wept against her bosom. I'd never seen Cindy cry in public before and it just killed me to see her in such pain.

Lorraine appeared at our table with a giant platter of Buffalo wings, placed them in front of us, and put a hand on Cindy's shoulder.

She said, "I don't think wings will take your

mind off a man who probably wasn't worth your time, Cindy, but the fact is they're delicious. And they're on the house."

Cindy smiled through her tears, and after Lorraine had gone, Cindy said, "Will someone else talk? Please?"

Claire kept her arm around Cindy and told us about the latest affront she'd suffered at the incompetent hands of Dr. Morse. She said emphatically that she would give up chocolate for a year if she could just get a decent lead into the recovery of Faye Farmer's body.

We batted the missing-body case around for a while, then Yuki took the floor to gloat— graciously—about the road trip to Bolinas, telling us how Brady reeled in Keith Herman and how insanely awesome it felt to have gotten that stupendous crud off the street.

Claire said, "I don't think I get Lynnette Lagrande. Did she want Jennifer Herman out of the way or not?"

Yuki shrugged and said, "How can you comprehend crazy? I spent a lot of time with that woman, so trust me when I say she's completely nuts. But her story is that she had nothing against

Jennifer. She loved Keith, and after being strung along for a couple of years, she was over it—but at the same time still pissed off. And she wanted Keith to pay."

I said, "Over it, but she still wanted payback?"

"Yeah," said Yuki. "That's what she says. So she set up the meeting for Keith with her new cop boyfriend, hoping Keith would be arrested for hiring a hit man. But Keith made the cop as a cop."

"So he decided to take out Jennifer himself?" Claire said.

"Right. Divorce by homicide. According to Keith, he didn't want his wife to end up with Lily. He's a psycho, but he loves his little girl."

I thought about Julie and looked at Claire. She had to be thinking about her little girl, Ruby Rose, too.

I sang a line from an old song: "Thank heaven for little girrrls."

I raised my mug and clinked it against Claire's.

Claire said solemnly, "And big girls, too. Getting bigger every day."

Cindy cracked up and hoisted her beer. Yuki raised what remained of her second watermelon margarita and we touched glasses across the table.

Yuki said, "To us." We said it in unison and with feeling. "To us."

EPILOGUE

A BAD DAY FOR PRO FOOTBALL

Chapter 111

AT EIGHT THAT morning, I was working at my desk across from Conklin when Brenda called to me from the far side of the bull pen.

"Sarge, I've got incoming from a sheriff in Nevada. You want the call?"

Brady was out of the building, so I was in charge.

"Transfer it over," I said.

The light on my phone console blinked. I picked up the receiver, tapped the button, and said my name and rank into the mouthpiece.

The man on the other end of the line said he was Sergeant Cosmo Rinker of the White Pine County, Nevada, sheriff's department.

He said, "Sergeant, we've got two DBs out

here, and you might be looking for them."

"How's that?" I said.

"Well," Rinker said, "what happened was, this UFO group saw a bright light on the horizon a couple of weeks ago, thought it was a close encounter of the little green kind. But when they got to it, turns out to be a vehicle completely consumed by fire."

I wondered what an incinerated vehicle had to do with us. But the sergeant had hooked me, and the man liked to tell the story his way.

"After the highway patrol called us, we got to see what was inside this burned-up Escalade. It was the cremains of two bodies in the rear cargo area, both of them female."

We were missing two female bodies, which was an inexcusable tragedy, an embarrassment to San Francisco law enforcement, and a very bad blow to a very good friend of mine.

"I'm listening, Sergeant. Please go on."

"Sure, sure; I'm getting there. One of the females had a bullet that went into her head and out the other side. The other female also had a gunshot to the head, but the bullet was fragmented and forensically worthless. But our lab did get a hit on the dental work of that first female and that's why I called you."

"What's the victim's name?"

"She's this Faye Farmer you're looking for, got stolen from your ME's office. We can't ID the other victim."

Rinker was still talking as I typed an instant message to Richie. **FAYE FARMER FOUND.** I sent it to his computer. He typed back !!!!!?????

I said, "Sergeant Rinker, where are the two bodies now?"

"They're at the ME's office in Las Vegas. But I think you should come see us here in Ely pretty soon. I think maybe we've got a lead on the doer."

"Put the coffee on, Sergeant. We'll be right there," I said.

Chapter 112

IT TOOK FOUR hours for Conklin, Claire, and me to get to McCarran Airport in Las Vegas. Then it was a four-hour drive in a rental car to a speck of a place fifty miles north of nowhere on a small track of road leading out into the desert.

The White Pine County sheriff's barracks were sided in white aluminum, with a line of small windows facing the road and a sign on the front reading PUBLIC SAFETY BUILDING.

We parked, stepped out into the blazing sun, and shielded our eyes with our hands so that we could view the distant blue hills at the farthest edge of the scrub and the endless open sky above us.

Moments later we went through the glass doors,

identified ourselves to the desk officer, then waited in the dark reception room until a lanky man in a tan uniform opened an interior door.

"Good to see you all," he said. "Come on back."

Rinker's office was lit with an overhead fluorescent fixture. File cabinets flanked his door, and his hat hung from a rack of antlers directly behind his chair. There was a framed picture of the Three Stooges in police uniforms and a dozen plaques on the walls.

We took seats around Rinker's desk, and after introductions were made, the sergeant opened a file on his computer and turned the monitor around.

"Can everyone see?"

We looked at photos of the torched Escalade from all sides, including a close-up of what looked like a red Frisbee in the backseat. That red disk had once been a plastic five-gallon gas container, and was likely the fire's point of origin.

Next Rinker showed us images of the interior of the cargo section at the back of the burned car. Along with the jack and the remains of the spare tire were two corpses, charred to the point of being what firefighters call crispy critters.

Rinker said, "Our ME removed the bodies.

Usually, when you take the bodies out, there will be carpet or something under them—clothes, maybe—that didn't burn. But this fire burned long and hot. All we got was ash and a few pieces of metal you can see in this picture here.

"Now, these are the reports from the ME."

He handed the records to Claire, who skimmed the forms, knowing just what she was looking for.

"'Jane Doe 91, cause of death, bullet to the head,'" she said. "'Manner of death, homicide.' May I see that photo of the artifacts again?"

Rinker pulled it up and Claire scrutinized the scorched litter until she saw what she was looking for.

"That buckle looks like it came from a gun belt. I'm just speculating, but until proven otherwise, I'm thinking this Jane Doe is Tracey Pendleton, still missing, still unaccounted for."

Claire put down the ME's autopsy report on Jane Doe 91 and picked up the second report.

She read, "'Faye Farmer, cause of death, gunshot to the head.' Uh-oh. Here's something interesting."

Claire looked over at me. "Faye Farmer was pregnant."

Chapter 113

I WAS VERY damned pleased that we would have the victims' bodies returned to San Francisco. That took away some of the stink from the abduction of Faye Farmer's corpse and the mysterious disappearance of the ME's nighttime security guard.

But it wasn't enough.

All of us, Claire included, were responsible for getting justice for Faye Farmer and Tracey Pendleton, and that meant finding their killer and gathering enough evidence to charge him with homicide.

Clearly, we were severely handicapped.

Whatever forensic evidence had once been on the bodies of Pendleton and Farmer had since gone up in a thousand degrees of gasoline-fueled flames. Faye Farmer's unborn child might lead to a motive—but it would be weeks before we'd know if there was viable DNA from the fetus's remains.

Conklin said, "Sergeant Rinker, what's this about a lead to the shooter?"

"I've got some crap-quality videotape. What other kind is there, right?"

As the sergeant punched keys on his computer, he told us that Ely was a small town, not much in it but a café, a few Western-style brick storefronts, something called the Frosty Stand, and a gas station called the Stagecoach that held down the intersection of the highway and the strip mall.

"The Stagecoach Gaseteria is your typical gas and food mart—three pumps and sandwiches to go. But here's the thing," Rinker said. "It's one of only a few gas stations around here for about a hundred miles.

"Here we are."

Rinker clicked his mouse to play the footage.

The so-called crap-quality video was grainy. Still, there was no mistaking the black Escalade when it pulled off the highway and parked at the pump.

Rinker said, "See, I can just make out two

numbers on the plate, but they're Ohio plates. Stolen off a car about three months ago."

We watched the driver get out of the Escalade, take his wallet out of his back pocket, and go into the gas station, presumably to pay. The angle of the camera showed us the back of his head.

I was pretty sure I knew who he was from that partial view, but it wasn't what you'd call a positive ID.

Conklin asked, "Is there footage from inside the store?"

Rinker said, "Would have been, but the camera was broke. So this is it. Now look, here he comes out of the store. And now he lifts his hand, waves to this guy parked out on the street."

There was a hulking guy standing next to a silver Audi that had pulled up on the roadside, just barely within the camera's range.

"That's Cal Sandler," I said. "Plays for the Niners with this man right here."

I stuck out my finger and stabbed the ghostly image of Jeff Kennedy, who was now filling up a red five-gallon gas container. I could make out Kennedy's face this time.

I thought anyone could.

Kennedy put the gas container in the backseat of the Escalade, got behind the wheel, and pulled out. His friend driving the Audi moved out right behind him.

Claire said, "Sons of bitches killing those women. A murder of an innocent person done to cover up the murder of an innocent person. Makes me sick."

"Three homicides," I said. "Baby makes three."

Chapter 114

IT WAS SUNDAY evening and I was alone in the bathtub with my thoughts.

I had just come back from a meeting with attorney George Fenn and his superstar client, the former football hero Jeff Kennedy.

Neither of them looked as self-assured in our little interview room as they had at Fenn & Tarbox's extraordinary conference room only a few weeks ago.

Today, Fenn blustered.

Kennedy denied shooting anyone, claimed that the man in the gas station video wasn't him, and that he was going to sue the city for defamation of character.

It was a nice try, but no sale. We had Kennedy

with the gas container, the Escalade, and we had a solid witness who wanted to keep himself off death row—Cal Sandler, Jeff Kennedy's best friend and accomplice.

It was a bad day for pro football.

But it was a good day to be a cop.

I was running more hot water into the tub when Joe brought Julie and Martha into the bathroom. It was a tight fit. Joe sat on the lid of the toilet seat and bounced our little girl on his knee. He asked me if I wanted reheated lasagna or if I wanted to go out to eat.

"Easy one," I said. "Please nuke the pasta."

Martha lowered her snout into the tub and lapped at the bathwater until, laughing, Joe pulled her away.

I wanted to savor these last few hours of the weekend, just soak them up. When the phone rang, I didn't answer it.

Whoever was calling could darn well wait until morning. But Joe looked at the caller ID, picked up, and said, "Hey, Richie."

I said, "Tell him I'll call him back."

"He said he'll wait," Joe told me.

I stepped out of my luxurious bath, threw on a

robe, and took the phone from Joe.

"I'm off duty, Richie."

"You want to hear this."

There was something in his voice that told me not to blow him off. He sounded bone-tired, or in shock, or simply at the end of his rope. Whatever the reason for his call, it was damned important to my partner.

"Then you'd better tell me," I said.

He said, "It's . . . it's . . ."

His voice cracked, as though he were going to cry.

"Rich. What's wrong?"

"It's Morales," he said. "She got herself out of the hospital. She escaped."

Acknowledgments

Our gratitude to these top professionals who were so generous with their time and expertise during the writing of this book: Dr. Humphrey Germaniuk, Medical Examiner and Coroner, Trumbull County, Ohio; Captain Richard Conklin of the Stamford, Connecticut, police department; attorney Philip R. Hoffman of New York City, New York; and Robert A. Wilson, MD.

We also wish to thank Andrea Spooner for sharing the experience of a lifetime.

As always, we are grateful to our excellent researchers, Ingrid Taylar and Lynn Colomello, and to Mary Jordan, who keeps it all together.

Turn the page for
an extract of

THEY SAY IT'S good luck if it snows on Christmas eve. I didn't usually buy into that kind of folk wisdom, but if it turned out to be true, well, this was looking like it'd be one of the best Christmases ever. A nor'easter was churning its way up the Carolinas at the same time as a cold front was diving south out of Ontario, all the makings for a monster storm along the Eastern Seaboard.

Sampson and I brought Lewis in and booked him. Since there were no arraignments scheduled until the day after tomorrow, it looked like the man of the year would be waiting for Santa in a holding cell this Yuletide season.

It was nearly eight by the time we finished up the paperwork and left.

"Merry Christmas, Alex," Sampson said outside.

"You too, John. Feel like stopping by for a holiday beverage tomorrow?"

"I'll check with my scheduler," Sampson said.

I took a cab home. As the taxi moved through DC, I looked out at the decorations glowing everywhere. The pace of the snow hadn't increased much yet, but the size of the flakes had. They were each about the diameter of a quarter, and thick, making the city look the way it does in those snow globes tourists buy at Union Station and the airports.

By the time I reached our house on Fifth Street in Southeast, it was close to eight thirty. The air smelled of pecan pie. Bree and the kids were busy finishing trimming the tree, which was in the alcove by the window at the front of the house. And of course, the official sergeant-of-all-holidays, Nana Mama, was supervising every little task on her to-do list.

"Don't put two green ornaments right next to each other, Damon. Show some style when you decorate a tree," she scolded with all the authority of the vice principal she'd once been.

Bree was hooking a faded crayon drawing of

the Three Wise Men up on one of the branches. According to legend, I had made that ornament when I was in kindergarten, and Nana always dragged it out on Christmas.

"Well, look who's come in from the snow-storm," Bree said, and she walked over and gave me a kiss on the lips. "Hello, sweetheart."

Nana decided not to look in my direction. All she said was, "Is there a faint possibility, Alex, that you might spend a few minutes of the holiday season with your family? Or are we asking too much?"

I should have had the wisdom to say nothing to Nana, to just give her a Christmas kiss, but I'll never learn. She pushes my buttons like nobody else on this earth.

"Thanks for the guilt! All wrapped up in a bow for Christmas," I said, dispensing hugs to my daughter, Jannie; my son Damon, who was home on winter break from prep school; and then Ava, the foster child Nana had recently brought under our roof.

"You're getting a dose of sense, fool," Nana Mama snapped.

"Nana, this morning, when I got that jingle

from Father Harris, he told me that *you* were the one who suggested he call me to help catch the poor-box thief," I said. *"Which I did."*

"Father Harris said that?" Nana asked.

"He did. He said that he hated to pester me on Christmas Eve, but you told him it would be no bother. Wouldn't take any time at all for your grandson to solve the case of the poor-box pilferer."

"Humph," she said, shaking her head. "Imagine a priest making up something that. Father Harris of all people. Then again, you never know." She reached in a box, turned to Ava. "Here you go, sweet thing. Put this porcelain Baby Jesus on a low branch, so if it falls, it doesn't fall far."

"So you're saying that Father Harris lied to me on Christmas Eve, Nana?"

She scowled, squinted at me. "I'm saying it's a pitiful state of the world when a man can't be with his family on Christmas Eve. Even a high-and-mighty homicide detective such as yourself needs to be home with his loved ones the night before Jesus's birthday."

Everyone was chuckling at Nana giving me such a hard time. I was holding back a smile myself. So was she.

"Kind of sucks Ali's not here," Jannie said, speaking of my six-year-old son.

"It does," I replied. "But his mom celebrates Christmas too."

Bree said, "I'll be right back," and left the room. I had to admit that the tree looked pretty great against the snowy picture window. Then Bree reappeared with a big glass bowl of homemade eggnog, another Christmas Eve tradition in our house.

The eggnog had big globs of nutmeg-sprinkled real whipped cream in it, so rich and sweet, each cupful would probably register a couple thousand calories. She set the bowl beside a plate of shortbread cookies that also probably registered a couple thousand calories each. But, hey, it was the Christmas season. I helped myself to two rounds of both. Damon got a Christmas-music station up on Pandora, whatever that was, and old Nat King Cole was crooning that all our troubles would soon be out of sight. Even though Nana wouldn't let up about me working on Christmas Eve, it was looking like it'd be a warm, wonderful night.

When the song switched to Mariah Carey's "All I Want for Christmas Is You," Jannie and Ava and

Bree started dancing. Damon began telling me about an incredible true story he was reading at school, about Teddy Roosevelt going up the Amazon River with his son.

Then my cell phone rang.

Not even Mariah's transcendent voice could stop that sound from sucking the joy right out of the room.

I hung my head, avoided eye contact, went into the hall, and answered. It was deputy chief of police Allen Chivers. "Am I interrupting Christmas Eve?"

"Yup," I said.

"Hate doing this, Alex. But we've got a bad one. The kind of thing that only you seem able to handle."

I listened another full minute, leaning my head against the wall, knowing just how silent the house had gone. "Okay," I said. "I'll get there." I clicked off, went back. Nana rolled her eyes. The kids looked away from me with here-we-go-again expressions on their faces.

Bree shook her head and said, "Well, there it is, then. Merry Christmas, Alex Cross."

AS I DROVE through the almost-deserted DC streets, the snow that had looked so beautiful an hour ago now seemed downright ugly. It was depressing to leave my house and family, and I didn't blame them for being angry and upset with me. Hell, *I* was angry and upset with me. And with my job.

Goddamn it, I thought. There was only one person in the world who should work on Christmas Eve. And he wore a goofy red suit and drank way too much fattening eggnog topped with nutmeg and real whipped cream. Damn it, and damn Santa too.

As I was driving into Georgetown on Pennsylvania Ave., the snow really began to fall.

A bus in front of me hit the brakes in a half inch of slush. I skidded and almost rear-ended it. Goddamned DC public-works folks were home with their families. Let the plows wait, right?

My windshield wipers were icing up as I looked for the address on Thirtieth Street in Northwest, a neighborhood in the city that was completely the opposite of mine. This was the land of milk and honey, and power and money, and the trophy homes to prove it.

Number 1314 was a beautiful limestone town house lit up like the White House Christmas tree. But I quickly saw that most of the lighting effects came from police cars, flashlights, floodlights, and TV-camera lights. I parked, opened the door, looked down at the slush, and cursed.

I had left home so quickly and in such a pissed-off state that I hadn't had the sense to bring along a pair of snow boots. As I slogged toward the crime scene tape, my ankles got cold, and little chunks of ice and wet snow wormed their way into my shoes.

I showed my badge to the patrolman working the barrier, ducked the tape, and started toward the two MPD vans parked on the front lawn of a Georgian brick mansion across the street. A car door on my side of the street opened. A middle-aged man in a green ski parka and a red ski hat got out and walked right up to me. He pulled off his gloves and held out a puffy red hand.

"You're Alex Cross, aren't you?" he said.

I thought I knew most cops in DC, but this one with the sea of freckles and bits of wavy red hair sneaking out from under his ski hat was new to me.

"I am," I said, shaking his hand.

"Detective Tom McGoey. Six whole days with the MPD. Originally from Staten Island."

"Happy holidays, Detective. Welcome to Washington. I got just a brief summary from Deputy Chief Chivers. You want to tell me all of it?"

"God-awful Christmas gift for you. And me."

I sighed. "Yeah, I already figured that much. Let's hear the gory details."

ROMANCE

Sundays at Tiffany's (*with Gabrielle Charbonnet*) •
The Christmas Wedding (*with Richard DiLallo*)

FAMILY OF PAGE-TURNERS

MAXIMUM RIDE SERIES

The Angel Experiment • School's Out Forever •
Saving the World and Other Extreme Sports •
The Final Warning • Max • Fang • Angel • Nevermore

DANIEL X SERIES

The Dangerous Days of Daniel X (*with Michael Ledwidge*) •
Watch the Skies (*with Ned Rust*) • Demons and Druids (*with
Adam Sadler*) • Game Over (*with Ned Rust*) •
Armageddon (*with Chris Grabenstein*)

WITCH & WIZARD SERIES

Witch & Wizard (*with Gabrielle Charbonnet*) • The Gift (*with
Ned Rust*) • The Fire (*with Jill Dembowski*) • The Kiss (*with
Jill Dembowski*)

MIDDLE SCHOOL NOVELS

Middle School: The Worst Years of My Life (*with Chris Tebbetts*) •
Middle School: Get Me Out of Here! (*with Chris Tebbetts*) •
Middle School: My Brother Is a Big, Fat Liar (*with Lisa
Papademetriou*) • Middle School: How I Survived Bullies,
Broccoli, and Snake Hill (*with Chris Tebbetts*)

I FUNNY

I Funny (*with Chris Grabenstein*) •
I Even Funnier (*with Chris Grabenstein*)

TREASURE HUNTERS

Treasure Hunters (*with Chris Grabenstein*)

CONFESSIONS SERIES

Confessions of a Murder Suspect (*with Maxine Paetro*) •
Confessions: The Private School Murders (*with Maxine Paetro*)

GRAPHIC NOVELS

Daniel X: Alien Hunter (*with Leopoldo Gout*) •
Maximum Ride: Manga Vol. 1–7 (*with NaRae Lee*)

For more information about James Patterson's novels, visit
www.jamespatterson.co.uk

Or become a fan on Facebook